BLOOD AND METAL

A DARK DESIRES NOVEL

BLOOD AND METAL

A DARK DESIRES NOVEL

NINA CROFT

Entangled Publishing, LLC
10940 S Parker Rd
Suite 327
Parker, CO 80134
rights@entangledpublishing.com

Amara is an imprint of Entangled Publishing, LLC.

Edited by Candace Havens
Cover design by Covers By Juan
Cover photography from Shutterstock

Manufactured in the United States of America

First Edition August 2015

For Rob—who I'm sure would donate his last drop of blood should I need it…

Prologue

"She'll burn in Hell's fires for this."

His father's words seared into his mind. Fergal swallowed a sob as his gaze fixed on the lifeless body of his mother. She looked almost at peace—if he ignored the blood pooled on the floor and the cuts like bracelets around her wrists.

He sniffed, digging his nails into his palms, until the pain dried his tears.

Since the last time they'd been brought back, she'd turned in on herself, shutting him out. He hardly saw her and never alone—his father made sure of that, using them against each other as hostages to ensure their good behavior.

That's why she'd done this. She'd known they would never get another chance to run. At least not together, and neither would leave the other behind. But wasn't that exactly what she had done in the end? Left him behind with his madman of a father?

Without her, he might find a way to escape, and a boy alone would have a far greater ability to stay hidden. She'd given him a chance at freedom. But he was only eight, and he didn't want his freedom. He wanted his mother.

"Have you nothing to say, boy?"

He shook his head. What was the point? His father never listened.

"For now, you will pay her penance." He snapped the strap at his side, and Fergal held himself very still so as not to wince. "Or would you rather burn in Hell's fires when you die?"

"No, sir."

A shiver ran through him. He didn't want to believe in Heaven or Hell or a god who would make a monster such as his father, but he'd had this beaten into him all his life. He resisted the urge to rub his arm where the old burn scar still itched. When he was six, his father had decided he needed an example of just how much the fires of Hell would hurt. It was something Fergal never forgot. That was when his mother had first tried to take him away. And failed.

"Well, boy? And how will you prevent it?"

He stared into his father's cold gray eyes, and heat surged inside him until his face burned as though already bathed in Hell's fires. He knew the expected reply; he'd be a good boy, follow the Church, obey his father.

He gritted his teeth. He had a much better answer.

"I'll make sure I never die, sir."

Chapter One

Someone prodded Fergal in the side. He didn't budge. No one had said anything for the last five years that was worth listening to, and he wasn't expecting that to change any time soon. The truth was, however gilded his cage, he was a prisoner and had been for a long time. His only trips out of this room were when they performed another set of intrusive and often painful tests on him. And he wasn't interested.

He should have left when he had the chance. Not that he'd ever had much of a chance. When he could have left, it would have been a death sentence without the anti-rejection drugs he'd been given on a daily basis. Once that had no longer been an issue, things had changed, and walking out was no longer an option.

Whoever it was nudged him again. "Wake up, Fergal."

That got his attention. No one called him Fergal anymore. Well, no one except Stefan. He rolled onto his back and blinked into the harsh light.

"Where the fuck have you been?" he snapped, sitting up and running a hand through his shoulder-length hair, rubbing his scalp. There was a dull ache in his head, but he was used to that now. It had been getting worse since they'd given him the final stage treatment two months ago. That had been the last time he'd seen Stefan.

Stefan was the head scientist at Cybercom, and this whole project was his baby. He was also the closest thing Fergal had to a buddy in this place—he'd never made friends easily, but they'd clicked.

"I'm being watched," Stefan said. "I didn't want to bring attention to you."

Fergal gave him a sharp look. His brain felt blurred, now he forced himself to concentrate, sensing Stefan had something important to say. "Who's watching you?"

Stefan didn't answer the question. Instead, he asked one of his own. "Do you know what's been happening outside?"

"Yeah, of course I do. *Not.*"

They told them nothing. It was enough to drive a nosy bastard like him insane. In the beginning, it had been okay—they'd had access to the comm streams, and he'd been able to keep up with what was happening on the outside. Back then he'd presumed his stay here was only temporary, that once he no longer needed the drugs they would let him out into the world. They'd monitor his progress, but he'd be free to come and go.

Then everything changed.

The last news he'd heard officially had been over twenty years ago. Callum Meridian, the leader of the known universe, was missing, the Collective was in disarray, and the Church was attempting a takeover. After that, everything had gone dark, their access to the comms cut off overnight. At first, Stefan had fed him what information he could. Although he'd refused to discuss company business, he'd kept Fergal up-to-date on what was going on. But for the last five years— nothing.

The only positive in this whole damn thing was that the treatment was obviously working. As far as Fergal could tell, he hadn't aged a day since he had walked into Cybercom all those years ago.

"When the Church came into power, the company tried to stay under the radar," Stefan said. "That was when we had the shutdown. It was considered too risky for any of the volunteers to be out there."

"So you locked us up. Like prisoners."

"You signed the agreement."

Yeah, he had. But back then, he would have signed anything to get into the program. "So what's changed?" He presumed something had precipitated this visit.

"Five years ago, the Church found out about our existence. At that time, they were still busy wiping out the Collective and the Rebel Coalition, but now they've turned their attention to us. I have every belief that within the next few days they will be taking control of Cybercom."

That wasn't good news. The Church of Everlasting Life claimed that all genetically modified beings, or GMs as they were known, along with all Collective members—the old ruling class—were abominations against God. He doubted that the products of Cybercom, including himself, would fare any better in the classification. But he still had no clue what Stefan wanted of him. "Come on, spit it out. Why are you here now?"

"I have an…offer I would like to make you."

"What sort of offer?"

He pursed his lips. "Let me ask you something first. How are you feeling?"

"Like shit."

A small smile flickered across his face. "Elucidate."

Fergal considered ignoring him—after all, that's what Stefan had been doing to him for the last five years. But his gut instinct was telling him something big was going down. It had been years since his gut had anything interesting to say, but he'd always relied on it in the past—it had led him to many a big story.

"My head aches. It started when you guys forced that last treatment on me, and it's been getting worse since."

"Like something is trying to take over your mind, perhaps?"

Fergal gave him another sharp glance. He didn't like the sound of that one damn bit. His body, okay, he could accept the changes. But his mind? He was happy with that the way it was. "Look, are you going to tell me what the fuck is going on?"

"Perhaps it would be better for me to show you."

"You'll let me out of here? What makes you think I won't make a run for it?"

"Because we're friends—I hope. And because you're curious. You were a reporter, you can't help yourself."

Fergal's eyes narrowed. So Stefan knew exactly who he was. That was surprising. He'd signed into this place with a false name and background. "How long have you known?"

"Since you made your initial application."

"And you still let me in."

"It was unimportant, and in every other way you were a perfect applicant. Besides, even back then I thought a reporter might come in handy one day."

Now he was definitely intrigued. It appeared Stefan had singled him out for a reason, and not because of his sunny personality. He pushed himself off the bed, pulled on a T-shirt over his black drawstring trousers, and he was ready to go. "Lead the way."

"Follow me," Stefan said.

Truth was he'd do anything to get away from this room.

Outside was a wide corridor, brightly lit with doors

on both sides every few feet. The doors all had little glass windows, like his, but when he peered inside one, the room was empty.

He hurried to catch up. "So Stefan, what's really going on?"

Stefan gave him a sideways glance as he halted in front of a set of double doors. "No one but the board has seen what I'm about to show you."

"I'm honored," Fergal said. "But get the fuck on with it."

That slight smile came again, but Stefan stepped forward and put his face to the retinal scanner. A second later, the doors slid open onto a huge room full of people. Except no one was moving. They all stood in ranks, row upon row. There must have been five hundred. Fergal peered closer and recognized one of his fellow volunteers. A frown formed between his eyes. "Are they drugged?"

"No. This is a result of the final phase of treatment."

"The final phase that I was given two months ago?"

"Yes. You've resisted longer than most. Only a handful of you are still functioning."

Fergal rubbed his head, where the dull ache had suddenly become a sharp stabbing pain. "So what's wrong with them?"

"The cybernetics have taken over their brains. In effect, they're mindless drones. We can input information via an external feed and they react, but they're unable to think for themselves."

"And that's what's happening to me?"

"Yes. I warned the board this might occur. I was still working on the auto-feedback suppressant. But they insisted we go ahead. I think there were outside forces at work, but I wasn't in the loop."

"Shit." Panic clawed at his guts. Being a mindless drone was not part of his plans. He breathed slowly, forcing himself to calm down. There was a reason he was here. Stefan wanted something from him. "So what are you doing about it?"

"Come with me and I'll explain."

Stefan led him through the ranks of men and women, and none of them even twitched as he passed. He recognized many of them. It was only in the last few years that the volunteers had been isolated. Before that, they'd been allowed to mix. He wouldn't say any of them were friends, but he did know them, and seeing them like this sent a ripple of primordial fear through him. To be mindless…

On the other side of the room, a smaller door took them into a laboratory. Stefan gestured to a chair, and Fergal sank down into it, trying to be patient. Stefan cleared his throat and began talking. "As I said, I've been working on an auto-feedback suppressant, which should result in the brain being able to override the cybernetics rather than the other way around."

"Sounds good. So why are there a whole load of mindless people in there?"

"The suppressant isn't ready yet. It still needs to be tested. And then it will take six months to complete in situ." And by that time Fergal would no doubt be one more mindless drone. "After that," Stefan continued, "it can be applied to the rest, and I'm hoping it will kick them back into…life."

"Hoping? You don't know?"

"No, I don't know." For the first time Stefan sounded angry. He took a deep breath, and Fergal could see him pulling himself together. "I'd normally have spent years testing this in vitro before the final phase was ever given, but it was taken out of my hands."

"Why are you telling me this now?"

"Because I've run out of time."

"And what do you want of me?"

"You'll help?"

"I don't have a lot of fucking choice, do I? Just promise

me that if I turn into one of those…things, you'll finish me off."

Stefan nodded.

Shit, he didn't want to die. While he had lost any belief in Heaven and Hell long ago, he still wanted to stand in front of his bastard of a father and say, *Look, I won. Your fucking devil is not going to get his hands on me.* "Tell me what you need."

"I expect this place to be taken over any day now. I want to input the suppressant into your system and get you out of here. It will either work or it won't. Then you have to stay out of trouble for six months."

"And after that?"

"You come and find me."

Some of his fear receded, replaced by a slow burn of excitement. He was getting out. "How will you get me away from here?"

"You're going to die. It won't be unexpected—a lot of people have died recently. The stronger the mind, the more it fights. Some have literally imploded rather than give in. After your death, your body will be disposed of, and I've arranged for someone to pick you up."

Sounded like Stefan had it all worked out. But once Fergal was away from here, he'd decide what happened in six months. Maybe he'd come looking for Stefan. Or maybe he wouldn't. "Let's do it."

Stefan nodded. "Good."

Fergal perched on the edge of a seat and watched as the doctor stuck a needle in his left arm and wired him up to a console and monitor. After pulling a pink vial from his pocket, he inserted it into the injector mechanism. Fergal held his breath as the liquid entered his veins. Icy cold flooded his system, shooting along his nerves, up his spine, into his brain. The dull ache shifted, and he had a moment of perfect clarity.

"What?" Stefan asked.

Fergal grinned. "My headache just vanished."

"Now one last thing." He took Fergal's wrist, stretched out his arm, and inserted a second needle into the blue vein. This time he felt nothing. "Time to get you back to your cell."

Fergal followed him back out through the room with the drones. He hadn't realized how dulled his brain had been. Now it was crystal clear, racing ahead. He had a chance. If this worked, he could still succeed, could still beat death. His pulse raced, excitement thrumming through him as Stefan opened the door to his room and gestured to him to enter.

"When will this happen?" he asked.

"Now."

As soon as Stefan said the word, Fergal's legs shuddered, and his knees gave out. He collapsed onto the bed behind him. "Shit."

Presumably, this was him dying. But there was one thing he was curious about. "So how do you know you can trust me?" he asked. "How do you know I won't disappear into the sunset and you'll never see me again?"

"I don't, but let's just say I've given myself a little insurance."

Fergal's eyes narrowed on Stefan as a tremor ran through the muscles of his arms. His brain might be clear, but his head was a weight on his shoulders. He needed to lie down. "You have?"

"That second injection was a poison I developed."

Fergal tried to stand up, but his legs wouldn't cooperate. "You've fucking poisoned me? I thought we were friends."

Stefan ignored the outburst and continued, "There's no cure, but there is an antidote. Which you will need to take every day. Listen to me, Fergal." He hunkered down in front of him, holding out a bottle of pills. "There's six months' supply. Keep them with you at all times. And take one every day, or you will die."

"Bastard." But the word lacked conviction. Fergal was actually impressed. Pissed off, but impressed.

"Then come and find me."

He tried to nod as Stefan reached across and slipped the pills into Fergal's pocket. The room was growing dim, the light shrinking to a pinprick.

"I'll see you in six months, Fergal. Don't let me down."

Then darkness.

Chapter Two

The bridge smelled of blood. Fresh blood.

Hot and oh so sweet.

Daisy's nostrils flared. If she closed her eyes, she could almost taste the sweetness on her tongue. She swayed in her seat as her mouth filled with a flood of saliva and her gums ached. Somewhere deep inside her, the darkness uncoiled sleepily, easing closer to the surface, wanting, needing... Placing her palms flat on the console, she pushed herself to her feet—

"Daisy!" Rico's voice broke through the fog of need.

Her eyes snapped open, and she plonked herself back down in her seat. "Sorry," she muttered. "But I'm hungry." She hated the whine in her voice and wished she could take the words back as six sets of eyes all turned her way.

Rico strode across the bridge, coming to a halt in front of her, his gaze narrowing on her face. "You okay?"

No. I'm not okay, I'm hungry, and I can't look at my friends without wanting to eat them. And I'm hungry. And they all pity me. And I'm hungry...

But she swallowed the words and choked down the darkness, though she knew from experience that it wouldn't sleep now until it was fed. Then she fixed a bright smile on her face. "I'm fine."

He quirked a brow. "Good girl. Your control is getting better, but don't leave it too long. We wouldn't want you ripping out the captain's throat. She needs it for ordering people about."

"Ha-ha," Tannis muttered. "But I second that—no throat ripping."

Daisy tried not to feel offended, but it was hard. After all, she hadn't actually done the throat-ripping thing since the first time.

The crew had made out some sort of roster and Tannis, the captain, was next on the feeding list. They were all immortal, and she couldn't kill them—even if she did rip out their throats—but she could weaken them if she fed too often.

She had to get her mind off food. Turning back to the console, she started searching through the incomprehensible mass of data.

"Do we have anything yet?" Tannis asked, as she had at least five times in the last hour.

"No," Daisy snapped.

"No need to get snippy."

"Well, sorry," she snarled, "but I'm not Janey." She curled her lip to show the tip of one sharp white fang. Janey had been their gorgeous and brilliant tech expert. She'd also been Daisy's best friend until she'd been murdered six months ago. Janey would have found the information they needed within minutes.

Daisy was a pilot—the copilot of *The Blood Hunter*—not a tech expert, but right now she was the best they had.

"We've been looking for six months," Tannis said. "Jon has to be there somewhere."

Jon and his wife, Alex, were crew members who had remained behind during *The Blood Hunter*'s recent trip through a black hole and into another universe. The plan had been to rendezvous with them on their return. Unfortunately, the ship's return had been...delayed. They'd taken an alternate route home through a wormhole, and by the time they got back, while only a few weeks had passed for them, over here more than twenty years had gone by. They'd gone to the arranged rendezvous only to discover Alex and Jon had been taken prisoner by the Church of Everlasting Life ten years ago. Alex was being forced into her old role as high priestess, while Jon was held as a hostage—a bargaining chip for her good behavior.

Now they had to find Jon and spring the pair of them.

Except they couldn't find him.

"Maybe he's already dead." Rico spoke the words everyone else was thinking.

"No. Alex would know if he was dead. They're using him to keep her in line. We just have to follow the trail."

Daisy muttered under her breath as she flicked through the continuous stream of information, searching for something...anything that might give them a clue, her hunger a constant distraction.

Rico had changed her six months ago in order to save her life, and she'd been hungry ever since. A deep, craving hunger that gnawed at her belly and kept her on edge. A hunger that had awakened the darkness deep inside her, so now she was never free of its presence, never free of the knowledge of what she had become—a bloodsucking monster. Feeding gave her a brief respite, but always the hunger came back like a live thing. Rico told her it would get better with time. But how long? He was over fifteen hundred years old—he didn't view time the same as the rest of them.

A hand came to rest on her shoulder and she jumped.

"Relax," Rico murmured.

Yeah, like that was going to happen.

He leaned down close to her. "You know, you need to get laid."

Even less likely. "Perhaps the crew could do a roster for that as well."

He grinned. "Never going to happen, sweetheart. But once we have this out of the way, we'll head back to Trakis Two and sort something out."

Rico had told her that the best way to get a grip on the hunger and keep the darkness at bay was sex. Unfortunately, everyone on the ship was part of a couple. She was happy for them, really, she was, but it did make her feel alone.

And what was she supposed to do on Trakis Two? She'd never found it easy to hook up. She was genetically modified, part plant, and the whole green thing had put a lot of men off. Though that was no longer an issue—in the months since Rico had changed her, the color had leached from her skin and hair as the chlorophyll died from lack of sunlight. Now, six months later, she was pale and boring; white skin, almost white hair. Even so, an average guy would very likely find the whole bloodsucking-monster thing a bit of a turnoff.

But there were more pleasure providers on Trakis Two than in the rest of the universe. Maybe she could pay someone. What a happy thought. This was what her life—or rather, her death—had come to. She was one sad excuse for a vampire.

Busy wallowing in self-pity, she almost missed the break she was looking for. She slammed her hand down on the console, then trawled back through the information and found the snippet that had caught her attention.

"I think I've found Jon."

His six months was nearly up. Only days to go. After that, Fergal Cain planned never to enter a prison again. He hated prisons, hated the stench of fear and despair that permeated the walls. The murmur of a thousand voices incarcerated behind bars. He'd been spending way too long in them lately, but if all went well, soon that would be over. A new life beckoned. Somewhere far away.

"So you're leaving us?" The governor's words broke into his thoughts.

"Yes, sir." His transfer had come through at last. Helped by a little strategic hacking into the prison system's database on his part. If his intel was correct, he'd found Stefan, and his transfer would take him exactly where he needed to be. He'd find his friend while keeping his cover intact.

And about time. This prison was worse than most. It had been rebuilt from the old Church headquarters, which had been destroyed over two decades ago by the Rebel Coalition. The parts of the prison aboveground weren't too bad, but the section underground, where the most dangerous prisoners were housed, was a noisome, dark precursor of the Hell the Church claimed the majority of the prisoners were heading for. Of course, they were given a last chance to repent…

The executions also took place underground. That was why they were here. At least the man had deserved to die. He'd been a rapist and a murderer. Fergal didn't think he could have stood by while they executed someone for their beliefs, or lack of them, but thankfully most of the "heretics" were long gone. Today, the prisoner hadn't taken up the Church's offer of repentance. Not that it would have saved him.

Was the bastard now in Hell?

Fergal didn't think so. He'd long ago gotten over his childhood indoctrination, or at least pushed it so far down it never bothered him. While he might believe that there was possibly more to life and death than he understood, no way was he buying into the usual crap people tried to pass off as religion. And certainly not the Church of Everlasting Life's even-crappier-than-normal version.

Up ahead the priest—there was always a priest present at executions—disappeared up the tunnel leading to ground level. "You go on," Fergal said to the governor. "I'll do a last check and lock up."

The man nodded. No one liked to spend longer than necessary down here. The place gave off an air of evil. "You'll be glad to get away from this place."

Fergal gave a noncommittal smile. "The prison on Trakis Five is said to be a better, if busier, place."

"Yes, the Collective may have been tough, but they weren't unduly cruel."

It was amazing how most people looked back on the reign of the Collective with something close to fondness and forgot the bits they hadn't liked. Five hundred years ago, when the human race had arrived at the Trakis system, they had also stumbled upon Meridian. Named after Callum Meridian, the ship's captain who had discovered it, the substance bestowed immortality—among other things—and the Collective had been born. Rich, immortal, telepathic, they soon ruled the universe with a ruthless hand.

Temperance Hatcher and his cronies made them look like total sweeties.

The Collective had fallen apart with the disappearance of their leader, Callum Meridian, and the destruction of the Meridian supplies on Trakis Seven. No one knew what had become of him—he'd supposedly been kidnapped and then disappeared without a trace. General opinion was Hatcher had arranged his assassination.

At the same time, the Rebel Coalition, the only other force that might have taken on the Church, had lost its own leader, Devlin Starke, and fallen into disarray. Starke was another who seemed to have vanished. Hatcher had obviously been busy. The bastard.

"It can't be worse," the governor said. He was a good man. They all did what they had to, to survive in these times. Or at least pretended to.

Fergal waited until the man had disappeared after the priest before heading down the tunnel, which took him deeper underground and finally opened out into the lower level control center. The room was empty, but the monitors were on, and nothing was moving. He exited down the tunnel opposite and checked the first row of cells. Most of the prisoners down here were awaiting appeal or execution for serious crimes. But there were also a few political prisoners. The farthest cell housed one of these. According to the records, he'd been here for twenty years. Why hadn't he been killed with the rest of the Collective? Burned in Hatcher's fires?

The cell's occupant had no name, but he was obviously Collective. In the dim light, his eyes glowed, inhuman and violet. He glanced up as Fergal peered through the glass pane in the cell's door, but no expression crossed his face— presumably drugged up to the eyeballs. He looked more boy than man; he must have been young when he took the Meridian treatment.

The other political prisoner was in the cell farthest from this one. At least he was categorized as political, though he actually looked more violent and more dangerous than the worst of the rapists and murderers. He paced the confines of his tiny cell, leashed power in his every move, his tall figure radiating pent-up fury. He glanced across as Fergal peered in and actually growled. Even safe on the outside, a frisson of fear trickled down his spine.

He stepped back. He'd done what was required of him.

Everyone was where they were supposed to be. Now he needed to get away from this stench and out into the fresh air.

Back in the control room, he checked the monitors one last time and headed toward ground level. He locked the door to the tunnels behind him with a sigh of relief and turned—

Something smashed into him from behind. A normal man would have gone down under the force of the blow. As it was, Fergal rocked on his feet. He snapped up straight and whirled around. A woman stood a foot away. Medium height, dressed all in black—tight pants, knee-high boots, a shirt, and a silver laser pistol at her hip. Had she shot him? That would explain the force of the blow. But her weapon was still holstered. A fall of waist-length silver-blond hair was pulled into a ponytail high on her head. She had the whitest skin he had ever seen, and dark green eyes. She was both seriously beautiful and seriously scary.

Her brows were drawn together. Obviously, she was wondering why he wasn't lying flat on his back on the floor after she'd hit him. Hard. Harder than she should have been able to hit.

Her mouth was wide and red and her upper lip curled in a snarl, revealing one sharp white tooth. Too big and too sharp. Where had he seen something like that before? It had been a while ago, over twenty years, but where…?

She moved fast, and he only had a second to brace himself. Crashing into his chest with the force of a blaster, she slammed him against the metal door behind him. Still clinging, her legs wrapped around his waist as her arms gripped his shoulders. Under different circumstances—very different circumstances—it might have been incredibly sexy.

He took a deep breath, gathered his strength, pried her fingers from around his neck, and hurled her from him. She smashed into the opposite wall, and he heaved a sigh. Then she was up again.

What the hell was she?

With a growl she leaped for him again, white ponytail flying out behind her. This time as she jumped him, she snarled, showing the biggest set of canines he had ever seen—on a human, at least. Shock held him immobile as she kept coming. Her head burrowed itself in the curve of his neck, and those sharp teeth sank into his throat. He felt the pump of his blood as the vein was severed, then his body's immediate repair response sending a flood of nanites to the damaged site.

He tried to tug her free, but she was locked on tight. She went still. Releasing her hold on his throat, she pushed away from his body and fell to her knees on the floor. She spat, and his blood was red against the white tiles.

"Ah, fuck, shit." She raised her head and spat again. "That is so disgusting."

He stared at her. What the fuck was going on? He edged around so he could reach the alarm switch on the door panel. If he used the alarm on his comm unit, they would want to know what was wrong, and he wasn't sure he could explain.

She straightened, swiping the back of her hand across her mouth and staring at him. A frown formed on her face, and she cocked her head to examine him. He inched another step sideways. Almost there.

Her eyes widened. "Holy Hell. Fergal?"

Shock held him motionless.

"Fergal? Is that you?"

He was sure he had never met her before. As he stared into those green eyes, some long-ago memory flickered in his mind, but he couldn't grasp on to it.

She obviously knew him. Or was it some sort of ploy? But she'd called him Fergal. He wasn't known by that name here.

He shook his head, trying to make sense of what was happening. Reaching up, he touched his neck. The wound was already healing. Her gaze followed the movement, narrowing on his throat.

Someone entered the corridor behind her, and Fergal tensed. The man was tall, dressed identically to the girl but with a laser pistol hanging loosely from one hand. He took in the two of them and shook his head. "Which part of 'take him down quietly' wasn't I clear on?" he said to the girl.

At the sound of the drawled words, Fergal remembered where he had heard that voice and seen teeth like that before.

"It's Fergal Cain," she replied.

The man cast him a sharp look. "Ah." Then he shrugged. "Sorry."

Fergal slapped his hand onto the alarm just as the laser pistol was raised to aim straight at his chest. As the shrill ring filled his head, the pistol flashed, thumping him in the middle. He crumpled to the floor, and everything went black.

Chapter Three

Daisy hurried across the room to where the downed man lay on the floor. Crouching beside him, she reached out and trailed a finger down his throat. The wound was almost healed, and his pulse was steady.

She glanced up at Rico accusingly. "You shot him."

"I wouldn't have had to if you'd taken him down like you were supposed to."

"I tried. But shit, he was strong." She frowned. "Hey, didn't he once take you down? If I remember, the captain had to save your ass."

Rico grinned. "Good point. But we needed him alive, and I was trying *not* to kill him at the time."

"You won't kill him now?" She stroked over the skin of his cheek; he was so warm to touch. She had fond memories of Fergal Cain. Even if the bastard hadn't recognized her. They'd once shared a torrid encounter in a very small shuttle. Though she supposed it had been less than a year for her, while it had been over twenty for him. And while he hadn't changed—presumably his not aging had something to do with the treatment he'd taken at Cybercom—she did look a little bit different than she had back then. Definitely less green. Even so…it was hardly flattering.

He was dressed in the uniform of a prison guard. Which meant nothing. More likely, he was undercover again. After all, that was how they had first come across him.

The alarm was still ringing. Rico had gone to peer down the way they had come, and now he returned to stare at Fergal while he considered her question.

"I'm not sure," he said. "I'm not even sure shooting him *would* kill him."

"He was strong," she said. Inhumanly strong. "And he tasted…ugh!"

Finally, the alarm went quiet. "Come on, we need to get out of here."

"We're aborting?" she asked.

"Well, I think it would be wise, don't you?"

"But we're so close. I hate to leave Jon here a moment longer."

"I know, but we'll be back." He pursed his lips and studied the unconscious man a moment longer. "We'll take lover boy with us. He might be of some use."

Fergal's lids flickered open, and he glared up at them. "Leave me the fuck here."

Rico rolled his eyes and blasted him again. "No."

"Did you have to?" Daisy cast him a look of reproach.

"Hey. It's only on stun. He'll live." Leaning down, he grabbed Fergal by the upper arms and hefted him over his shoulder. "*Dios*, he's heavy. Lead the way."

As Daisy headed to the corridor they'd entered by, running figures appeared around the corner, firing as soon as they saw her. Heat singed her arm, and she whirled and raced back the way she'd come, Rico close behind.

Well, that had gone well. Not.

The breakout should have been easy. Rico had let her do the takedown because it was unlikely she'd get such an easy chance to test out her new abilities again. It was supposed to prove that she could do it without giving way to the ever-present blood hunger. Well, she'd screwed up there. God, but he'd tasted disgusting. Sort of harsh and metallic. While he still looked human, he was obviously changed somehow.

She paused as she came to a choice of left or right.

"Left," Rico yelled from behind her, and she ran on.

She couldn't hear any sound of pursuit. They'd left them far behind. Sometimes she wasn't sure about the changes she'd gone through, the hunger could be a pain, but she loved the superhuman strength and the speed.

Up ahead she spotted a metal double door. The scent of fresh air teased her nostrils, and without slowing, she pulled her laser pistol and blew the lock. The alarm sounded again, harsh in her ears, but she ignored it, kicking the doors open, and she was out into the cool air. She loved the night, and she breathed in deeply, clearing her lungs of the obscene prison smell as she made her way around the outer perimeter before taking a right angle and heading into the forest.

A shot blasted from behind them, and a tree burst into flame.

But they were nearly there.

"*Mierda*," Rico said from behind her.

He'd been hit but was still moving, so she didn't slow until she was running up the ramp and onto the shuttle. "Open," she shouted, and the double doors slid apart. She threw herself into the pilot's seat before Rico was even inside, strapping on the harness. "Engines to emergency takeoff mode."

The seat vibrated beneath her as the shuttle flared into life. She cast a glance over her shoulder as Rico lowered the still unconscious Fergal onto the floor and took the seat next to her. "Go!"

"Take off," she said, and the sudden force thrust her down into the seat. She loved this moment, all the power of the ship at her command. "Back to *The Blood Hunter*," she told the shuttle, and they left the planet behind.

Yes!

Exhilaration filled her as they shot into the sky.

The adrenaline rush quickly faded.

We failed, and it was my fault.

If she couldn't get control of herself, she was always going to be a liability.

Of course they would try again. They wouldn't give up. Couldn't give up. Tannis would never leave a member of the crew behind—it was one of the unspoken laws on *The Blood Hunter*. Probably the only law. They weren't much into rules.

"Well, that was a load of crap," Rico said. "No thanks to your boyfriend down there."

"He's not my boyfriend. Bastard didn't even recognize me."

"Well, sweetheart, that's not entirely his fault. You were a little greener last time he saw you."

"Yeah."

It was weird, but she hadn't realized until she lost it how much being green had been part of her. Like a badge of honor, revealing what she was to the world, and she'd been proud of it. Now, only her eyes remained green—presumably their actual color.

Fergal Cain hadn't minded her being green. He'd seemed to quite like it.

She swiveled her chair around so she could study him where he lay unconscious, taking up most of the floor space in the small shuttle. She found it hard to believe they'd ever actually had sex. Though it was less than a year ago for her, it seemed like another life. They'd kidnapped Fergal that time as well, and her skin flushed at the memory. They'd needed intel for another prison break, and Fergal was the only source they could find. He'd been a reporter, specializing in going undercover and exposing corruption wherever he could find it, and he'd spent some time in the Collective's maximum-security prison on Trakis One. The Collective hadn't been too happy about the piece and had pulled it from the comms, so talking to Fergal in person had been the only reliable source of information regarding the internal security of the prison.

When they'd caught up with him, he'd been undercover again. This time at a company called Cybercom. Apparently, he'd cut off his own arm in order to get entry into the company. He'd been fitted with a cybernetic arm and at the same time gotten himself inducted into the company's more secretive and far less legal program. She didn't know what they'd done to him there, but something extreme—she'd felt his inhuman strength when she'd attacked him.

He was stunning, with a narrow bony face and well-shaped lips that had kissed her so passionately. His dark blond hair had been shoulder length the last time she'd seen him, but was now cropped short. He had a long, lean body, broad at the shoulder, narrow at the waist and the biggest... Her gaze shifted to his groin, and heat coalesced low down in her belly.

"You're drooling," Rico murmured from beside her. She glanced up to see the lazy smile on his face and looked away. She shouldn't be having such thoughts with Rico next to her. He was almost like a father to her now—it was improper. Her lips curled at the thought of Rico in a fatherly role. It definitely didn't suit him. Though he had made her. Turned her into a vampire to save her life. Of course, he had also been responsible for her life needing saving, but that got complicated, so she avoided thinking about it too much.

She'd had a crush on Rico ever since she'd woken from

cryo and found herself on the old *Blood Hunter.* They'd discovered her escape pod floating aimlessly in deep space. It had been damaged when she'd fled from the massacre that had killed her family. Something else she tried not to think about. Her parents had been good people and hadn't deserved to die.

Tannis, the captain, had taken her in, and Daisy loved her for it. But she'd been fascinated by Rico. He was gorgeous, with his black hair, golden skin, and dark eyes. He was also different than anyone she had ever met—he was the first vampire she had ever laid eyes on. Rico was also a pilot, and Daisy had dreamed of flying for as long as she could remember.

She'd sort of had these fantasies about him biting her and doing a whole load more, but she'd known they were nothing more than fantasies. Rico wouldn't touch any of the crew— he'd promised the captain, and anyway, now he had Skylar.

Strangely though, since he'd turned her into a vampire, she'd ceased to think about him like that. Apparently, vampires didn't tend to get up close and personal to each other.

"He is pretty," she said, turning her attention back to Fergal. "But his blood was disgusting."

"Yeah, I remember."

Her gaze flew to Rico's face; his expression was bland. "You fed from him?"

"No, just got some on my knuckles during that little fight we had."

"Is it the cyborg thing?"

"Must be. I've never tasted anything like it." He considered her for a moment, his head cocked on one side.

"What?"

"You know we talked about sex."

"Yeah." Rico knew she'd been having problems

controlling her hunger. Sometimes it was like a pain inside her, a deep, dark need that threatened to consume her. Much of the time, she could pretend she was the same person as before, but in those darker moments, she knew there was very little of Daisy the green girl left. Rico had told her that the best way to subdue the darkness was sex. So far, she hadn't tried it. She didn't dare. If she relaxed and lost control, bit someone, she could drain them dry before she could stop.

"Well," Rico continued, "it occurs to me that our friend here"—he nudged Fergal with his toe—"might be the perfect candidate for you."

"How do you work that out?"

"You said it yourself. He tastes like shit. You lose it and bite him by mistake, you're not going to take more than a mouthful."

Her brows drew together. "That's a strange reason to go after someone—they taste horrible."

Rico rolled his eyes. "Sweetheart, we're not talking relationships here, we're talking fucking."

Fucking with Fergal. There was a little twinge in her nether regions.

"Like that idea, don't you?"

The amusement was clear in Rico's voice, but she didn't try to deny it. He knew her too well. There was a connection between them now.

"It doesn't matter. He's hardly likely to want me. This is the second time we've kidnapped him."

"Then perhaps you don't give him a choice."

"You're not suggesting I force him, are you? I'd have to tie him up—he's stronger than I am."

Rico rolled his eyes. "Use your feminine wiles."

"I'm not actually sure I have any. I haven't exactly been drowning in offers, you know. Even before the whole big teeth thing."

"You just haven't made an effort yet." He was studying her again. "You could have just about any man if you put your mind to it."

"I could?"

"The green was a little distracting, but now it's gone, and you are really quite beautiful."

Wow.

"Of course, you're also pretty terrifying, but some men get off on that."

Great.

Somehow, she doubted Fergal was much into terror—probably impervious to it. Tannis had reckoned he had balls of steel to chop off his own arm just for a story, so she couldn't rely on that to attract him.

Green makeup? He'd liked her green. But a little messy.

Maybe she'd tie him up after all.

Fergal was moving, so at least he was alive. Unfortunately, he was not moving under his own steam. Instead, he was hoisted over someone's shoulder with his head hanging down. Nausea roiled in his stomach, and he had to swallow before it was safe to speak.

"Put me the fuck down," he growled.

They stopped moving, and he was tossed to the floor. He landed on his ass with a jolt, which did nothing to improve his mood.

He sat for a moment, patting his pocket to ensure he still had the bottle with his last remaining antidote pills, doing an internal check. When he found no damage, he pushed himself to his feet and looked around.

He was on the bridge of a space cruiser—easily the biggest bridge he'd ever seen. Screens lined the walls, showing the views from external monitors, so he had a 360-degree panorama of space. From the look of it, they were in a high orbit above Trakis Four. At least they hadn't left yet.

A man and a woman stood in front of him, both in identical positions, legs braced, arms folded across their chests. He recognized them from the prison, though their most distinguishing features—those impressive teeth—were hidden now. The man he also recognized from over two decades ago; Ricardo Sanchez, pilot of *The Blood Hunter*. Like Fergal, he hadn't aged a day. No doubt a vampire thing.

"Fucking asshole. You fucking kidnapped me. Again."

Rico's lips curled into the semblance of a smile. "You remember me. How sweet."

"Yeah, I fucking remember you, and as I said last time—take me the fuck back."

"And as I said last time…maybe." Rico flung himself into a chair. Stretching out his long, booted legs, he regarded Fergal through narrowed eyes. The woman took the chair next to him and did the same. There was something familiar about her, but he couldn't put his finger on it. A sound from behind distracted him, and he turned.

A second woman stood in the doorway. He recognized her. Skylar, who'd also been present last time. She was tall, athletic, with blond hair cut military short and the inhuman violet eyes of the Collective.

"That's not Jon." She waved a hand in his direction. "What happened?"

"He did," Rico replied, pointing a finger at Fergal. Rising to his feet, he strode over to the woman and kissed her. For a long time. Fergal looked away and caught the other woman's gaze. She was slumped low in her chair, a scowl on her face.

"Get used to it," she muttered.

He had no intention of getting used to anything. At least not anything on this ship. What he needed to do was find out if his cover was blown. If it wasn't, then he had to get back to the prison. If it was blown…he was royally fucked.

When he looked back, the two were still kissing. He cleared his throat loudly, and at last, the woman pulled away.

"Welcome back," she said to Rico.

"You can welcome me properly when we have this mess sorted out."

Fergal frowned. Was he the mess? And how did they plan to sort him out? And what was he doing here, anyway? And where was here? Because it definitely wasn't the same ship as last time.

"So you didn't find Jon?" Skylar asked.

"We didn't get a chance. Mr. Undercover Reporter over there interrupted us and set off the alarm."

"Only after she"—Fergal waved a hand at the woman still seated behind him—"nearly ripped my throat out."

Skylar turned to her. "Did you?"

She nodded, her expression rueful. "I lost it a little."

"Undercover reporter?" Skylar turned to study him. After a second, she laughed. "Hey, it's Fergal, come to pay us another visit."

"Yeah, right. Because I had so much fun here last time." Actually, it hadn't been so bad. There was the sweetest little green girl he'd ever come across. Well, the only green girl, but she'd definitely been sweet. Was she still around? Daisy— he remembered now. "Anyway, why don't you drop me back where you found me and we'll call it quits?"

"Not going to happen," Rico said.

"And why the fuck's that?" He clenched his fists at his side. Could he take them all? Skylar's hand was resting on the butt of her laser pistol, and it looked very at home there.

"Don't try it," Rico said. "Unless you're looking for another laser blast. She's good."

Fergal rolled his neck, stretching his back muscles to ease

the tension. One way or another, he needed to persuade them to take him back. And why wouldn't they? Unless they were after the bounty—there was a price on anyone who'd been involved in Cybercom. Glancing around, he chose a seat, sat down, and surveyed his captors. "Well?"

Rico raised an eyebrow and gave a small shrug. "We need to break someone out from the prison. At least we hope he's there." He returned to his own seat, studied Fergal for a moment. "You know all the prisoners?"

"Not all, but I do know the ones in the maximum-security section."

"He'd definitely be in maximum." He was silent for a moment as if trying to decide whether to trust Fergal with more information. He gave a quick nod. "His name's Jonathon Decker."

Fergal frowned. He knew the name, but then, he did have almost perfect recall. Even before the enhancements, he'd been good. Now his mind was like a computer. "The guy who assassinated Aiden Ross? The one who was broken out of the maximum-security"—ah, something came together in his mind—"prison on Trakis One by you guys. But that was twenty years ago."

"For you, maybe," Rico replied.

What the hell did that mean? He filed it away to ask later. "I'll tell you what I know, and you take me back."

"Maybe. If he's there, we're going in again, probably tomorrow—they won't expect another attempt so soon. We might consider taking you with us."

That was probably the best he was going to get. He'd decide later if it was enough. "There's nobody listed by that name, but that means nothing—the political prisoners don't keep their names. They get numbers. What does your friend look like?"

"Probably angry."

"A little more might be useful." But his mind flashed back to the tall, dark-haired man pacing his cell. Yeah, "angry" described him.

Skylar answered. "Six-four, big, dark hair, golden eyes."

The description fit perfectly. Should he tell them, or would it work better in his favor if they didn't know? If they took him back tomorrow, his cover would most likely already be blown. It would be better if they took him back now. He could say they'd knocked him out and he'd come around outside the prison walls. He might even be believed.

"Spit it out, Cain," Rico said. "I can see your mind working. Which means you think you have options. You don't."

"There are always options."

"Yeah, and yours are tell us what you know now, or tell us in ten minutes after I've *persuaded* you."

"You'd torture me?" He was curious as to the answer.

"Hell, yeah. Or I'd let Daisy do it. I don't think she's feeling too happy with you right now."

Fergal latched onto the name, and a smile tugged at his lips. "Daisy? She's on board?"

Amusement quirked in Rico's eyes. "You could say that."

Again—what the hell did that mean? God, the guy could be irritating. "Are you going to explain that?"

Rico shrugged. "Daisy, do you want to try and explain? Preferably in words with one syllable."

Fergal frowned then turned his head to see whom the vampire was speaking to. The blonde from the prison. She'd slumped even lower in her seat, the scowl still on her face, one hand tugging at her long ponytail. "No," she replied.

Normally, he wasn't this slow. He studied her, the shape of her face, the sweet curve of her lips, down to the swell of her breasts above a tiny waist.

She was the right size. The right shape. But totally the

wrong color. He raised his gaze back to her face. Except the eyes. They were deep, dark green and narrowed on him. She also looked no older than the girl he'd met all those years ago—this was doing his fucking head in.

"Daisy?"

"Hardly complimentary, Fergal," Rico said, amusement clear in his voice.

Daisy had been a good thing in his life. Something he remembered when times got hard or painful. At one point he'd considered trying to find her, but by the time he was in any shape to leave Cybercom, he was a fugitive and in hiding.

Besides, he was a loner. Always had been.

He shook his head and looked some more. Yes, he could see it now. The green had sort of overshadowed everything else. And those rather large and scary fangs hadn't been there—he would have noticed.

When they'd met before, he'd thought her pretty. She was in fact extraordinarily beautiful, even with that scowl on her face.

"Actually," Skylar said, "I think it's an understandable mistake."

That was kind of her, but he wasn't sure Daisy agreed. He rubbed his forehead. The pain reminded him it was time for his medication, and however sweet this reunion was, he had a job to do—find Stefan—or he was dead.

"So," Rico said, "can we get back to our friend? We need to contact the others. Tell them it's off for the day, but I'd prefer it if we could give them some good news at the same time."

Fergal scrubbed a hand over his chin. He was sure he could withstand torture, and part of him was curious to discover if they would actually do it. But what the hell, this was probably his best bet. He nodded. "There are two political prisoners. I think your friend is one of them."

"Good. That didn't hurt at all, did it?"

"So we go in tomorrow?" Daisy asked.

Fergal turned to look at her. She was leaning forward in her seat, eager.

"As soon as it's dark," Rico said. "But maybe you should stay behind this time."

"No, I want to come. I can control it."

Control what?

"Hmm." Rico studied her then turned to Skylar. "Is Devlin back?"

"Yeah," she answered. "Arrived an hour ago and went straight to bed."

"Not alone, I presume." Rico pursed his lips and gave an abrupt nod. "Okay," he said to Daisy. "But you feed before we go. You almost lost it today. And we take Skylar and Devlin with us in case we have to fight our way out. We're not leaving without Jon a second time."

"That will leave just Saffira on the ship. Can she cope?" Skylar asked.

"Yeah. She can handle her. In fact, we should get her and Devlin out of bed and down here. They need to be in on this. They can sleep—or whatever it is they're doing—when we have a plan." He pressed the comm unit on his wrist. "Devlin, you're both required on the bridge now." His lips twitched as he listened to the answer. "Hey, if I can wait, so can you."

Rico got up and paced the room. Pausing, he leaned down and pulled a bottle from below one of the seats. After taking a swallow, he handed it to Fergal.

Fergal took the bottle and lifted it to his lips with caution. He had a vague memory of accepting a drink from the vampire last time. It had nearly blown his head off. Taking a sip, the liquid burned down his throat and heated his belly. Deciding it wasn't going to kill him, he took a gulp and almost choked.

Everyone was watching him. Was it a test? He caught

Daisy's gaze and held it while he took another swallow. This time he felt it in his brain, like a warm buzz. He walked over and handed her the bottle. She didn't look away as she raised it to her mouth—her lips red against the whiteness of her skin.

An image flashed in his head of those red lips wrapped around his dick, causing a jerk in his pants. It had been a long time since he'd experienced desire. He'd worried that was a side effect of the cybernetics, or the medication, or some of the weird shit that was happening in his body right now. But it appeared everything was working. Nice. But did he really want those fangs anywhere near his dick?

She swallowed and handed the bottle back. Their fingers touched and a jolt of electricity shot through him. Her eyes narrowed as she sat back in her seat and wiped her hand down the side of her pants. Fergal looked away to find Rico watching him, cool speculation in his eyes. The vampire opened his mouth, no doubt to make some wiseass comment, but at that moment the doors slid open and a couple appeared. The man was tall, with streaky black and gold hair loose on his shoulders. He had the violet eyes of the Collective and a scar that ran down his right cheek from his eye to his lip, lifting his mouth in a perpetual sneer. Devlin Starke. Fergal recognized him from the files. The head of the Rebel Coalition and once the most wanted man on the Collective's most-wanted-dead list; it looked like now he had become one of them. He'd disappeared over twenty years ago. Where the hell had he been?

Fergal turned his attention to the woman. At last, someone he didn't know. Medium height, with long, dark red hair, but the same violet eyes. She had an air of…difference about her, even more than usual with the Collective.

"So what's happening? You didn't find him? And who's this?" Starke's gaze locked with Fergal's and his eyes narrowed as he took in the prison guard's uniform.

"This is an old…friend, Fergal Cain, who interrupted us but is now about to redeem himself by giving us the lowdown on the security system. Jon's in there, and we're going back tomorrow night. You and Skylar will be coming this time. We're getting him out if we have to pull the place down and kill everyone in it."

Fergal presumed he was serious.

"Oh, and are you okay for Daisy?" Rico asked Starke. "I don't want her hungry going in."

Starke tossed a look at Daisy, who squirmed a little, but he nodded abruptly. "Of course."

"Good." Rico turned back to Fergal. "And this is Devlin and Saffira," he completed the introductions.

"Devlin Starke." Fergal stepped forward and held out his hand.

Starke's eyes narrowed on it for a moment, then he took it briefly. "Yeah. So?"

"Everyone presumed you were dead."

"Well, obviously *everyone* was wrong."

"And weren't you committed to taking down the Collective?" He waved a hand in the general direction of Starke's violet eyes. "After you took down the Church, of course."

Starke turned to Rico. "Is he always this nosy?"

"He's a reporter. He can't help himself."

Fergal hadn't actually been a reporter for years, but he'd keep quiet about that. If they believed he was undercover trying to get a story, they were unlikely to probe his real reasons for being at the prison.

"Well, try," Starke suggested.

Chapter Four

Daisy slouched low in her seat and watched the interactions. She'd seen Devlin's look when Rico had asked him about feeding her. They were all so good to her, but she hated using her friends as food. Rico had promised to teach her to hunt once they were back on Trakis Two, but only if she managed to get some control and wouldn't kill her prey. He didn't think she was ready to do that.

Too right.

Whatever Rico said about what she had become—she was no killer.

Fergal was shaking hands with Saffira now, while Devlin looked on. As Fergal murmured something, Saffira laughed. Devlin took a step toward them, his lips tight.

"Okay, the introductions are over."

The comm unit on the screen beside her was flashing. "Rico?"

"Yeah?"

"Tannis is on the line."

Tannis and Callum were hiding out down on Trakis Five

waiting for the go-ahead to pull Alex out. "Tell me you've got him," Tannis said.

"We don't."

"Jesus, Rico. Was he not there? Our intel is crappy these days. Shit, I miss Janey."

Daisy missed her as well. But Janey had been murdered by that bastard Temperance Hatcher six months ago. Along with Devlin's brother, *The Blood Hunter*'s engineer.

"No, he's there. The intel is good. We just hit a slight problem."

"We need to get the hell off this freaking planet. It's giving me the creeps. It's crawling with Church people."

"Hold tight until tomorrow and we'll have him out of there."

Tannis was silent for a moment, but Daisy could hear her rapid breathing. "Okay. But call as soon as you're done."

"You think you can pull Alex out."

"Yeah, she's not a prisoner. She can come and go as she pleases, but that's going to change if they get word Jon is free."

"We'll comm you the second we have him."

"We'll be standing by." Tannis ended the comm.

"Who's Alex?" Fergal asked.

Rico shrugged. "You might as well know—you won't be talking to anyone else before tomorrow. Alex, aka Lady Alexia, the high priestess of the fucking Church of Everlasting Life."

"The somewhat reluctant high priestess," Skylar added.

Fergal's eyes narrowed. "Didn't she vanish for a few years? There's a lot of that going on."

"She did, but they got her back. The man we're breaking out tomorrow is her husband—"

"Husband? Isn't she supposed to be the virgin bride of blah, blah, blah?"

"It's a long story. But essentially, Jon has been kept as

a hostage for her good behavior. As long as they have him, she's going to behave in a priestess-like manner. And after ten years, I'm guessing she's ready to explode. So we have to get him out of there. Then Tannis will pull Alex from Trakis Five."

Jon and Alex had chosen to stay behind when *The Blood Hunter* had made the potentially disastrous trip through the black hole at Trakis One. Alex had been pregnant and hadn't wanted to risk the baby—babies, as it turned out; she'd had twins. That had been twenty-two years ago. At least for Alex and Jon. For the rest of them on *The Blood Hunter*, it had only been six months, due to that slight miscalculation on Saffira's part when bringing them through the wormhole.

Saffira was a time-mancer and could manipulate time and space. But she was new to her abilities and didn't always get it quite right. When she'd called up a wormhole to bring them home, she'd managed to lose a few years, but she had saved them all from certain death, so no one had complained too loudly.

"Okay," Rico said. "Explain the security systems. How hard is this going to be?"

"It should be easy. While they'll be on alert after today, I doubt it will be high alert. They don't expect trouble. I don't think there's been a breakout in the fifteen years the prison has been there. The Church has everyone so cowed no one will risk it."

"Except us. So…details."

Why the fuck not tell them? He certainly owed the Church no loyalty. "Twenty guards each shift, most of them not particularly efficient or loyal—unlikely to risk their lives trying to stop a prisoner escaping."

"What about the rest?"

"The tech stuff is old. No biometrics, just codes changed on a weekly basis. That isn't normally due for a couple of days, but they'll change them after today. I can get into the system and pull out the new ones—"

"You can do that?"

"Yeah, providing you get me to the main control room."

"Should be easy enough."

Daisy let the conversation flow over her as she studied him. He looked even better awake than he had unconscious on the floor, and things tightened low down in her belly.

The last time they'd been together, he'd taken her fast and hard, with her bent over the pilot's chair. Followed by him sitting on the chair with Daisy straddling his lap, riding him, while he played with her breasts. Her nipples peaked at the memory. But that was a long time ago and the last sex she'd had. As Rico kept pointing out—she needed to get laid.

Fergal glanced toward her, and she looked away, not wanting to be caught ogling. For a second, when he'd first realized who she was, he'd looked at her as though he liked what he saw.

"Okay," Rico said. "That's it for now."

Fergal stretched, arms above his head, then rubbed the back of his neck. "I don't suppose there's any food?"

"I'll take you," Rico said.

Daisy jumped to her feet, meaning to go with them, but Rico shook his head. "You stay here and do what you have to do with Devlin. I'll look after your boyfriend and bring him safely back to you."

She watched as they disappeared out the door, leaving her with Saffira and Devlin. Saffira took herself off to one of the consoles and started reviewing star charts—she did that a lot. She was searching for something she'd seen in one of her visions, though she hadn't shared the details.

It was probably best. It was partly Saffira's fault that Daisy was now a vampire. The result of another of her not-totally-successful adventures in time travel. If she hadn't taken them back in time and back to Earth, Daisy would never have had her throat ripped out by a newly turned Rico back in 1499. The whole time travel thing still did her head in.

She shifted restlessly as the hunger flared to life inside her, choking the air from her lungs. Her gums ached with the need to feed, and her vision tinged with crimson.

She paced the room, trying to ease the restlessness, but it was futile, and eventually she sank back down onto her seat, taking slow, careful breaths. Right now, she had to eat on a daily basis. Rico had told her the first years were the hardest. Later she would get control and not need to feed so frequently. Rico hardly had to at all, but he was over fifteen hundred years old. He really only fed from Skylar now, and mainly for recreational purposes. What would it be like to feed from someone like that—someone who wanted you to bite them, pleasure them?

Will I ever find out?

Unlikely.

From across the room, Devlin caught her eye. He looked at her for a moment then came on over. "You okay?"

She nodded quickly.

"You want to do this now?"

She nodded again, wishing she could say no, but she knew from experience that the hunger would only get worse, and the darkness would build and build until it obliterated all else. "Do you really hate this?" she asked.

A startled expression crossed Devlin's face. He took the seat beside her, sat back, and considered her question. She was glad he hadn't said an automatic no. Because she wouldn't have believed him.

"It makes me a little…uncomfortable."

"I hurt you?"

"No." He shifted in his chair. "If you must know, it turns me on."

A frown tugged her brows together, while heat flushed her cheeks. "Oh." She couldn't think of anything more intelligent to say.

"And it doesn't feel right. You're a friend. And I feel guilty and…" He grinned. "If it makes you feel any better, Saffira tells me it does the same to her."

No, it didn't make her feel better. She chewed on her lip. "It's a vamp thing, I suppose."

"Yeah. I fed Rico once—when he was changing you and he needed blood. I got a fucking hard-on and it totally creeped me out. At least with you it's understandable and a little more acceptable."

She forced a smile. "Thank you. I think." She took a deep breath. "So where…?"

The neck was best. For some reason it healed quicker than the wrist, but it was maybe a little too intimate. Rico had told her there was also a vein at the groin, but that would definitely be too intimate. Devlin usually went for wrist, but he didn't hold out his arm as she'd expected.

"We might be fighting tomorrow. I'll need both my arms. You'd better go for the neck."

She kept her expression blank, not letting her excitement show until she had risen to her feet and moved behind him. She closed her eyes, ran a calming mantra though her mind, and got a grip on her hunger. She was getting better at this.

A wave of need washed over her as she lowered her head. The blood pulsated in the vein in his throat, so close to the surface, the tantalizing scent drawing her in. He was afraid. Probably not something Devlin experienced very often, but he held himself very still.

She swept his hair away, breathed in deeply, and ran her tongue over the pulse point. Devlin shifted as though he couldn't stay still, and she rested her hands on his shoulders as she sank her fangs through the flesh of his throat. The first spurt of warm blood filled her mouth, and she battled down her bloodlust.

Keep it together.

Just for a few seconds, and she would be okay. She swallowed convulsively, the blood flooding her system with warmth and power. Devlin's pulse slowed to a heavy throbbing beat. He relaxed back in the chair, the tension draining from him.

For long minutes, she fed, her body growing warm and full, but still she wanted more. Craved the last drop.

Stop!

She could do this. She had to. While she couldn't kill him, taking too much could seriously incapacitate him. Still, the urge to keep going, to take everything from him, filled her.

No!

I can do this. I am not a killer.

Daisy tightened her hold and forced her jaws open, raised her head, and licked a last drop of blood from the wound on his neck.

Yay!

She'd done it.

She looked up and straight into Fergal's silver eyes. He stood in the doorway, his gaze fixed on her and Devlin. She could read nothing into his expression. Her attention shifted to Rico at his back. He pushed his way past and threw her a grin. "Good girl."

"Thanks, Devlin."

He nodded, blinked a couple of times as if coming awake. "You're getting better at controlling it."

"Yeah, Rico might even let me out in public one day soon."

"Maybe when we get back to Trakis Two. Right now, I have important things to do."

She was guessing important things involving Skylar.

"Me too," Devlin said, getting to his feet and heading over to Saffira. He kissed her lingeringly, and Daisy felt something close to jealousy rise up inside her. She hated that. She didn't begrudge her friends their happiness, but it seemed like everyone had someone. Except for her. Sometimes she longed for someone to hold her. But if she ever got that close, the hunger rose.

It sucked sometimes being a vampire.

Her glance went to Fergal. But he wasn't the answer. Maybe he'd sleep with her, but ultimately, he was a loner. She'd learned that much about him at their last meeting.

Besides, she was hardly perfect girlfriend material.

"Keep an eye on our guest here," Rico said. "I don't want him to have any opportunity to call anyone. Not that I think he will, but to be sure…stick to him. And remember what I said."

"Which bit?"

He didn't go quite so far as to waggle his eyebrows in an exaggerated leer, but near enough.

"Yeah, I remember."

His gaze shot from her to Fergal and back again. "You want to borrow the handcuffs?"

"Thanks, but…no, thanks."

Chapter Five

"Handcuffs?" Fergal asked, strolling across the room, hands shoved in his pockets.

He felt better after the food—his faster metabolism meant he needed more than two normal people, and he'd also managed to slip in his medication. Already he could feel the poisons clearing from his system.

Daisy looked better after her meal, as well.

She was a goddamn vampire. She drank blood.

He should have been repulsed, but he found it an enormous turn-on. Coming into the room and finding her hunched over Devlin Starke, her fangs buried deep in his throat, had sent his own blood straight to his cock.

Fucking crazy.

When she'd looked up and caught him watching, he'd felt like some sort of voyeur, but turned on as all hell.

Starke hadn't been fighting, either. He'd had a sleepy, almost sated look on his face, and no guesses what he was up to now.

Now she was studying him, her lips in a small pout as she

considered her answer. "Rico suggested I tie you up and have sex with you."

The image of him tied to the bed and Daisy riding him hard sent blood straight to his groin.

He shook his head to dispel the picture. "Is that a vampire thing?"

"Sort of. Give me a moment to check the auto-systems and we'll go and rest up for a while. It's been a long day."

"Do vampires sleep?"

"No. But I do get tired, and it recharges me to rest."

She crossed to the big pilot's chair. While she looked tiny in the huge seat, she appeared competent.

"Everything's good," she said after a moment.

He peered around him. "I've never seen a ship like this. Does she work totally on voice control?"

Daisy grinned. "Better than that. She works on mind control. At least for the Collective people. It pisses Rico off that there's something he can't do. She can also be flown on manual, which is good, because she can be tricky. But Devlin keeps her in good condition."

"I can't believe the most wanted man in the universe is hiding away as a ship's engineer." Fergal moved closer so he could see her face while they talked. She had a beautiful face, but her green eyes now held flecks of crimson. "Where did she come from? The ship, I mean."

"Callum had her built."

He went still. "Callum?"

"Callum Meridian. You know, the leader of the universe."

"Ex-leader. He vanished. Just like a whole load of other people."

"He's here. Well, not actually here right now. He's with the captain on Trakis Five, waiting to pull Alex out."

"Callum Meridian has been with you all this time?"

"Not quite. It's complicated, but we sort of went through

this wormhole and lost a few years."

"You went through a wormhole?" His mind was going into overload.

"Saffira is a time-mancer. She can sort of control them, just not very well."

"What the hell is a time-mancer?"

"You'd better ask Saffira. It's complicated."

"I bet." He studied her closely. Was she telling the truth? But why make up something so totally unbelievable?

She grinned. "You don't believe me? I don't blame you. Like I said—it's complicated."

"But the bit about Callum Meridian is true? He's alive? There were all sorts of rumors—most people believe the Church had him assassinated."

"Nope. He's in love with the captain."

He cast his memory back to his visit to the earlier *Blood Hunter*. The captain had been the sort of woman to make an impression—genetically modified with snake DNA.

"She's Collective now as well. Or maybe not Collective, but she's taken the treatment."

"How? The Meridian source was destroyed years ago."

"Another long story." She gave the console one last look and jumped to her feet. "She's good. Come on."

Fergal wondered if she was actually going to try to tie him up and have her evil way with him. Would he let her?

Daisy today was a vastly different proposition from the earlier version. Back then, all she'd wanted from him was simple, straightforward sex. She'd been uncomplicated, carefree, happy even. This Daisy had to be about the most complicated woman he'd ever come across. And her eyes were shadowed. Something bad had happened to her, and it was more than being turned into a vampire.

"What happened to the redhead from the last time I was here?" he asked as she led him across the bridge and into a transporter bubble.

"My room," Daisy commanded. The doors slid closed, and they drifted upward. "You mean Janey? She was murdered by the Church."

"I'm sorry."

Crimson sparks flashed in her eyes, and he had to fight the urge to step back. "*They* will be. Temperance Hatcher will pay the price for Janey."

He went still and then shook off the feeling; Temperance Hatcher was nothing to him. They were welcome to kill the bastard. The bubble opened onto a wide corridor. The whole ship was built on a large scale.

She came to a halt outside a door. "Open."

Her room was big, with a huge bed in the center and not much else. The walls were white and so was the floor, the only color a throw of crimson on the bed. To hide the blood, perhaps?

She turned as he hesitated at the door and raised one arched brow. "I'm not actually going to tie you up. But I do have to keep my eye on you, so you might as well come in and relax."

He stepped through the door, and it glided silently shut behind him. "Why did he suggest it?"

"The sex or the tying up?"

"Both."

"Let me clean up first. I got some of your blood on me back there at the prison. Black clothes are great—they hide the blood—but I find the smell a little...distracting."

"Go ahead. Wouldn't want you distracted."

She disappeared through a second door. Fergal sank down onto the bed and kicked off his shoes. He could do with a cleanup, but he lay back and closed his eyes. Kidnapped by a couple of bloodsucking monsters, and it was actually the first time he'd relaxed in years. The last of the tension drained from his limbs, and he slept.

Fergal opened his eyes. Daisy sat at the top of the bed, her back against the wall, her knees drawn up, and her chin resting on her hands as she watched him. Her hair was loose, a fall of silver around her shoulders. She'd dressed in a black jumpsuit, but her feet were bare.

He pushed himself up and ran a hand through his hair. "I can't believe I fell asleep."

"And in the vampire's lair."

At least she sounded amused. "Yeah. And that. Weren't you tempted to snack on me?"

Her lips curled into a smile. "Not even a little bit."

What the hell did Devlin Starke have that he didn't?

She seemed to read his mind. "Your blood tastes like crap."

"What?"

She wrinkled her nose. "Sort of harsh and metally. Ugh."

Well, it was hardly going to be normal, was it? "So back to the conversation we almost had before I fell asleep—why did Rico suggest you have sex with me?"

"It's a vampire thing. He thinks the best thing to keep the darkness at bay is sex."

"The darkness?"

"Do you always ask this many questions?"

"Yes. Now tell me about this darkness."

She shrugged. "I used to think Rico was just this guy who drank blood. But it's not like that." A visible shiver ran through her, and she rubbed her arms. "I died and came back to life, but I'm not the same. Right in the center of me there's this dark place, and sometimes it tries to crawl up and come out. It's worse when I'm hungry. That's why I try to feed regularly. Anyway, Rico thinks the best way to keep it firmly locked inside is sex."

"And you can't just pick up some guy."

"I'd probably rip out their throats." She sounded so matter-of-fact.

"Why did it happen?"

She shifted on the bed. "I was dying. It was the only way Rico could save me."

"And are you okay with it?"

"Most of the time. I liked being green, though—made me sort of unique."

"It sure did, but so does being a vampire."

"I guess. And there are some good things. I'm super strong, and I get to live forever."

"So Rico suggested you have sex with me because I taste disgusting and you won't be tempted to drain me dry."

"Something like that. Rico said he'd killed hundreds, probably thousands, in his early years, and not all of them on purpose."

"Shit." He frowned. "So what's with the tying up, or is that just personal preference?"

"I don't know. I've never tied anyone up before. But I guess he thought you might try to run away or fight me off."

He studied her across the bed. The jumpsuit was open at the neck, revealing the swell of her breasts. Her legs were long, her hips rounded, and she had the sexiest lips—when she wasn't flashing her fangs—that he had ever seen.

His dick pulsed in his pants, and he savored the feeling. It had been so long since he'd experienced desire for anything but survival. Scary monster or not, he wanted her, and his dick jerked again in agreement. Wanted to push himself deep inside her and forget everything for a while.

"I don't think I'll be running." He watched her face as he spoke. Her eyes widened. "Why so shocked?" he asked.

"You're a beautiful woman."

"I am?"

"You must know it."

She looked away. "I was green. You saw me. It didn't do it for most guys."

He picked up her hand, played with her fingers. "It did it for me."

"You're hardly normal."

"Hey, I'm…normalish. And you're not green now."

She grinned, her eyes flashing. "No, but I've hardly been dating, either. We've been hiding out most of the time since we got back."

"Got back from where?"

"Another long story. I think I intimidate most guys. And I might have messed up one or two people. I'm getting better, but I used to completely lose it. That's why Rico has me feeding from immortals—so I can't kill them."

"Back to the sex thing. It's not as though we haven't done it before, and from what I remember, it was pretty damn good."

"It was."

"So…?" When she didn't say anything else, he released her hand, wrapped his fingers around her ankle, and tugged her down so she lay on her back, her breasts rising and falling rapidly in time with her breathing. Her silver-gilt hair spread out across the crimson cover, and her mouth parted slightly. He could see the tips of her sharp white fangs, and a brief pang of something close to primordial fear jabbed him in the belly. It wasn't as strong as the throbbing of his dick or the ache in his balls, so he ignored it and came up over her.

Balancing on his arms, he lowered his head and put his lips on hers. The briefest of kisses. When she didn't protest, he kissed her again, stroking his tongue along her plump lower lip, dipping inside. For a second, she kissed him back, her tongue flicking against his. She tasted different, but not unpleasant, sweet and coppery, no doubt from the blood she had taken.

Reluctantly, he left her lips, dropping kisses along her jawline, and she moaned low in her throat. She tipped her head back, baring the line of her neck, and he kissed down, lingering on the frantic pulse point before moving even lower. He buried his nose in the V of the jumpsuit and between her breasts, his nostrils filling with the sweet, slightly musky scent of her skin.

Balancing himself on one hand, he used the other to pull down the fastener, baring her to the waist. Her breasts were full, her skin flawless, white with pale pink nipples that puckered under his watchful gaze. The blood shot to his groin, and his balls hurt.

He lowered his head, took one nipple in his mouth and suckled gently. Her back arched beneath him as he increased the pressure, scraping the taut peak with the edge of his teeth. She pushed herself against his mouth, urging him on.

His dick was rock hard now, and he shifted, trying to ease the pressure. Cupping one breast in his palm, he transferred his attentions to the other nipple, licking it slowly, watching as it tightened, darkened to deep red.

She was moving restlessly now, twisting on the scarlet cover, and quite the most erotic thing he had ever seen. He kissed lower, over her flat white belly, pushing the fastener down with his teeth, and burrowing his face in the curls at the junction of her thighs. The clothing prevented him from getting any farther, and he paused for a moment before coming up on his knees beside her. He slipped the jumpsuit down over her shoulders, and she lifted her hips from the bed so he could slide the garment from her and toss it on the floor. It was all she wore, and now she lay naked in front of him. Perfection. Flawless, and his breath hitched. He trailed a finger down from her throat, over the swell of one breast, down the flat plane of her belly, dipping into her navel so she squirmed, and into the silky curls.

The hair was the same silver gilt as on her head. He ruffled his fingers through its softness, and then rubbed one along the line separating her sex. Her thighs fell open, giving him access, and he parted the folds. He found her swollen and wet. He teased a lazy circle around her, flicked her with the tip of his finger, and a shudder ran through her.

"No, stop," she moaned. "I can't—"

"Of course you can. Relax." She was going to come so sweetly for him. He stroked over the nub, increasing the pressure slowly. She'd gone silent and was holding herself very still, a strange tension radiating from her. Pausing, he peered up the line of her body as her eyes fluttered open.

Everything stopped.

They were crimson pools of darkness.

Her nostrils flared.

Something told him to move, get away from her, but he was locked in place. Then it was too late. She reared up, faster than he could have thought possible. Her hands gripped his shoulders, and the momentum knocked them both off the bed, so they crashed to the floor. He landed on his back with a naked woman sprawled on top of him. She came up, hands still hard on his upper arms, and lunged for his throat.

Shock held him still as her teeth ripped into the flesh at his neck, sucking frantically at the vein. Fergal gathered himself to throw her off, but he didn't get the chance. She released her hold, came up on her hands and knees, and threw up.

All over him.

Chapter Six

Daisy crouched on all fours, head hanging like an exhausted dog as she fought the urge to throw up again. But there was nothing left. The contents of her stomach were splattered all over the floor and all over Fergal. The scene looked like something from a slaughterhouse.

He was still on the ground but up on his elbows, regarding her with a wary expression. Who could blame him? She'd lost it completely. If he'd been an ordinary human, he'd be dead.

It had felt so good. As she'd relaxed into the feelings, eased up on her control, something had woken inside her. But by the time she'd recognized the danger, it was too late and the darkness had taken her over, filled her.

Only the foul taste of Fergal's blood had brought her back.

She was naked, a pulse throbbing between her legs.

Crap. Bet he thinks I'm sexy now. Not.

Finally, she sat back on her heels, forced herself to look into Fergal's face. "Sorry." He snorted but didn't speak, and she gave a small shrug. "You probably have naked girls puking on you all the time."

"It's my technique."

He looked so serious, lying in his blood- and vomit-spattered uniform, that a giggle rose up inside her.

His eyes widened as she laughed, but a grin curved his lips, followed by a look of resignation. "Well, that didn't go as planned. You know how long it's been since I was with a naked woman? Too fucking long. Shit, my dick's still hard even after all that."

She glanced down at his groin. Definitely still hard. God, she wanted that erection. Life—or she supposed death in her case—sucked sometimes.

She forced her gaze upward. There was a ragged wound in his neck. "Does that hurt?"

"Hell, yeah. But not as much as my dick right now." He sat up, pushing himself to his feet. "I need to clean up."

"Through there." Nodding toward the bathroom door, she waited until he disappeared before calling one of the cleaner drones. She wrapped the scarlet cover about herself and perched on the bed while it cleared the floor.

Fergal probably thought she was some sort of cross between a lunatic woman and a bloodsucking monster. Rico had warned her that she wasn't the same person. He'd told her that she had to accept what she was.

They were predators, killers.

But this was the first time she had caught a glimpse of what he really meant. Before, when she'd been consumed by the need to feed, it had been as though she was controlled by something outside herself. This time the darkness had awoken, and it was part of her. She craved blood and death.

You're evil. Suck it up and accept it.

Damn it. She didn't want to be evil. In which case, she was screwed.

Rico said she had to come to terms with what she was.

Learn to control it. But she still had a free will. She could choose to resist the bad things eventually, though it would be hard.

Right now, it seemed impossible.

Crap.

Why *had* Rico changed her?

Once, he'd told them that he'd sworn never to change anyone again, and having met his last attempt, she could understand why. But he had gone against his beliefs and changed her.

He should have let her die. Now her life stretched out ahead of her. A constant fight. Alone.

God, she was a miserable bitch.

A tear welled up in her eye. She blinked, and it rolled down her cheek. As she swiped it away, crimson stained the back of her hand. Shit, she couldn't even cry like a normal person anymore.

She hadn't actually cried since it happened. No way was she about to start now. She was tougher than that. She scrubbed at her cheek then thumped the wall beside the bed, leaving a crimson smear.

Damn it.

She'd needed this thing with Fergal.

If only she hadn't tried to eat him.

It hadn't even been so much the sex—well, maybe a little bit. She'd just wanted to feel close to someone for a while. To connect on a level not involving food or being obligated or…

She felt like crap. Her stomach was raw and empty—she'd lost most of the food she'd taken from Devlin—and the occasional spasm tightened the muscles of her gut. She pulled the cover around herself as a shiver ran through her.

Rico's silver flask sat on the small table beside the bed, Fergal must have brought it with him. She grabbed it, unscrewed the top, and took a deep swallow. The liquid warmed her from the inside, and she took another gulp.

Maybe it was bad to lower her inhibitions, but she had an idea that Fergal was safe from her. A shudder ran through her as she remembered the taste of him. Ugh.

She took another drink, the whiskey easing into her brain.

Life was unfair. Or should it be death was unfair?

Whatever.

She drank some more. Pictured the moment she'd thrown up all over Fergal.

"Hey, did you know you've got blood on your face?" Fergal leaned in the bathroom doorway.

She shrugged. "I thought about crying. But don't worry, I changed my mind and decided to have a drink instead."

"Your tears are red?"

"Yeah."

He was naked except for a towel wrapped around his hips. And he was stunning. Broad chest, with the smooth swell of muscles, wide shoulders, sculpted arms. She glanced at the right one, the cybernetic limb, but she couldn't see any difference.

His clothes were in his hand. "Can I get these cleaned? I'll need them tomorrow."

She nodded to the cleaning unit on the far wall, and he crossed the room and shoved the clothes inside. As he stood with his back to her, she could see pale lines crisscrossing from his shoulders to where the towel wrapped around his hips. Old scars, but from where?

He turned, casting her a wary glance, before heading over and frowning down at her. "So why were you thinking about crying?"

She sniffed. "I bet you hate women who cry, don't you?"

"Believe it or not, I don't actually reduce many of them to tears. Wait here." He disappeared into the bathroom, came back a few seconds later carrying another towel. He sank down on the bed beside her and slipped a finger under her chin, raising her head. After studying her for a moment, he slowly wiped the towel over her face. She held herself very still. His hand curved around the back of her skull, and he held her steady, but she wasn't going anywhere. His touch felt so good.

"There, clean," he said, releasing her and sitting back. "You going to think about crying some more?"

She shook her head. "No. That's me finished—monsters don't cry. How's your throat?"

"Hardly hurts at all." He touched a finger to the wound on his neck. It was already knitting together. He healed faster than the Collective. Must be part of the cyborg thing.

"Good."

He dropped his hand from his throat. "So what happened? Why did you decide to bite me?"

"It wasn't actually a conscious decision." She plucked at the cover still wrapped around her. "I lost it. I think I came face-to-face with the darkness Rico keeps going on about. I never really believed him. Not every day you get to meet your own personal monster."

"That what upset you?"

"Maybe. Maybe I'm just due for a good blub and you're lucky enough to be here."

"Yeah. I'm a lucky guy." He tossed the towel on the floor. "Budge up."

She shifted over on the bed, and he sat down beside her, insinuating one arm around her shoulder. "So, I'm guessing sex is out."

She was on a bed with a gorgeous, nearly naked man plastered along her side. Life was so unfair. She exhaled loudly. "You guess right."

He squeezed her shoulder. "Tying me up wouldn't do any

good, but you know what might work?"

She twisted her head so she could see his face. "No."

"Tying *you* up."

She had an image of herself spread-eagle on the bed, her wrists and ankles tied to the corners. Heat flooded her sex, and warmth flushed her face.

"So you like the idea?" he murmured with a grin. "I can see you're thinking about it."

She wrinkled her nose. "No, I'm not."

"Think. You can go all dark and monsterish, and you won't be able to touch me." He leaned in close and whispered in her ear. "I could fuck your brains out and you could do nothing about it."

She stared straight ahead.

"On your back or on your front. Either works for me." He shifted. "Shit, I'm hard again."

She cast him a sideways glance. "You're a brave man to even think of sex after what just happened." But the earlier image was replaced by one of her on her belly, tied to the bed, Fergal crouched between her open thighs.

Fuck.

She bit back a moan.

"Desperate times call for desperate measures," he said. "I want you."

God, she wanted him, too, but really, tying her up wasn't an option right then. "There's one problem with that plan," she said.

"I can't think of one."

"Well, I don't think you're thinking with your head right now," she said, staring at the bulge under the towel wrapped around his hips.

"Probably not. So this problem...?"

"I'm supposed to be keeping an eye on you. Can you imagine the reaction when I tell them you escaped because I was tied to the bed? I'd never live it down."

He pressed his hand to his heart. "You don't trust me? I'm hurt."

His silver eyes gleamed with a mixture of lust and mockery. Did she trust him? Hell, no. Who knew what he was really after? Why had he been undercover in that prison? She doubted he was after a story. So what was he after?

He leaned in closer, close enough to kiss her, and for a second she swayed toward him.

Stop right there.

Swallowing, she forced the words out. "No, I don't trust you."

"Pity." He sat back and ran a hand through his short, damp hair. "Show me some fang."

"What?" She shook her head. "Why?"

"I need to get this hard-on under control. So show me a fang."

"You mean you don't find my teeth sexy? Now *I'm* hurt." But she twisted to face him fully and curled the corner of her upper lip, revealing the tip of one fang. She remembered the feel of the darkness embracing her and felt the humanity bleed from her eyes.

Fergal swallowed. "Okay, job done. Now let's get some rest."

He tugged her down, one arm still wrapped around her, and snuggled her against his side. She lay stiff for a minute.

"Relax," he murmured. "I won't bite."

A small laugh escaped her. "Neither will I."

"Good."

Her head rested on his chest, and soon his breathing evened out as he slept. Daisy breathed in the scent of him, warm man with just a hint of metal, and tried to unwind. But when she closed her eyes, an image flashed in her mind. Fergal lay beneath her, blood dripping from his ripped-out throat, and she relived the moment when the darkness had overwhelmed her, taken control.

More crap.

Tremors shook her body, and she blinked open her eyes to banish the vision. Fergal's nipple was right in front of her nose, and the memory of the darkness was ousted by a flashback to how good it had felt before everything had gone to shit. His mouth on her breasts. His clever fingers working between her thighs. She'd been so close.

Bloody, sodding darkness.

Why couldn't it have waited a few more seconds?

She pulled away gently and rolled over onto her side, pressing her back against him. Staring at the wall, she listened to the steady throb of his heart. Finally the tension seeped out of her limbs, and she relaxed.

Hours later, her comm unit buzzed.

"Meeting on the bridge in ten minutes," Skylar said and switched off. She'd never been one for small talk.

Daisy lay for a minute longer. A sense of unease nagged at her mind and body. Inside she had a new awareness of the darkness coiled and slumbering, but always present. She didn't think she would ever be unaware of it again.

Beside her, Fergal lay motionless, but when she twisted her head to look, his eyes were open, and he was watching her. He stretched his arms above his head. "That's the best night's sleep I've had in years. Thank you."

"Day's," she said. "Day's sleep. It's coming up to night. I can feel it."

"You can? Even in space?"

"Only if we're close to a planet. We're in stationary orbit right now, and the sun is going out of our range." She got out of bed, dragging the crimson cover around her. "Come on, meeting in ten."

She pulled his cleaned uniform out and tossed it to him,

then found herself some clothes. After tugging on black pants, she reached for a black shirt but changed her mind and picked a purple one. Boots and her weapons belt, and she was ready to go.

She felt jumpy, on edge, hungry—she'd lost most of her last meal—but she forced the feelings down. They had a prison to break into, a friend to rescue, and presumably Fergal to say good-bye to. It was going to be a long night.

A pang of regret prodded her in the gut at the thought of leaving Fergal at the prison to continue whatever nefarious plots he was involved in. Would he tell her if she asked nicely? Doubtful.

He didn't trust her. Or any of them.

She didn't trust him, either. But he'd given her what she needed—some human warmth, closeness, a feeling that for however brief a time, she wasn't alone in the world.

And she liked him.

Rico gave her a strange look as they came through the door of the bridge. She tried to keep her eyes blank, but his narrowed, and he sauntered on over.

Searching her face, he pursed his lips. "What happened?"

"Why?"

"Well, let's just say there's a change, but it's not the one I was hoping for."

Rico saw everything. She hated that. "I attacked him, bit him, then threw up all over him."

Rico's lips twitched. "Romantic." He turned to study Fergal, who'd taken a seat away from the others and was watching them both as he ate a bowl of stew they'd picked up on the way down. "So was it his sexual technique or something else?"

She folded her arms and glared. "Actually, I lost it. Totally."

"Tell me."

"We were"—she lifted one shoulder—"taking your advice, and it was okay, until…" She closed her eyes and remembered. "The darkness awoke. And it was hungry, not only for blood but for life. It wanted to drain him dry until the life force was mine."

"It's an amazing feeling," Rico said.

She bit her lip. "I don't want to be a killer."

"Darling, you already are."

"No." She almost stamped her foot. "I haven't killed anyone. And I won't. But it felt so good with Fergal and I relaxed and…it won't happen again."

"Maybe you're the one who should be tied up."

She'd been watching Fergal, now her gaze flashed to Rico's face to see if he was serious. There was nothing to show otherwise. "Fergal suggested that."

"Did he? And you said…?"

"That I doubted anyone would be happy if I allowed the prisoner I was guarding to tie me up."

"Good point. But something to keep in mind for the future. He's obviously willing, and you might even enjoy it."

"Great. I can be a killer or a pervert. What a choice."

"Nothing wrong with a few harmless perversions, but do you need to feed again?"

Actually, she could feel the hunger low down in her belly. But she didn't want anyone else to have to feed her so soon. She shook her head. "I'm good." She hoped it was the truth.

She took the seat beside Fergal. Across from her, Devlin and Saffira sat close together, Saffira's small white dog, Devil, on her lap. Daisy could scent their blood, almost hear it pounding in their veins, taste it on her tongue.

I'm hungry!

Daisy was watching the couple across the room, a dazed, hungry look on her face. As she licked her lips, despite their recent disastrous attempt at sex, blood shot to his groin.

He reached across and squeezed her knee. She blinked, giving a little shake of her head as she dragged her gaze away and turned to him.

"You okay?" Fergal asked.

She gave a quick nod, opened her mouth, but Skylar started speaking and she closed it again.

"We have two options," Skylar said. "We go in using Fergal as a hostage, threaten to kill him if they don't give us Jon, or—"

"Won't work," Fergal interrupted. "They'd let you kill me first."

"You sure of that?" Skylar asked.

"Yup. Zero fucking tolerance. Plus I don't have any friends down there."

"What a surprise," Rico muttered. "Must be your charming nature."

Skylar came to a halt in front of Fergal, hands resting on her hips. "So option two: you go in on your own."

Fergal definitely preferred that idea.

"You say we took you with us as a hostage," Skylar continued, "but dropped you off when we were safely away, or you escaped…whatever."

"I like it so far."

"You get into the control room, turn off the alarms. Let us in."

From their point of view, the plan should work. He wasn't so sure it would suit him. "Might work for you. But it will blow my fucking cover wide open."

She turned those inhuman violet eyes on him, examining him as though he were some vaguely interesting specimen. "And we care about this why?"

Fergal gave his best charming smile. "Because you're caring guys."

She pursed her lips. "I'm sure you can work it so you're left in the clear. You're a resourceful man or someone would have killed you long ago." The implication being he was annoying as hell. "If you're careful, you can wipe the surveillance tapes afterward and we can shoot you so it looks realistic."

He was sure there would be plenty of takers for that job. He considered the plan. She was right. It could work. And it wasn't as though there were a lot of options. "Okay. Then what?"

"We come in. You get the new codes for the maximum-security section. We get Jon out and leave quietly."

The plan sounded fine in theory, but those were the sort that usually went to shit. He searched his mind for alternatives but came up blank. The plan might be crap, but it was his best bet. "When do we do this?"

"Now would be good."

He cast a sideways glance at Daisy. His hand was still on her knee. He liked to touch her. If this worked, he wouldn't see her alone again, wouldn't get to touch her more than this. His chest tightened, and there was a heaviness in his stomach.

Liking people made you weak.

Made you want to keep them safe. Want that over anything else.

And they left you anyway.

Like his mother. The old emotion flooded his body. *Betrayal.* From the one person who was supposed to be on his side. Who'd promised to never leave him.

Daisy turned her head to look at him. A sweet smile curved her lips, and some emotion he didn't want to examine kicked him in the gut.

He snatched back his hand. "Now sounds excellent."

Chapter Seven

Skylar had wired him up so they could listen.

Fergal didn't blame her, but it limited his options. If he said something they didn't like, they would move to plan B, which would involve a full-frontal attack on the prison. And no doubt the first place they would blow was the control room. With him in it.

The guard on the front gate let him in. Fergal said he needed to report to the governor, but the man didn't seem concerned. Apparently, everyone had presumed Fergal was dead and the implication was that nobody had been particularly bothered. Well, he'd known he wasn't popular.

Instead of going to the governor's office, he made his way to the main control room on the ground floor. Through the glass window, he could see two men inside, which was normal. So far, so good. He tapped on the door, and one glanced up, then came over and let him in.

"We thought you were dead."

"Sorry to disappoint," he said, strolling into the room.

"So what happened?"

"They knocked me out, took me as a hostage, but let me go once they were clear of the prison."

"You did good getting the alarm off. We all would have lost our bonuses if they'd succeeded." The thank-you was grudging. "Do you know who they were after?"

"No. But the governor has asked me to review the security tapes for clues, jog my memory, see if I can remember anything else."

"Nothing much to see. Just you being taken down by some little girl."

"I was shot." His eyes narrowed; he couldn't believe he'd risen to the gibe. "Well?"

"Help yourself." The guard nodded to the console behind them and sat down again.

Fergal pulled the laser pistol from where it was tucked under his shirt and glanced down to check it was set to stun. He shot the first guard in the back of the head and the second before he even had time to move. Turning back to the console, he pulled up the surveillance and wiped the last few minutes before disconnecting.

When this was over, he'd come back here and one of the *Blood Hunter* crew would be kind enough to shoot him in the head to look like they were all shot at the same time.

If all went well.

And his gut feeling told him it would.

Next, he disarmed the alarms and unlocked the rear entrance to the prison. "You can come in now."

He started working on the codes. Five minutes later, he had them. He'd always been good with computers—it was how he'd been so successful at going undercover—but these days they talked to him, spilling their secrets with the minimum of effort.

A tap came at the door, and he glanced up as Rico peered through the glass window. He hurried across and let them in.

Daisy gave him a quick grin, but he ignored it along with the hurt expression that followed.

"Are we good?" Skylar asked.

"Yeah. Just need to check the maximum-security section."

He went back to the console and tapped in a few codes, pulling off the wire from under his shirt and handing it to Skylar as he worked. "Shit."

"What is it?"

"Your friend is scheduled for execution."

"When?"

"Now."

"*Dios.*" Rico scowled. "We need to contact Tannis, tell her to get Alex out of there immediately."

Skylar nodded. "I'll do it. I'll get Callum—he's clearer at this distance."

"Do it on the way," Rico said. "We're moving now." He turned to Fergal. "Take us there."

Fergal hesitated. If they interrupted the execution, chances were his cover was blown.

"Move," Rico snarled.

The order put his back up. He was pissed off with assholes telling him what to do. He stiffened. As he locked eyes on the vampire, his hand tightened on the pistol at his waist.

"Please, Fergal," Daisy said. "He's our friend."

Her words broke the tension, and he forced his muscles to relax. Truth was, he couldn't stand by and see an innocent man executed. He gave her a quick nod and whirled around. He left the room at a run, the others close behind him, and headed down toward the maximum-security section. A guard stood at the door. Rico drew his pistol and shot the man without slowing.

Fergal punched in the code and pushed open the heavy doors. All the executions were carried out in room C, away from the cells. A narrow, bare stone corridor led deep below the ground, and he headed down there.

"You get through?" he heard Rico ask.

"Yes," Skylar said. "They're going in now. You think they mean to kill Alex?"

"Why else would they execute Jon at this point? Because they don't need him anymore. How much fucking farther?"

"We're there."

Fergal skidded to a halt outside a black door.

He paused before he pushed it open. If he hung back, maybe there was still a chance he'd get away with this. "There'll be the governor, a priest, and two guards."

Rico gave a curt nod. "I'll go in with Devlin. Skylar, you stay out here and listen for Tannis. Daisy, keep an eye out for incoming."

Devlin moved up to stand beside him. Rico kicked out, and the door gave way. They were shooting as it opened. After thirty seconds, all went silent, and Fergal peered through the doorway. The guards and governor were down. Stunned or dead, he didn't know. The priest remained upright, but not for long. Devlin shot him in the head, and he crumpled to the stone floor.

The tall dark-haired prisoner stood chained to the wall, still alive but with a slightly dazed look on his face. The priest clutched the full needle, so he hadn't yet administered the lethal injection, though the oven behind him was already stoked, and sweat beaded the prisoner's forehead.

"Alex?" he asked, and Fergal could hear the tension in his voice.

"They're pulling her out now," Rico replied. "Skylar, what's happening?"

"Wait a second." She was silent for a moment. Fergal's back itched. He needed them out of here before reinforcements arrived. There was still a chance.

Skylar grinned. "Tannis has her. She was at the church,

so they pulled her straight out. They're heading back to the shuttle, but no one's after them."

"Thank Christ." The tall man—Jon—sagged against the chains that held him. He closed his eyes for a moment. When he opened them, they gleamed feral. "I'm going to rip that fucker Hatcher's throat out."

"Get in line," Rico said.

Narrowed golden eyes turned on the vampire. "Well, it took you fucking long enough," he said. "Twenty fucking years. Where the fuck have you been?"

Rico grinned. "It's a long story."

There were a lot of long stories about. And one day, Fergal would really like to hear them. Just not now. "Can we move this along?" he suggested.

Golden eyes turned on him, filled with savage intent. Where had he seen eyes like that before?

Jon's nostrils flared, and he breathed in, his gaze running over Fergal's uniform. "Why is he alive?" he snarled.

"He got us in here," Rico said. "So it would have been a little ungrateful to kill him. Jon, meet, Fergal Cain, journalist and…actually, I'm really not sure what else." He studied Jon for a moment. "You want to hold yourself away from the wall and I'll shoot those chains off?"

"Or how about I unlock them," Skylar suggested. She was crouched down beside one of the guards; now she straightened and waved a key in their direction. Crossing the small space to Jon, she unlocked the cuffs about his wrists. They dropped away, and he rubbed the reddened skin. "She's really safe?"

"Really."

"Shit." He closed his eyes, ran a hand through his shoulder-length hair. "I could have shifted, escaped, but not while they had Alex." He looked around. "It's been a long time. I need…"

"Go ahead," Rico said.

Jon dragged the T-shirt over his head. His feet were bare, and when he kicked his pants off, he was naked. The move took Fergal by surprise. He glanced around, but no one else appeared to find it odd.

A ripple ran through the man. Fergal stood, his mouth hanging open, as Jon dropped to all fours and a change flowed over him. One moment a man, the next a huge shaggy black…dog? As tall as Fergal's shoulder.

"What the fuck…"

"Did we forget to mention he's a werewolf?"

"Shit. Yeah—I think I would have remembered."

The great beast stretched, then raised its head and howled. The sound filled the room, echoing off the walls.

"Right," Rico said. "You might want to cut that out." The howl was cut short. "Okay, we're out of here." He turned to Fergal. "You still plan on staying?"

He hesitated, but only for a second. He wouldn't last much longer without finding Stefan. He really did have no choice. "Yeah. If we can go back via the control room. And if one of you would be so kind as to shoot me."

"My pleasure." Rico headed to the door and peered out. "All clear?"

"Nothing moving yet," Daisy replied.

That couldn't hold out for long. "Let's go."

"Wait a minute," Skylar said.

"What is it?" Rico came back toward her. "Have you heard something?"

"Yes, but not from Tannis or Callum." She turned to Fergal. "The other political prisoner—is he Collective?"

"Yes. So?" He glanced at the door. They needed to move now.

But Skylar turned to Rico. "It's the colonel."

"Your old boss? The head of the Corps?" She nodded.

"And that's a problem why?"

Her eyes narrowed. "We need to get him out, Rico."

"We do?" But Rico sounded resigned.

"He's a good man," Skylar said. "And besides, he's Callum's friend. You know he's been looking for him."

"You sure it's him?"

"Yes, the signal is weak. They must have him drugged, which is why Callum's never picked him up, but it's definitely him."

"Okay."

"Not okay," Fergal said, taking a step toward Rico. "You need to get out of here now. I signed on to get one person out of here. Not two."

A low growl came from the wolf. Its upper lip curled, showing fangs that rivaled even Rico's and Daisy's.

"You don't mean that, Fergal. You really don't want to upset Jon."

"Goddamn it." He didn't give a toss if he upset Jon, but maybe they could rescue this guy and still get out. He snorted. Of course they could. Why not rescue the whole fucking prison while they were at it? "You three head up to the control room." He waved a hand to encompass, Rico, Devlin, and the wolf. "I'll take her"—he nodded at Skylar—"and go get her friend. Then you shoot me and you're out of here."

"Sounds like a plan."

As he stalked out of the room, Daisy turned from where she'd been watching the corridor. "What's happening?"

"Skylar wants to rescue someone else," Rico said.

"She does?"

"Fergal's taking her. We'll meet you above ground."

"I'll go with them. Watch their backs."

Rico studied her for a second. "Okay."

"Let's go," Fergal said, frustration clawing at him. His good feeling had evaporated, replaced by a very bad feeling.

Beside him, Skylar still had her pistol drawn and he had the distinct impression she'd be quite happy to use it on him. Shit, she'd been Corps. He hadn't known that. The Corps had been the Collective's own private army, drawn from the Collective itself, ruthless, highly trained, and virtually indestructible. She wouldn't hesitate to shoot him.

Once again, he had no fucking choice. And he was getting sick of not having options.

He led them to the lower level control room to access the codes to open the cell. Daisy waited in the doorway, keeping an eye out, but Skylar stood at his back, and he could sense her tapping her foot behind him. "Do you mind stopping that?" he snarled. "I'm trying to concentrate."

Finally, he had the codes, and they headed down to the cell. He tapped the panel next to the door. If they were wrong, they were fucked, because he was out of ideas. But the door slid open.

He stepped back to allow Skylar to enter, and Daisy came up beside him.

"Thank you," she said.

"For nothing," he replied. "It's not as though I have a lot of choice."

"You have to help your friends," she said. "If not, what's any of it worth?"

"I don't have friends."

She rested a hand on his arm. "You have me."

For long moments, he gazed down into her eyes. "You don't want to be my friend. I'm trouble."

"Maybe I like trouble. And hey, I'm a vampire, I can deal with trouble." She went still and sniffed the air.

"What is it?" Fergal asked.

"Blood." She shook her head. "People coming. Skylar, we have company."

Inside the cell, Skylar was crouched beside the slumped

man. She glanced up at Daisy's words, nodded and spoke quietly to him.

"I'm okay," he mumbled. "I can make it." He staggered to his feet, swayed, but then straightened. "Let's get out of here."

"Great idea." The thud of booted feet was growing louder by the second. They'd never make it.

Skylar supported the prisoner across the cell. It was obvious they weren't capable of moving fast. Beside him, Daisy drew her laser pistol. "You go ahead. I'll hold them off."

"Alone?"

She cast him a grin. "There are only five of them, Fergal. I can manage."

"Give us ten minutes," Skylar said to her. "Then meet us at the control room as planned.

He took a step after Skylar and stopped.

Shit.

What was he—a fucking savior of the world? These weren't his people. They'd kidnapped him and coerced him into this. He owed them nothing. Then he had a flashback to waking up in Daisy's arms. Her softness.

Fuck!

He gritted his teeth and turned back. "I'll stay."

A grin tugged up the corner of her lips.

"Ten minutes," Skylar said. "No longer. Or we'll be coming back. And comm if you have a problem."

Daisy nodded. "We will. Now go."

Skylar disappeared around the corner, supporting the colonel with one arm around his shoulder. Fergal turned back to Daisy, where she stood close to the wall peering around the corner. "Here they come." She stretched out her arm and shot a continuous burst of laser toward the oncoming guards. A loud crash reverberated down the corridor as one hit the ground, and then they were shooting back.

The scents of scorched flesh and fresh blood filled the

air. Beside him, Daisy went still. She sniffed, and a glazed expression slid down over her eyes. Her lip curled, and her tongue stroked over one sharp white fang.

He'd seen that expression before. Last night, just before she'd jumped on him and tried to rip out his throat.

Shit, this wasn't good.

Should he grab her? But that would leave neither of them able to shoot. Before he could decide, an alarm sounded. They must have the systems up and running.

Not good suddenly turned to *fucking catastrophic.*

Then the long continuous shrill changed to a pulsated ring. And things got even worse.

"Daisy!" he yelled. "We have to get out of here."

She ignored him. All her attention focused on the group of men crouching ahead. They knew what the alarm meant. After shooting off a couple of blasts, they were up and running in the opposite direction.

He had about two minutes to get Daisy out.

There was one other way. They might make it. Except Daisy wasn't paying any attention to him. He was about to grab her arm when she leaped forward. She flew through the air, slamming into the man at the back of the small group. As he crashed to the floor, the rest didn't even look around.

"Daisy!"

Wrenching back the man's head, she lunged for his throat, and blood sprayed from a severed artery. She swallowed frantically until the man was no longer struggling, just the occasional jerk from his feet.

"Shit." Fergal couldn't look away.

Finally, she glanced across at him, her eyes glowing red. Crimson covered her chin, and she swiped it away with the back of her hand.

He hurried across, grabbed her arm, and pulled her to her feet. She tried to look back, but he hauled her after him.

They weren't going to make it.

Almost there, but as they reached the final intersection, the steel shutters slid down from the ceiling, blocking the way out. All around him, he heard the *clang* as they were cut off. The whole of the maximum-security section was sealed, and any second now, gas would be released.

Final protocol in the event of a break-in.

He lifted Daisy's arm—she was still almost totally unresponsive—and pressed the comm unit on her wrist. "Skylar? You out of here?"

"Yeah, I'm back at the control center with the others. What's going on?"

"We're sealed inside. Get out of here. I'll get Daisy out another way."

"Can you do that? We have explosives—we can blow the place."

"No. They're going release gas any moment. The whole place will blow."

"Cain." Rico's voice.

"Yeah."

"Get her out of there or we'll find you."

"Go fuck yourself." He switched off the comm unit and turned to Daisy. A little awareness seemed to have slipped back into her expression. And she didn't look happy.

"I killed someone."

"You sure did."

"You could lie and tell me he might live."

"With half his throat gone, I don't think so. But right now we have bigger problems. Any moment they're going to release poisonous gas. It might not kill either of us, but it will most likely knock us out, and I don't think you want the Church getting hold of you—I'm thinking they might consider you a little…"

"Evil?" she said in a small voice. "They referred to Rico

as son of Satan. That makes me…"

"Dead if we don't get out of here. And then your protector will hunt me down and make my life miserable. You can wallow in self-pity when we're out."

She stuck out her lower lip, and he was pretty sure she was going to wallow some more, but instead, she drew back her shoulders. "What do we do?"

He looked around. They were in a tunnel, one side—the side heading up to ground level—blocked off by the steel shutter. And he was betting what guards were left would be securing the main exit. So there wasn't much point in heading that way.

He cast his mind back to the plans of the place.

"Come on." He grabbed her arm again and ran back the way they had come, down another tunnel, and into the cell they had taken Skylar's friend from.

He stood for a moment orienting himself. If he was correct, on the other side of the wall should be the older section of the place, bricked off when the prison was built.

"What are we doing?" Daisy asked.

At least she sounded vaguely normal, but a quick glance showed that while most of the blood was gone from her face, her whole body was tense.

"There should be an old tunnel, not part of the prison, behind that wall. We get into that and it should lead us out without banging into the welcome party I'm sure is waiting for us."

"So all we have to do is get through that wall. No problem then."

He was glad to hear the sarcasm in her voice. It proved she really was getting back to normal. "Watch and admire," he murmured.

Chapter Eight

Oh God, I killed a man.

His blood sang in her body, buzzed in her brain.

The exhilaration of that last draw of blood, when his life force had become hers, thrummed through her body. Rico was right. There was nothing to compare.

But I killed a man.

She'd been clinging to the dream that she wasn't a killer. Now she could never go back. Though maybe she wouldn't get the chance anyway.

They were in a small cell about nine feet by nine feet with bare stone walls. Solid walls. How the hell did Fergal think he was going to get them out of here? Had he led her to a dead end on purpose?

Already, the gas hung heavy and acrid on the air, drifting around them, tendrils tugging at her consciousness. Would this be the last she would see? Would they stake her before she awoke?

She searched Fergal's face for any sign of a plan. One eyebrow lifted, as though he sensed her skepticism. He raised his right arm between them. For a second nothing happened. Then silver ran over his skin, seeping from beneath his shirtsleeve, flowing over his hand, encasing his fingers in metal. The hand formed a fist, and the fingers fused.

He stepped toward the far wall, raised the fist, and smashed it into the stone at shoulder level. Dust flew, but nothing much else happened. He stared for a second, raised the arm again, and the fist flowed into a point. This time when he punched the wall, the point sank in.

He yanked it free, tearing stone, and punched twice more.

Daisy coughed, trying to clear her airways, but the gas was thickening, clogging her lungs, fogging her mind.

Fergal's hand shifted to hook shaped, and he dragged the stones from the hole, enlarging it. Sweat gleamed on his forehead, but he didn't slow until there was a hole big enough for a person to squeeze through.

Clean air flowed into the room, and her brain cleared, relief washing over her. "That was impressive," Daisy said, admiring his appendage. "Can you make that thing any shape you like?"

He cast her a grin. "As long as it's the same overall size, then yeah."

"Cool."

"It is. Come on, let's get the fuck out of here."

He waved a hand to the gap, and Daisy stepped up and then sideways to squeeze through. She found herself in another tunnel. The air was a little stale but clear of gas, and she breathed deeply. There was no light apart from what came through from the cell, but she could make out a passage leading in two directions, one heading up, presumably toward ground level, and the other down.

Fergal swore as he squeezed through the small gap, his shirt tearing on the sharp stones. He grabbed her hand as soon as he was through and headed off up toward the surface, pulling her behind him.

Soon they were in total darkness. Daisy's vision had improved since she'd been changed—vampires needed to be able to see in the night—but even she couldn't penetrate the stygian darkness.

Fergal slowed to a walk. "Put your hand out. Feel the wall. We're looking for a turnoff to the left. If we keep in this tunnel, it will take us up to the main prison, and we don't want to be there right now."

She stretched out her arm until her fingertips brushed the rough stone of the wall, keeping the contact as they walked, slowly now.

The dark didn't frighten her, but she could feel the weight of the rock above her pressing her down. She squeezed Fergal's hand and held on tight. Finally, the wall at her fingertips vanished, and she halted. "Here."

They entered the new tunnel. This climbed more steeply and eventually the darkness eased until she could make out the cobbled floor and the stone walls on either side. At the end of the tunnel was an iron grille with an old-fashioned padlock. Fergal drew his laser pistol and shot out the lock then kicked down the grille. The other side was overgrown with vegetation, but he pushed through and she followed, the branches stinging the skin of her face. Finally, they were through and into the clear air.

A moon hung lazily in the sky.

She was alive. Well, sort of. Unlike the man she had killed.

Who had he been? Good? Bad? Did he have children, people who loved him and would miss him?

"Stop thinking," Fergal said from behind her. "We're not out of this yet."

"Where are we?" she asked.

"Around the side of the main building."

"It's lucky you knew about the tunnel."

"Not lucky. It occurred to me that I might need a quick way out one day, so I studied the plans. This was used by the Church, but closed off when the place was turned into a prison."

If she listened hard, she could hear a general commotion far off to the right somewhere. The noise of a shuttle engine rose above it. One appeared above them and headed into space. Then another.

Her comm buzzed, and she raised it. "Yes?"

"It's Skylar. Are you two okay?"

"We're outside the prison."

"Can you lie low for a while? We have someone on our tail right now. We need to lose them before we head back to *The Blood Hunter*."

Fergal spoke. "Don't worry—just get away from here. We'll follow you."

"You will?" Skylar sounded skeptical.

"Well, you managed to fuck up my cover, so there's not much point in me hanging around. I have a shuttle stashed for emergencies. We'll take that."

Skylar was silent for a moment, or she'd switched off the comm while she consulted someone else—probably Rico. "Okay. Daisy knows where to rendezvous with us. We'll see you soon. And Rico says remember what he said and bring her back safe. Just a minute…" She went quiet again. When she came back, her voice held a hint of amusement. "He says ropes won't hold her, metal cuffs are best in his experience."

Daisy snatched her arm away. "Piss off," she said and closed off the comm.

They needed to keep moving, because if she stopped she'd have to start thinking again. That wasn't a good idea until she was somewhere safe and quiet and preferably where she could be alone. Because she had a weird notion she was going to crack and break. Then she'd have to put herself back together again. She'd already nearly cried in front of Fergal once, and she didn't want to do it again—properly this time. It would not be pretty.

"You okay?" he asked.

"Yeah." She hesitated. "The man I killed—did you know him?"

"As well as I knew any of the guards."

"What was he like?"

Fergal considered her, his head cocked to one side. "A complete and utter bastard—used to torture helpless prisoners, probably puppies and kittens as well." Her eyes narrowed on him, and he shrugged. "What do you want me to say? He was just a guy, no better, no worse than a whole load of others. But you really don't want to know him. Stop torturing yourself. He's dead and you're alive."

She gave a rueful smile. "Sort of alive."

"Yeah, sort of. Now let's get out of here. You can have a breakdown once we're away."

"I will not break down."

He definitely looked doubtful. "Good."

"Where is this shuttle? And what sort of range does it have?"

"She's a couple of miles away. And she should be good for anywhere in the system. If you want to go farther out, we'll have to find something bigger."

"No, that will work." She considered telling him where they were headed, but she wasn't quite sure she trusted him yet. Though the fact was, he didn't have to take her anywhere. He could dump her here, fly off without her, and get on with his own business. Whatever that was.

He hadn't needed to tell Skylar he would take her. He could have let them organize something else. They wouldn't have left her here. They never left crew behind. It was an unwritten rule. But perhaps Fergal didn't know that.

Should she ask him why?

Did she really want to know?

Maybe it was better to wait until they were away from this place before she started with the interrogation. Once in space, he was unlikely to dump her out the air lock, but he might still leave her here if she annoyed him enough.

"Thanks for getting me out," she said. "You could have left me when I went all bloodsucking monster in there."

"I thought about it."

"Not for very long."

"I'm no hero, but even I can't sleep with a girl one night and leave her to die the next."

"We didn't exactly sleep together."

He raised an eyebrow. "Actually, that's all we did."

He set off walking, and she followed. The track was narrow and overgrown, and she stayed behind him, which was no hardship. Fergal Cain had a great ass. She watched it as an alternative to thinking.

His metal arm had returned to normal. That had been seriously impressive. Last time they'd met, he'd told her that he was only beginning the changes, and that Cybercom was doing some real advanced stuff involving cybernetics and the combination of man and metal. How else had he changed?

He was super strong.

She was pretty sure from what she had seen that his brain was far from normal, and he could commune with computers almost as if he was one himself. He tried to hide it, but she'd spent enough time trying to dig out intel since Janey died to know that what he did was in no way normal.

They would have a couple of days to make it back to Trakis Two—more if the shuttle was old and slow. Maybe he would open up a little then.

The shuttle stood in a clearing surrounded by thick vegetation. Obviously old, but solid and big—she'd carry ten people with ease. Inside, she had a food dispenser and a small bathroom off the single cabin. Two seats faced the console with a further eight around the edges. And a couple of bunk beds built into the wall.

"Can you fly this thing?" he asked.

She glanced at him. "Can't you?"

"In theory. But I've never actually tried. I paid some smugglers to get it here."

Maybe that was why he had brought her along. The thought sent a pang of something—disappointment, maybe—running through her. "I can fly anything." While she'd never flown one of these models before, it was close enough to the old *Blood Hunter* shuttles not to be a problem.

She sat in the pilot's seat and flicked on the engines.

"Are you okay now?" he asked, taking the seat beside her.

"I guess." She wasn't totally convinced. She'd killed someone, but she was doing her best not to think about it until they were both out of danger.

"Not going to go all scary monster on me again?"

She closed her eyes and found the darkness sleeping, and for once, the hunger wasn't clamoring to be fed. Her body was satisfied, more so than in a long time, probably since before Rico had changed her.

Guilt flickered across her mind.

She'd killed and she felt good. That seemed totally wrong, but she had a flashback to the sensation of the life force flowing into her and residual pleasure bathed her whole body in warmth.

"Daisy?"

She blinked. "Sorry. No, I'm good. I'll be fine. Strap yourself in—this might get bumpy until I get the feel of her."

She strapped her own harness and waited until Fergal was ready in the seat beside her before switching on the main thrusters. They rose smoothly. Leaning across, she hit the switch to turn on the external monitors. The planet was below them now, and she could see the clearing where they had taken off. All was quiet.

As she hit the boosters, they shot off, heading for space, and the same sense of exhilaration filled her that always took hold when she flew. Right from the first time, she had loved flying. She'd made Rico's life a misery badgering him to let her take the controls. It was a wonder he hadn't snapped and bitten her head off. Finally, Tannis had suggested that it might be useful to have a copilot on board, just in case anything happened to Rico—something Tannis considered likely with his innate ability to piss people off—and her life had been complete. She would have been happy with that life forever, but everything had changed when Skylar had come on board. She'd made them an offer they couldn't refuse, setting in motion the events that had resulted in Janey's death and everything else that had happened.

Daisy didn't blame Skylar, though, and she was glad that Rico had found someone. They were perfect for each other. Maybe if she survived sixteen hundred years she'd find someone. By then she'd have the control not to rip their heads off while they were making out. And they'd love her enough not to be put off by the whole scary monster thing. But that was way off in the future. With a sigh, she cast a sideways glance at Fergal. He was slumped low in his seat, rubbing at a spot on his forehead, his eyes closed.

"How about you?" she asked. "Are you okay?"

He turned to her, and his eyes opened. "No."

The answer took her by surprise. "No?"

He rubbed a hand through his hair. "There's something I need to do. I'm not going to explain what right now. But it doesn't involve you or your friends, and it's better you don't know."

"Mysterious," she muttered.

"Yeah, I'm good at that. Anyway, I just got a whole lot farther away from doing it."

"Sorry."

"Don't be. It was my decision. And for once, I did have a choice."

"Are you regretting it?"

"Not yet. I'm telling you this because I can't stay with you. I take you to this rendezvous and then I need to be out of there."

"Don't worry. I'm not the clingy sort." But she couldn't deny the pang of loss that shivered through her. She didn't want him to go.

This thing with him was new, but the truth was she'd fancied him from the first time she'd seen him all those months ago on the old *Blood Hunter*. She'd wanted him back then. Hell, she'd had him back then and the memory had sustained her for a long time afterward.

No, she didn't want him to go. But she had no way to keep him, and no right. She was a monster with nothing to offer a man right now. Better to accept that.

"What happens if you don't do this…mysterious thing you have to do?" She studied his face while she waited for an answer. He sat back in his seat, and his brows drew together. Was he deciding what to tell her? At least he was thinking about it and not shutting her out.

"The truth? I don't know. But nothing good."

"And if you do this thing, you'll be okay?"

He turned his head and gave her a wry grin. "Again—I don't know."

"Well, that's honest anyway." She took a deep breath. "The rendezvous is on Trakis Two."

"The planet that never sleeps. So how long to get there?"

She checked the monitors. "About thirty hours, give or take."

He cast her a long, slow look, his gaze drifting down over her body, so heat flushed her skin. "Thirty hours locked in a small room with a bloodsucking monster," he murmured.

She swallowed her rising excitement. "Well, I think we've already decided your blood is safe."

"Hmm. I don't suppose you suck anything else?"

She snorted. "I haven't actually risked it."

"Can you set to autopilot?"

Something hot stirred in her belly. He was a brave man to be willing to try again after she'd nearly ripped his throat out, but a sideways glance told her he was watching her out of sleepy eyes. She dropped her gaze lower and saw the bulge in his pants. When she looked back at his face, a rueful smile curved his lips. "There's something about danger that makes my dick hard."

"Really?" She swallowed again and reached across, her fingers almost fumbling as she set the coordinates and checked again that there was nothing behind them. Likely any available ships were following Rico. They were alone in the vastness of space.

Sitting back, she tried to ignore the fluttering in her belly, the wetness between her thighs. While she wanted this desperately, she didn't want to hurt him again. She bit her lip and turned to him. "You sure you want to risk it again?"

His gaze dropped down over her, lingering on her breasts, where her nipples pressed urgently against her shirt. "Sweetheart, I don't plan on there being any risk involved."

Suddenly she struggled to get enough air into her lungs. "You don't?"

"Strangely, I don't have any cuffs on board—I'll have to remember to pack them next time—but I'm sure we can come up with something that will do the job."

"The job?" Her voice was breathy.

Would she really let herself be tied up? Put herself totally in his power? Last time she'd been worried he would escape. This time he had nowhere to go.

Heat flooded her sex.

"I'm going to tie you up and fuck you until there's no room inside you for any darkness. No room for anything but me."

"You think you can do that?"

He gave a smirk. "Oh, yeah."

She chewed on her lip.

"You're thinking too much. Wouldn't you like to stop thinking for a while?" He gave another rueful smile. "I know I would."

For a second, she caught a brief glimpse into his mind. Saw a loneliness bordering on despair. She'd felt alone for six months, and it was hard. Fergal had been alone for much longer. What had made him cut himself off so completely? She suspected it went back way before Cybercom.

And she could help him. If only for a little while. It was that thought, more than the blood thundering in her veins, throbbing between her thighs, that made up her mind. She gave a quick nod, and the tension drained from him.

"Good, because I'm about to explode here."

"You are?"

He unfastened his harness, reached across and took her hand in his. Drawing her closer, he pressed her palm to his groin so she could feel the steely hardness of his erection.

"It's like an unstable laser pistol, likely to go off at any second."

"I hope not. That would be a...waste." She gave him a squeeze. If anything, he got harder. Like...metal. "Hey, you can't do that thing"—she waved at his arm—"you know...

turn other bits of your body into metal?"

He grinned. "No. Just the arm, and that's because it *is* metal."

"Oh."

"Don't sound so disappointed. Believe me, it will be hard enough."

He gave a tug on her hand to pull her into his lap, but she was still harnessed into her seat. He dropped her hand and rose to his feet, to stand staring down at her through those strange silver eyes. She squirmed in the seat. "You know, I actually like you all tied up." Reaching down, he tweaked the strap. "I don't suppose these would hold?"

She shook her head. She was pretty sure she could snap through the harness straps if she put her mind to it.

"Pity."

He turned away and crossed to a cabinet on the wall, riffled through the contents, tossing stuff onto the floor. Finally, he made a triumphant, "Yes!" and turned back to her. "Tow cable. Guaranteed not to give under the most arduous of conditions." He held a roll of thick cable in his hand. Flexible but strong, she knew it would hold her. Her heart rate picked up. This was going to happen. Her legs trembled as she pushed herself to her feet.

"You want this now?" He waved the roll, and she knew he meant did she want him to tie her up now. "Or you want to play a bit first?"

She shook her head. Excitement was bubbling up inside her. She was holding it under tight control because beneath the excitement she could sense the darkness stirring sleepily, as if to say, *what's going on?*

"Now."

Chapter Nine

Fergal grinned. "Shit. I've been thinking about tying you up ever since you first mentioned it."

"Is that why you saved me back there?"

His grin widened. "I'm not that shallow." He looked around the room. "Hmm, lying down or standing? Standing, I think." His eyes lit on something behind her, and she turned to follow his gaze.

"Come here," he said.

She took the three steps to close the space between them, licked her dry lips.

"Did you know there are little red flecks in your eyes?" he asked.

No, she didn't, but she sensed the darkness awakening. "Better hurry up then."

"Hold out your hands."

Palms pressed together, she held them out as he wrapped the end of the cable around her wrists, looping it a couple of times. She wriggled her fingers. The cable was smooth and thick enough not to cut into her skin even if she struggled.

His gaze drifted from his handiwork to her face, and she curled her lip, revealing a fang—just to remind him exactly what she was. She didn't want him too complacent.

"Fuck," he murmured. "I think maybe this time we're going to play it safe. Turn around."

A frown tugged at her mouth. She wanted to look at him while he made love to her, but she saw the sense of it. There was no way she could bite him if he was behind her.

She turned, and he looped the cable over a metal bar that ran around the room above her head. As he pulled on the cable, her arms were raised. He tied it off.

"How does that feel?"

Daisy pulled at her wrists; she was held firm. "Good. What next?"

He chuckled. "You sound eager."

Throbbing and eager, she ached with the need to have him inside her. At the same time, the darkness was rising. For a few seconds, she fought it. But wasn't that the whole point of this exercise? She could relax her hold on the stupid darkness, and it wouldn't be able to do any harm to anyone while she was tethered like this. Taking a deep breath, she loosened the tight grip on her control. Immediately, the choking sensation eased; the darkness seemed to relax and accept her. Maybe that's what Rico had meant. Only by relaxing her control could she come to terms with what was inside her, learn to live with and accept it.

She reached deeper inside herself, trying to understand this new thing, and she found it wasn't separate after all, but a part of her. And there was no sense of evil. She'd stood before evil, and this wasn't the same. While maybe without conscience, it wasn't intrinsically bad. And it had wants and needs. She had a brief flashback to the guard's dying moment, and the darkness sighed inside her.

"Daisy?"

Fergal's voice pulled her out of her internal contemplations. She twisted her head so she could see him at her side.

"You still with us?" he asked.

She nodded. "I'm good." She tugged at her wrists. "I think you're safe to go."

"Relax then."

"You're joking. I'm so keyed up, I'm about to self-combust."

"Well, let's see if we can make that happen."

He stepped back, and she strained to see what he was up to. He studied her for a moment, a frown forming between his brows. "Perhaps we should have done a little prebinding preparation. Sorry about this…" His hands slipped into the neckline of her T-shirt, and he ripped it down her back.

"Hey, that was a present."

"I'll buy you another." His palms slid around under the tattered edges and cupped her breasts, and she didn't care anymore. He rubbed, and her nipples stiffened. As he tweaked them between his fingers and thumb, pleasure shot to her groin.

Her gums ached, but she ignored the feeling, concentrated on Fergal's hands massaging her breasts.

Then they were gone.

And back, to slide down over her stomach, inching inside the waistband of her pants, tugging them over her ass and her hips, down her legs. Kneeling beside her, he pulled off her boots one by one and yanked her pants the rest of the way, and she was naked but for the tatters of her T-shirt.

She closed her eyes, rested her head against her arms. The darkness was wide-awake, so powerful she instinctively fought the sensation.

"You're tensing up again," Fergal murmured. "Let it go. You can't hurt me. Just be whatever you want to be."

She released the breath she was holding and sagged

against the bonds. With an effort of will, she relaxed her mind. Fergal was on his knees behind her now. He leaned in close and his warm breath feathered against the skin of her ass, sending frissons shivering through her.

"That is so, so pretty." His lips touched her, kissing lightly over the swell of one buttock and down to her thigh.

At the same time, his hands moved to her hips, and he shifted her back slightly, spreading her thighs so she could feel the cool air against her sex. He kissed her again, this time on the inside of her thigh, then his tongue glided upward, hot and wet.

His palms massaged her buttocks, alternately squeezing and releasing so her hips jerked in time with his ministrations. She was holding her breath again, waiting for him to touch her where she needed him the most.

"Slow down," he whispered against her skin. "We have two days."

"Fergal…" Her tone held an obvious warning, but he chose to ignore it. Instead of moving higher where she needed him, his mouth trailed down her legs to lick the back of her knees, and she moaned.

"You asked me to do that last time," he said. "Now, to the good bit."

He burrowed his face between her legs and nuzzled her right where a pulse was beating between her thighs. With gentle hands, he parted the folds of her sex, and finally, his firm mouth was on her.

The ache in her gums was forgotten, darkness forgotten, everything faded to nothing except the sensation of his tongue gliding along the folds of her sex, finding its way between, pushing inside her, filling her with slick wet heat.

One hand parted her farther, and his tongue slid up to find her clit, swollen with need, throbbing and almost painfully engorged. He teased lazy circles around it while two fingers pushed inside her, rubbing the internal walls of her sex, finding the sweet spot as he finally relented, took her clit between his lips, and sucked gently.

Everything clenched up tight inside her. She hovered on the edge.

He stopped. His mouth drew back.

"How are you doing?" he asked. She gritted her teeth and peered over her shoulders. He was sitting back on his heels, looking up at her. He licked his lips. "Gone all scary monster on me yet?"

She bared her teeth. But realized that the ache in her gums was gone, replaced by something more insistent. "No, but I might very quickly if you don't—"

"Don't what? This...?"

He pushed a finger inside her then rubbed over her clit.

"Oh God, that feels so good."

"More?"

She nodded.

As he massaged the swollen bud, the sweet tension built inside her, rising up from the place the darkness lived. She closed her eyes and sank into the sensation, lost in a place where colors whirled red and black, swirling, spiraling out of control. Then he pinched her clit between his thumb and finger, and she exploded.

Her knees gave way, and she sagged against the bonds, the sharp pain bringing her back. He ran the pad of his thumb over her, pinched again, and the pain vanished along with everything else, leaving her there in that dark place, but at one with the blackness.

They merged as stars flashed in her head.

She came back to herself to find Fergal standing behind her, his arm wrapped around her waist, supporting her weight.

He kissed the back of her neck. "You all right, baby?"

Was she? She gave a weak nod.

"Ready for the next bit?"

She didn't think she'd ever be ready. She felt unraveled, taken apart. But she gave another nod and stiffened her knees as he stepped back. She wobbled but then stood firm. Behind her, she heard the rustle as he shed his clothes.

Fergal released her slowly, making sure her legs would hold her before he let go completely. He could taste her on his tongue. Sweet. Unique. His dick was screaming for relief; this was going to be hard and fast. Her sweet ass was pointed up, her legs parted so he could see the curls of her sex.

He tore open his shirt. He wouldn't need the prison guard uniform again—he was done with prisons. Then he kicked off his boots and unfastened his pants. The relief was amazing, and he groaned. Daisy must have heard the sound. She twisted her head so she could look at him. Her eyes were dark but normal, widening when she found him naked. Her mouth parted, and she licked the pouting lower lip with a pointed tongue. His cock jerked as his head filled with a vision of her lush mouth wrapped around him.

Would he ever trust her with his dick in her mouth? Not likely, and not in the time they had together. She must have gotten what he was thinking—a grin curved her lips, and she flashed him one sharp white fang. His dick didn't care. It jerked again, and he grabbed it in his fist and squeezed. His balls ached; he needed to be inside her soon. He tried to tell himself that it had been a long time and that's why he felt so driven, but he knew it was more than that. Daisy touched him somewhere no one else ever had. It made him uneasy, but he'd worry about it later.

She finally raised her gaze from his cock.

"You want?" he asked.

She nodded, the movement jerky.

"Then hold on, baby."

When she didn't move, he released himself and slapped her ass. He remembered from the first time they'd been together all those years ago that she liked it rough. Her ass lifted a little, and he slapped her again, then rubbed at the red mark. She finally turned so she was facing the wall, braced her hands as well as she could.

He used both hands to massage her cheeks, parting them, his mouth going dry as the scent of her arousal filled the air. Shifting one hand to her hip to steady her, he used his other to part the lips of her sex. He rubbed the head of his cock over the slick heat a couple of times, found her entrance, and shoved inside with one hard push. She took him with a sigh, her muscles clenching around him.

He withdrew and pushed back inside, the sensation perfection, pleasure rippling through his cock and his balls, up his spine.

He leaned his head close. "Are you okay?"

She gave a small nod, and he increased the speed, flexing his hips, filling her all the way. She was moving with him now, her movements jerky as though she was fighting for control.

"Let it go," he murmured. "You can't hurt me. Just give in…"

He shoved again, and the tension snapped.

"Oh God, I can't…"

Then she was fighting the restraints, twisting and turning, trying to get free, while at the same time she pushed back against him, urging him to move faster, harder.

He didn't want to hurt her, but he wasn't dealing with an ordinary girl and she was amazingly strong. He fisted one hand in her long blond hair and used his arm to push her shoulders into the wall, used his own strength to pin her there while he pumped into her.

He was close, and he slid his free hand around her, over her belly and between her thighs. Finding her swollen clit, he rubbed and pinched until she threw back her head and screamed her release.

She wasn't fighting him now, and he shifted both hands so they rested on her hips and increased his speed until he exploded in an orgasm so powerful, lights danced before his eyes.

He couldn't seem to stop moving, and she came again, her muscles tightening around him, sending another wave of pleasure crashing over him.

Finally, he collapsed against her, his face burrowed in the curve of her shoulder. He stayed like that for long minutes, his breathing ragged, his pulse racing. Beneath him she was calm.

He raised his head and kissed the side of her neck. "How are you doing?"

She turned to look at him, and her face was tranquil. "I'm good. In fact, I don't think I've ever felt better.

A smile tugged at his lips. "You going to bite me if I let you go?"

She shook her head. "No, you're safe."

He pushed himself away from her. His legs were shaking, and he stood for a second, breathing deeply. Taking a step toward her, he reached up and untied the cable. Her arms dropped to her sides and she rubbed her wrists, but the cable had left no marks. She turned to face him, and he tensed, watching her warily, but she seemed almost peaceful, a sleepy, sated look in her eyes. No sign of the monster lurking within.

Deciding the risk was low, he took a step toward her, bent his head, and kissed her lips. Then he wrapped his arms around her, picked her up, and carried her to one of the bunks lining the room. Sitting down, he pulled her onto his lap and snuggled down.

"Sleep."

"Vampires don't sleep," she mumbled. But her eyes closed and her breathing evened. She wriggled once or twice getting comfortable and finally lay still.

Fergal closed his own eyes, feeling at peace for once. He knew it wouldn't last, couldn't last. This could only ever be an interlude—if he didn't find Stefan, he would run out of antidote and be dead within days. But he had learned to take his pleasures where he could, and right now, he wanted nothing more than to sleep with Daisy in his arms.

He woke long hours later. Daisy sat at the end of the bed, her legs crossed, her chin resting in one hand as she examined him. She'd found his stash of spare clothes, because she was dressed in a black T-shirt that reached mid-thigh. He was sprawled naked on top of the bunk, but he felt too lazy and satisfied to care. Let her look. She could even have him again if she wanted, as soon as he could get the strength to tie her up.

"So did it work?"

She straightened, stretched her legs. "I think so. I feel good. It's twelve hours since I fed, and I feel fine."

"Twelve hours. I've been asleep that long?"

"Yeah. I didn't like to wake you. You're kind of cute when you're asleep."

"I'm cute when I'm awake."

"No, you're not." But she smiled to take the sting from the words.

"I'm glad it worked. Now you just need a few people into bondage and you're good."

"What about you?" she asked.

He knew what she meant but answered a different

question instead. "I don't mind it now and again."

He should have known she wouldn't accept his evasive answer. She was one of the most straightforward people he'd ever met. "You know what I meant. Will you be around? I'm not sure I trust anyone else to tie me up."

"And you trust me?"

"Yes."

The unequivocal answer twisted something inside him. He looked away for a second. "I won't be around for much longer. I'll drop you at Trakis Two. Then I have to be on my way. Nothing has changed."

"Why can't you stay? Just a little while?"

For a second he thought about telling her. But he still didn't know what she and her friends were really up to. When he'd first met them, they'd been pirates, mercenaries for hire to the highest bidder. Why should things be any different now? He couldn't trust them. But it worried him that he wanted to. "I have things to do."

She opened her mouth, closed it again, and shrugged. "Well, I guess I'll have to find somebody else."

He didn't like the sound of that. Not at all. He wasn't going to be here. So why did he give a shit? But he did. Enough to point something out to her. "You fought me at one point. If I'd been ordinary human, you'd have thrown me off."

She studied him, her head cocked on one side as if trying to see into his mind. He was glad she couldn't—it was a mess in there. Even he didn't understand what was going on.

"Maybe one of Thorne's people," she said.

"Who's Thorne?"

"He's…a little hard to explain. But he and his people are Collective…sort of. But much older."

He frowned. As far as he was aware, Callum Meridian was the oldest of the Collective, as he'd been the first to take the treatment. It had been Callum who had discovered

Meridian five hundred years ago when mankind had first arrived at the Trakis system and his ship had crash-landed on Trakis Seven. "How can they be older?" he asked.

"Long story. But they all have wings, like Callum. They're actually pretty cool. I'm sure I could find someone willing to give me a go. Some have already volunteered to feed me."

Shit. Ultra strong, cool wings, and they wouldn't make her puke if she bit them. He gritted his teeth; he was starting to feel inadequate.

"What's wrong?" she asked.

"Nothing. I'm glad you've already got some candidates. I'm surprised you haven't given any of them a try before now."

She shrugged. "I didn't really feel in the mood. Just hungry."

Until he'd come along. Then she'd gotten in the mood pretty damn fast. That had to mean something. Just nothing that should mean anything to him. He had things to do.

He swung his legs around and stood up, felt her eyes on him, and stretched. His dick was already semi hard, ready for another go, and it jerked under her stare. He crossed the room, picked up his pants and pulled them on. She might be able to subdue her hunger through sex; he needed food and lots of it. And coffee.

He got a bowl of porridge from the dispenser and wolfed it down while standing. After refilling the bowl, he took it back to the bed.

"You eat a lot," she said.

He was lean, bordering on skinny. It took a lot to keep him going these days. "My metabolism is a little weird from the change."

"How changed are you?"

"This"—he waved his artificial arm in the air—"and a few other things."

She regarded him, her brows drawn together. "What

other things? What did they do to you at Cybercom? You're super strong, your brain's like a computer, you—"

"—are an amazing lover with exhausting stamina."

She blew him a kiss. "Of course you are. That doesn't all come from your arm. So what else is different?"

Secrecy was ingrained in him. Truth was, he hadn't confided in anybody since he was eight years old and his mother had died. He'd also signed a confidentiality agreement when he'd been admitted to the secret program at Cybercom. He'd gone in there ostensibly to get an artificial arm. He hadn't bothered to tell them that he'd actually had a medic friend amputate the limb so he'd have an excuse to get into the company. Because it hadn't been artificial limbs he'd been interested in—well, not until he needed one, anyway—but the extras that Cybercom had been rumored to be working on. Cybernetics at the genetic level, a new form of micro engineering that changed DNA into a self-regulating, self-repairing new form. A form that would improve the human body, make it virtually indestructible and self-renewing.

Daisy was looking at him expectantly, and he realized that nearly all the people with any interest in that confidentiality agreement were dead. All the chief executives of the company had been executed soon after they were taken. It was amazing that Stefan hadn't been killed along with them, and Fergal had no clue why. He was only grateful. With Stefan alive, there was still a chance.

"Cybercom was developing a microchip that could be inserted into the bloodstream to combine with the DNA. It became self-replicating."

"But what does it do?"

"Hopefully, it makes you immortal." No point in telling her the downside—that it might also turn him into a mindless drone.

Back when he'd joined the program, the Meridian

treatment had still been available—at a price—but over the years, Fergal had come to realize he was never going to earn enough to get immortality that way. Besides, he'd heard a rumor that Meridian was running out. He heard a lot of rumors in his profession. So Cybercom had seemed like the only answer. His plan had always been that one day he would stand in front of his fucking father, laugh in the bastard's face, and tell him the devil was never going to get his hands on Fergal. A shiver ran through him, and he automatically rubbed at the old burn scar on his arm. He no longer believed in the devil or God, but that fear had been instilled in him at such a young age, he doubted he would ever be totally free of it.

"Wow."

"I don't know about 'wow.' Immortality seems to be pretty common around you."

She pursed her lips. "I never wanted it, you know. Immortality, I mean. I could have gone with Callum and Tannis, gotten the treatment but—"

"I thought Meridian was gone, finished?"

"It's a—"

"Long story?" he interrupted. Soon she was going to settle in and tell him some of those long stories. "Why didn't you want immortality?"

She traced a pattern on the mattress with her finger while she considered her answer. "I'm not sure. I wasn't in a good place. Maybe I thought everyone dies. My friends, my parents... Maybe I didn't want to be alone forever. I don't know. Given more time, I might have changed my mind. I was still young—hard to think seriously about dying when you're only twenty-four."

He frowned. She did look young—it was one of the things he'd noticed when he first recognized her—but he'd put it down to some sort of vampire shit. But how could she be only twenty-four? That would have made her three years old when they first made love, and he would have noticed that.

"No way are you only twenty-four. You know, I think it's time for one of those long stories."

She studied him, head cocked on one side. "Why not? I'll try and make it a quick long story, but you might as well get comfortable."

He placed his dish on the floor and patted the bed beside him.

Daisy sank down, wriggled, and settled back with a sigh. "So, you know the black hole at Trakis One?" He nodded, and she continued, "Well, six months ago, we went through there and into a whole different universe. There were these aliens, and Thorne's people, including Saffira. Anyway, it turns out she can do this time travel thing. She took us back to Earth before it was destroyed and saved everybody, and afterward, she brought us back here through a wormhole. But she's still learning how, so we lost a few years. And that's it—here we are, two decades later but only six months older." She grinned. "Hey, not such a long story after all."

Fergal sat with his mouth open. He had a thousand questions but couldn't decide which to ask first, so he snapped it shut. Okay, just one question. "Why did you go through the black hole at Trakis One?"

"Tannis was dying of the Meridian poisoning—you know the only cure is to take the treatment?"

He nodded.

"Well, there was none left here, but we found out that there might be more on the other side of the hole."

"Okay. Makes perfect sense. Not." His head was spinning. Maybe he shouldn't have asked. "I need more food."

He got another bowl of food and ate it while he was standing, studying the room. The cable he'd used to tie her up lay coiled on the floor, and blood drained to his groin. He'd had enough talking. He picked the cable up on his way back. The bunk was attached to the wall with sturdy metal posts. He tested one as he got back.

"If you don't want that T-shirt ripped, I suggest you take it off."

She looked from the cable in his hand to the bunk, then gripped the hem of her shirt and pulled it over her head, baring her breasts. Her nipples were already tight.

She glanced at him and raised one arched brow as if to say, *what next?*

"On your back," he said.

"Are you sure?"

He nodded. If he tied her tight enough, she wouldn't get at him. "I want to watch your face this time." He grinned. "And your breasts. You have amazing breasts."

Without waiting for an answer, Daisy lay on her back and stretched her arms above her head, and he got to work. After looping the cable around both her wrists, he wound it through the bars that held the bunk to the wall. "That is seriously hot. Did I mention the amazing breasts?" They were thrust upward, and he trailed his knuckles over one, then the other, until she squirmed on the thin mattress.

What next? Threading the end of the cable underneath the bunk, he wrapped it around one slender ankle before fastening it to the corner support.

Daisy raised her head from the pillow and peered at him through narrowed eyes. "What are you doing? I'm hardly likely to bite you with my feet."

"Hey, whose fantasy is this?"

She kicked out as he grabbed the other ankle, but she was giggling, so he presumed she wasn't totally against the idea. He tied her second foot to the opposite corner and stood back to admire his handiwork. He let out a low whistle. "Holy. Mother. Of. God."

She was stretched out before him, legs parted. He forced his gaze upward to her face. She'd stopped giggling, her expression serious. Had that darkness thing woken up inside her? She shifted restlessly, breathing hard, her eyes gleaming with little glints of crimson. Her lower lip was caught between her teeth, and she looked ready to snap, she was wound so tight.

Perhaps this hadn't been such a good idea, but as he watched, she shut her eyes and took control of herself.

He didn't want her in control. He considered her for a moment then reached out and stroked his fingers from her elbow over the soft skin to her armpit and tickled her.

Her lids flew open. "Stop that."

"Make me." And he tickled her again. "Death by tickling."

A small giggle escaped her, and she struggled against the bonds, the movements making her breasts jiggle. He liked that, a lot, and he repeated the process on the other side until she twisted and turned.

"You'll be so sorry for this," she muttered as he gave her a moment of respite.

"No, I won't."

He stripped off his clothes and crawled onto the bunk between her thighs, fisting his already rock-hard dick in his hand. Glancing up, he found her gaze fixed on him, eyes wide but clear of the darkness.

"You ready?" he asked.

She nodded. "Fergal?"

"Yeah?"

"If I forget to tell you, I…" She gave a little shrug.

"Come on, out with it. I have an agenda here." He waved his dick in her general direction.

"I don't know what's going to happen when we get back, but whatever it is, I want you to know that I like you, and that

I had…fun. And there hasn't been too much of that lately."

He grinned. "I like you, too."

Placing a hand on the bunk on either side of her, he lowered his body until his chest brushed the tips of her breasts and slowly pushed inside. "Fan-fucking-tastic."

This time he was going to take it slowly.

Twelve hours later, they made landfall on Trakis Two. Not in the city, as he'd expected, but in some weird-shit fortress a few miles from the capital. A huge place built of black rock that merged into the darkness.

Trakis Two was known as the planet that never sleeps—despite being a land of constant night. No daylight ever touched the dark side of the planet. It was a cesspit of vice with every perversion known to man available—for a price. It was also rumored that other things flourished in the darkness.

Things like vampires, maybe?

Fergal's curiosity stirred as the top of the black fortress opened, and Daisy lowered the ship gently down. For so long, he hadn't cared enough to be curious about anything. The change was down to Daisy. Maybe she was restoring a little of his faith in humanity. He'd lost that so young that he hadn't even known it was missing. Strange that he should learn about humanity from a woman who wasn't even human.

Though she was trying. Which was maybe a mistake. There was no turning back. She needed to accept what she was and not try to find a way to control or ignore it.

Helping her do that was in no way a hardship. He only had to look at a piece of cable to get a hard-on these days.

He'd tied her to the bunk, bent over the pilot's chair, stretched out on the floor, on her front, her back…and a few other variations. Even with his increased healing, his dick was sore. But she'd gotten jittery after the first day was over—hungry—and sex seemed to calm her.

He watched as she strolled down the ramp, her nostrils flaring, no doubt at the scent of all that fresh blood just wandering about the place. All those willing donors with tasty blood and cool wings.

The place was buzzing. People moving about with purpose in the great cavern, and at least fifteen ships were docked in the space. He recognized *The Blood Hunter*—by far the biggest, baddest ship there—parked up in the far corner.

"It's a goddamn army," he muttered, coming to a halt beside her at the base of the ramp.

"Yeah. People have been joining us from all over. Thorne's people, what's left of Devlin's rebels, even some of the Collective—Skylar put out a call."

He looked around. "What are you planning?"

She grinned. "We're going to attack Trakis Five. We're going to take out the Church once and for all, destroy them completely. And Temperance Hatcher is going to die."

He turned to her abruptly. "Why Hatcher in particular?"

"He killed my friends."

A sick feeling rose up in his throat. More people dead at Hatcher's hands.

Did they have the power to destroy the Church? Looking around he suspected that they might. He wouldn't care if the Church was torn down. And Hatcher…he cut off the thought.

But Stefan was on Trakis Five, and if Fergal's intel was correct, he was in the prison at the Church's headquarters. If they attacked, in all likelihood Stefan would be killed. And if Stefan died, then Fergal's future did not look bright.

Shit.

He needed to get Stefan out of there. Would they even let him go now he'd seen this place? He had to find a way.

"You could stay and help," Daisy said. "We need a good techie person."

He wanted to. And he couldn't believe it. When had he ever wanted to work with anyone else? But it would mean he could stay with Daisy for a while. He scrubbed a hand over his face,

Fucking impossible.

He had no choice but to go. Well, maybe he did have a choice, but it was one that would end up with him dead. Or worse.

After he'd found Stefan... He didn't know. Truth was, he'd never cared, either. Until now.

He didn't want to put Daisy on her guard, but at the same time, some part of him needed her to know that whatever he did—he didn't do it lightly.

"I can't stick around for long." Just long enough to find out what they were planning and whether it would affect his hunt for Stefan. "I have to go."

"Why? What's so important?"

"I have to find a man. And if I don't find him very soon, I'm dead. Or worse."

Chapter Ten

The usual cynical twist to his lips was gone. He appeared deadly serious.

Daisy glanced away, trying to ignore the tightening in her chest as she struggled to keep her expression blank and not reveal her disappointment.

He was leaving, and she was an idiot.

But an idiot who didn't want him to go.

At least not yet.

She ransacked her mind for some way to make him stick around. "Maybe we could help you?" she said. "Find this man, I mean. After we've finished with the Church, we could help you search for this person."

"That will be too late."

"Why?" She searched his face, but he gave nothing away.

"They're not my secrets to tell, but I'm running out of time."

"Oh."

"Besides, I've never been a team player."

"Things can change." God, she was starting to sound

desperate.

"People can't change. Not in my experience." He pinched the bridge of his nose and exhaled. "I don't like relying on others and don't like them relying on me."

The words sounded like a warning. Why was she pushing this? She should let him go before she got even more attached. The truth was, she wanted him to stay because he'd known the old Daisy, and he made her feel a little bit like that girl still existed somewhere deep inside. That she might even come back. But the old Daisy was dead and gone. She was a monster, and she had no right to forget that. "Well, don't worry—I'm not relying on you."

He gave her an odd glance. Maybe his comment hadn't been aimed specifically at her. But he was leaving. Soon. Time to stand on her own two feet. He'd helped her, shown her that she could get a measure of control. She couldn't expect anything more from him. And he was right; ultimately everyone was on their own.

"Let's go find out what's happening," she said with a bright smile. "Then you can go."

Some emotion flashed across his face, and he reached out a hand to her. "Daisy—"

"It doesn't matter." She took a step back. "Hey, we had fun, and I never expected true love or any of that crap. I'm a goddamn bloodsucking monster. We don't do true love or any other kind." Except Rico had found it with Skylar, though it had taken him nearly two thousand years. "I'm not going to get all clingy or anything."

He reached for her again. This time she held herself still, and he slid his hand behind her neck and pulled her to him. As his lips touched hers, something twisted inside her. She wished he hadn't done that, because she really didn't want to get clingy, but she could feel her fingers curling into the hard muscles of his shoulders, holding him tight.

"I hope you two have been practicing safe sex," Rico said from behind them, and Fergal went still against her. He drew back slightly, and she forced her fingers to unclench from his skin.

"Well, he's still alive, so I'm guessing so." Rico studied her for a moment, a lazy smile curling his lips. "You look good."

"I feel good. A little hungry, but nothing I can't handle."

"We'll sort something out after the meeting."

"There's a meeting?"

"We're waiting for Tannis to get here."

"The captain isn't here yet?"

"No, they had a tail they needed to lose first. But they're only a few minutes behind you. Which is good, because if I have to put up with Mr. Lovesick Werewolf any longer, I might lose the will to live." He waved a hand across the cavern, and she caught sight of Jon. He was pacing the sandy black floor, his figure radiating tension. Every few seconds, he'd pause and stare up at the ceiling and a low growl would emerge from his throat.

"Is he okay?"

"Physically, yes. Or he was after he'd shifted a couple of times. Mentally, he's a mess."

"He'll be okay when Alex gets here. Where are Candy and Angel?"

"Angel is around, that calmed Jon a bit. But fucking Candace is missing. Again. Apparently, she left pretty much after us. I guess she was pissed off that we wouldn't take her along. Thorne's gone into Pleasure City to find her."

"Who are Candy and Angel?" Fergal asked.

"Jon's kids," Daisy said. "Well, not kids. They're twenty-one now. She'll be okay, won't she?"

Candy and Angel, Jon and Alex's twins, were the reason they'd stayed behind and not dived headfirst into a black hole with the rest of them. Angel was a darling. He was the responsible, sensible twin. Candy was a nightmare. Daisy loved her dearly, but she was wild. She'd been looking after herself and Angel since they were twelve and their parents had been taken by the Church. She was convinced they didn't need anyone else.

"Yeah, she'll be fine. I'm not so sure about anything she comes up against, though—bloodthirsty little bitch."

At that moment, the ceiling above their heads started to move. The two sections slid apart, exposing a star-strewn sky and a medium-size space cruiser, which lowered itself lightly to the black sand. The engines hadn't even died before Jon was racing across the sand and leaping for the emerging ramp. The double doors opened, revealing Alex's diminutive figure. For a second Jon halted his run and stood and stared. Then he threw back his head and howled.

Alex was dressed in long black robes, but her head was bare, showing raggedly cut dark red hair. She flew down the ramp and leaped into Jon's arms.

Daisy blinked away a tear. What would it be like to be loved like that? She cast a sideways glance at Fergal. His attention was fixed on the open doors of the space cruiser, where two figures had appeared. They swaggered down the ramp, edging around the embracing couple, but both were smiling.

Tannis was dressed in black pants and boots, a scarlet shirt on top, a laser pistol at her hip. Beside her Callum wore the same, but his shirt was purple to match his eyes. Both their eyes. His wings were furled tightly at his back.

"Callum fucking Meridian," Fergal murmured.

"You've met him?" she asked.

"Interviewed him once. And he saved my life. The Collective would have killed me after I did that piece on the maximum-security prison. He stepped in and stopped them."

"He's an okay guy once you get past the whole leader-of-the-universe crap."

"Is the plan to put him back up there?"

Daisy frowned. "I don't know. We've never spoken of it." She turned to Rico. "Does he want to go back?"

"I doubt it. He was bored out of his mind, and somehow I can't see Tannis as first lady."

Daisy tried to picture the captain in a crown or something. She giggled, and Rico cast her a sharp look. "What?" she asked.

"Just haven't heard you laugh in a long time. Lover boy must be good for you."

Fergal ignored the comment. "So who will be in charge? You know, after the revolution and all that?"

"Frankly, I don't give a fuck," Rico said. "As long as it isn't me and it isn't Temperance Hatcher."

Daisy had never thought that far ahead. She didn't think any of them had. This wasn't so much about putting the good guys in power as getting rid of the bad guys. But she supposed someone would have to rule. Otherwise it would be chaos.

Tannis came to a halt in front of their little group, and her smile faded.

"You took your time," Rico said.

"Freaking bastards stuck to us like glue. We eventually realized they must have bugged their little priestess. Once we sorted that out, we shook them off pretty quickly. But I'm not sure they won't have guessed where we were heading. They tailed us for a while before we picked them up."

"Is Alex okay?" Daisy asked. She wanted to go and welcome her friend back, but she didn't want to interrupt the reunion.

"Once we told her we had Jon, she was fine. Had to stop her going in and trying to kill Hatcher herself, though."

They all turned to look as Jon scooped Alex up in his

arms and headed for *The Blood Hunter.*

"I'm betting that's the last we'll see of them for a while," Tannis said. "Let's go get this meeting over with. We need a plan." She glanced around; her gaze settled on Fergal and recognition sparked in her eyes. "Well, if it isn't our old friend the crazy reporter."

"Crazy?" Callum asked from beside her.

"Yeah. Chopped off his own arm to get a story."

Callum studied him for a second. "Fergal Cain." He held out his hand, and Fergal stepped forward and shook it.

"You two know each other?" Tannis asked.

"We met. Cain interviewed me a while back—made me sound quite nice."

"He's a clever man," Rico said. He turned to Fergal. "So are you staying or going?"

Daisy held her breath.

"Staying for now."

And she released it.

Fergal followed them across the cavern floor and up the docking bay into *The Blood Hunter,* his eyes fixed on the sway of Daisy's ass as she walked up ahead with Rico.

Maybe he should have left. But he really did need to know what they were planning.

The meeting was being held in the main conference room on board *The Blood Hunter.* The room was big enough to hold fifty people easy, even if some of them had wings—and there were a few who did, as well as Callum.

"Okay," Tannis yelled across the room, cutting through the medley of voices. "Can we get this moving? I have people to shoot." Nothing happened, and Tannis drew her weapon and fired a blast toward the ceiling. "I said, shut the fuck up."

An immediate hush settled over the room.

"Thank you." Tannis holstered her weapon.

Fergal crossed to where Daisy had taken a seat at the edge of the room and sat beside her. "I like your captain," he murmured.

"Yeah, she gets things done."

Everyone was shuffling now, finding a seat or leaning against the wall facing the center of the room where Tannis stood tapping her booted foot.

"Right," Tannis said. "The plan. Basically we're going to go blow the fuckers up."

"Nice and simple," Rico said. "I like that."

Fergal didn't. As far as he was concerned, it was the worst possible scenario. What the hell chance would Stefan have of surviving an outright attack on the Church's headquarters? Though the prison was a few miles away from the main building. If Stefan was being held there, he might have a chance. But there were also cells beneath the main headquarters. A direct hit would take them out as well.

He was very nearly all out of the antidote and had no source of any more. He'd tried. He'd had the pills analyzed at a lab, but they hadn't been able to reproduce them. Some unidentifiable ingredient. Fergal had known it was pointless—Stefan wouldn't have given him something easy to cure.

No, his only hope was finding Stefan and seeing this through. Before his friend was blown into tiny little pieces.

"When?" someone asked.

"As soon as we can get everyone in place. We're going to do simultaneous attacks on the stronghold on Trakis Twelve and Four. So there's no fear of backup."

"Do we give them warning?"

"Hell, no. We—"

There was a commotion at the door. A girl entered, followed by a tall man with wings close behind her. The girl wasn't short, but he towered over her, radiating a palpable tension the girl seemed oblivious to. She was beautiful, and Fergal guessed who she was immediately. She had her father's midnight-dark hair hanging halfway down her back, and her mother's silver-gray eyes. Pale skin and full lips.

"Wow," he muttered.

"Close your mouth," Daisy snapped from beside him.

He did as he was told.

"Are they here?" the girl asked. "Did you get them?" Her gaze searched the room before coming back to Tannis. "Thorne told me you had them. Was it a fucking lie to get me back here?" She whirled around to face the winged guy who flanked her. "You fucking bastard. You lied to me."

She swung back her fist, but before it could connect, he gripped it in his huge hand and held her still.

"I did not lie," he ground out.

"That's Candy," Daisy whispered from beside him. "Sweet, isn't she?"

"Candace!" Tannis snapped. "Your parents are both safe."

Some of the tension drained from her, and she sagged. She tugged her hand free, and it dropped to her side. "So where are they?"

"They're having a little…alone time."

"Ugh!" She turned and stomped from the room. Thorne watched her go and then came forward. He heaved a huge sigh and threw himself back into a seat. He was big. Tall and broad with short, dark red hair and the violet eyes of the Collective.

"That's Thorne," Daisy said. "He's ten thousand years old and in charge of a planetload of people. He isn't used to people not doing what he says. I think Candy came as a shock."

He did look a little frazzled. He sat slumped in his seat,

long legs stretched out in front of him.

"So," Tannis said. "Can we move on? As I was saying—we go in there and we blow the fuckers up."

"Isn't that a little simplistic?" Thorne asked.

"Why complicate matters?"

"Matters have a way of complicating themselves. Do you even know Hatcher is there?"

Fergal cast him a sharp glance. Was this *all* about Hatcher?

"We've been trying to get into their internal systems," Tannis replied. "But so far we've failed." She ran a hand through her hair. "God, I miss Janey."

"Fergal could do it," Daisy said from beside him.

For a second, he wanted to hiss at her to shut up. But maybe this was a good thing. He needed to try to discover Stefan's exact whereabouts, and if he could hack into the Church's internal files, then maybe he could find out. He could have done it before, but hadn't wanted to risk alerting anyone, and he'd believed he would have more time. Now time was running out.

All eyes turned to Daisy and then most—well, the ones who actually knew who he was—shifted to him. He decided to stay silent and wait until he heard the response.

"He could?" Tannis sounded skeptical.

"He's brilliant," Daisy said.

"Really?"

"Just who is Fergal?" Thorne asked.

"That would be me," Fergal muttered.

"And you are?"

He wasn't sure how to answer that. There were a whole lot of things he could say. He was a reporter? He wasn't even sure that was true anymore. A cyborg? He quite liked that one. Daisy's lover? Sounded good.

"He's thinking too hard," Thorne said. "Anyone who has

to think that hard about who they are is unlikely to actually be who they say they are when they eventually get around to saying it."

"He's a reporter," Tannis said. "He's helped us out a couple of times."

"How does a reporter help you out?"

"Well, there's maybe a little more to him than that, but that's what he was when we first met."

"Can he be trusted?"

Tannis studied him, eyes narrowing, and Fergal held himself still. "I don't know," she said after a minute's scrutiny. "But Daisy seems to like him."

"And he did help us get Jon and the colonel out," Skylar added.

"I'd give him a maybe," Rico said. "I'd still like to know what he was doing in that prison in the first place."

"Looking for a story?" Fergal suggested.

"Nah, I'm not buying that. Then there's the whole not-quite-human thing."

"In what way?" Thorne asked.

"We're not actually sure," Rico replied. He turned to Fergal. "Just how human are you, Fergal?"

Chapter Eleven

Fergal shrugged. "Fifty-fifty at a guess."

"And what's the rest?" Tannis asked.

"Little bits of metal and a few big bits of metal." He flexed his right arm. He'd punched Rico with that arm once.

"The question is—can he do it?" Tannis said. "Can you hack into the Church's systems?"

"Probably."

"I like a man with confidence." Tannis grinned. "Let's see you do it."

Fergal glanced around the room. Did he want to reveal what he could do in front of all these people? Everyone who had anything to do with Cybercom had been rounded up in the last six months and executed. He felt uneasy exposing his secrets to so many people.

"Not here. Not now."

Tannis stared at him, her smile fading, her boot tapping on the floor, then she shrugged—he was guessing she knew all about people who liked to keep secrets. "Okay, after the meeting. Let's presume Hatcher is there. Do we just blast the place or do we want to make sure he's dead?"

"Make sure he's dead," Devlin said. "I don't want the slimy bastard slipping away."

It occurred to Fergal that this was as much a personal attack on Temperance Hatcher as it was on the Church. He wasn't sure how he felt about that. He should feel nothing. But that obviously wasn't the case. And he wasn't happy about it.

"Are you okay?" Daisy asked from beside him.

"Yeah. Why shouldn't I be?"

"I don't know. You looked a little weird for a minute."

"No, I'm fine." He glanced sideways at her. "You guys really hate this Hatcher, don't you?"

Her expression hardened. "He killed our friends. That made it personal."

"Yeah, I guess it would."

"So," Tannis continued, "We send a small team in—Me, Rico and Devlin. We kill the bastard, get out of there, and blast the place to pieces."

"Why not me?" Callum asked.

"Because you're a little conspicuous, sweetie." Tannis patted his wings.

"And what happens afterward?" Thorne asked.

Tannis frowned. "Afterward? Who gives a toss?"

"So you destroy the Church and afterward, you just leave everything in chaos?"

"I like chaos."

"We can't remove the old rulers and leave nothing in their place," Thorne said. "We have responsibilities—"

"You might have responsibilities," Tannis said. "We don't. If you're so fucking concerned, you take over. You're pretty good at telling people what to do yourself, if I remember."

Beside him, Daisy shifted restlessly, dragging him from the conversation. "What's the matter?" he asked.

"Just hungry. All these people…"

"All this blood," he finished for her. "Can you control it?"

"I think so."

They were still bickering among themselves. Finally, Rico stepped forward. "*Madre de Dios,*" he muttered. "Enough. Let's kill the bastards first and worry about who's in charge afterward. One thing at a time."

Thorne didn't look happy, but he settled into his seat, a scowl on his face.

"Okay," Rico continued. "Everyone who doesn't belong here—out."

Fergal wondered if that included him. He'd never really belonged anywhere before, and now wasn't a good time to start. And certainly not here. He needed to work out his next move, and he was very aware that it might involve betraying these people. But he kept his seat.

The room cleared quickly, leaving just the crew of *The Blood Hunter* and Thorne.

Tannis crossed to them and hunkered down beside Daisy. "You okay? I'm next on the roster if you need to feed."

Daisy gave a jerky nod. "Sorry."

"Don't be. It's not a problem. Come on, let's do it now, then we can get your boyfriend set up and see if he has anything to offer other than the obvious uses."

Daisy flashed him a quick smile as she disappeared out of the room with Tannis. Restless, Fergal stood and wandered over to where Rico talked quietly with Devlin and Skylar. He glanced up as Fergal approached and met him halfway.

"How long will Daisy be like this?" Fergal asked.

"Like what?"

"Needing to feed so often."

"I don't know. Maybe years, but she's doing very well. I was still ripping people's throats out at this point. I think the blood she's getting is a bit more potent than normal. It's changing her. But she'll be okay. She's stronger than she looks. Actually, incredibly resilient."

"Good."

"You care about her?"

"She's a friend."

Rico studied him for a moment longer and shrugged. "Let's get you set up and see what you can do."

"I'm hungry."

"You're always hungry. You're worse than Daisy." But he called over to Skylar. "Can you go get Fergal some food? He's feeling faint."

"What am I the goddamn maid?" But she headed for the transporter bubble.

"Come on," Rico said and led him to where Saffira was sitting at a console, tapping away.

"Any luck?" Rico asked.

"No. I keep hitting a wall."

"Okay, let's see if iron man here can do any better."

Saffira stood up, and Fergal took her seat. He sat for a minute, thinking how best to do this. Did he want to reveal what he was becoming? But he needed the information himself and was pretty sure they weren't going to leave him alone while he tried to get it.

Taking a deep breath, he closed his eyes. He'd only done this a few times. Mainly because he wasn't sure what sort of alarms his intrusions would set off. Also the ability had been a side effect of that last phase he'd received a few weeks before Stefan helped him escape Cybercom. The final phase that had turned everyone else into drones or dead men. He'd had to work it out on his own as well.

Reaching inside, he flipped the internal switch. His brain clicked into another mode like a load of lights flashing on, until the whole of his head was lit up. The people around faded out of focus, but the machines came into harsh relief. The ship was a living, breathing thing. He could sense the hum of her workings like the beat of a heart. The console in front of him was buzzing. He needed to focus. Resting a hand on the keyboard, he pressed a few keys, not because he needed to but because it might make it a little unclear to those watching exactly what he was doing.

Then he opened his mind and spoke to the computer. Immediately his brain flooded with information. He didn't try to slow it, just set his brain to sorting. He delved farther inside, found the wall that Saffira had spoken of, thought about knocking it down, but it dissolved before him.

All the information in the universe was there for him.

He was vaguely aware of Daisy returning, standing behind him, and resting one hand on his shoulder. The touch anchored him, brought him back to himself a little, and he realized he'd been in danger of getting lost in the maze of information.

Someone placed a bowl of food in front of him, and he ate it absently, the flow of information not slowing down. He sorted through it, sifting at lightning speed. Finally, he latched onto the files he needed and informed the machine in front of him to output what was required. He was dimly aware of it flashing up on the screen in front of him for the others to read.

He searched some more for the prison records. Forgot to switch off the external feed and swore as the details whizzed out to the monitors. Finally, he withdrew, closing down the links, pulling out. When he was sure he'd shut off everything behind him, he clicked off his internal switch and heaved a sigh.

Everything was quiet.

He swiveled his chair so he was facing them.

"Fuck," Saffira said. "What the hell did you just do?"

Daisy squeezed his shoulder, and he glanced up. She looked good, her cheeks flushed with color. Tannis, on the other hand, looked pale, but okay. She was reading through the information on the monitor, flicking through quickly. "Jesus, you've even got what Hatcher had for breakfast."

"Dry bread and water?" he asked.

"Yeah, how did you know?"

Fergal could have said because that's what the man always had, but he didn't. Instead, he shrugged. He shouldn't have said anything, but it was taking a minute for his brain to come back to itself.

"Well, he's definitely there, and we have all his security details as well. They're not very heavy."

"He probably believes God will protect him," Devlin said.

That's exactly what he believed, but this time Fergal kept the information to himself. He was coming around.

"We've got the fucker," Tannis said and punched him on the shoulder. "Crazy or not—you certainly have your uses. And not only getting information, according to Daisy." She gave him a sly look.

What exactly had Daisy been saying? He cast her a glance, but she just smiled.

"What's this other stuff?" Tannis asked. She'd gone back to reading the screen. "It's the prison records for Trakis Five. What did you get those for?"

"No reason. I'm not too good at controlling the output yet." He reached forward and deleted the file. He didn't need to read it. He already knew that Stefan wasn't listed as in the prison. Which presumably meant he was at the Church's headquarters. Though he hadn't found any reference to him. At least not under that name.

Shit.

Somehow, he had to get Stefan out of there before the crew of *The Blood Hunter* blew the whole place, and Stefan, into little pieces.

For a moment, he considered asking for their help. But only for a moment. It wasn't in his nature. And they were too determined to kill Hatcher and destroy the Church. Why would they let what he needed stand in their way? He was nothing to them.

That caused a little jolt of something. He just wasn't sure what. Daisy might be upset if he dropped dead on her, but she would be the only one.

He looked up and found her watching him, her brows drawn together. What was she thinking?

But even Daisy would no doubt turn against him if she learned exactly what his connection to Temperance Hatcher was. No, he was on his own, as he'd always been. He'd have to find a way to get Stefan out. But he hoped he could find a way that wouldn't mean the end of the crew of *The Blood Hunter*.

He was lying about something. Daisy just wasn't sure what it was.

He'd gone all shifty-looking when Tannis had mentioned the prison records. He'd said they were a mistake. She didn't believe him. Earlier he'd told her he was looking for a man. Had he been searching in the prison? If so, had he found him?

He didn't trust them, that much was clear.

And why should he? Trust had to be earned. But she'd thought they were coming closer. Given time, she knew he would come to trust her, at least. How could you not trust someone who let you tie them up? He could have killed her at any time.

But they didn't have time. Things were coming to a head.

There'd also been a minute tic in his cheek every time Hatcher was mentioned.

Did he also have reason to hate the man? She sensed

it was more than that. What was clear was Fergal Cain had secrets he wasn't ready to share.

Perhaps she should tell someone of her concerns. Maybe they would all be safer if they had Fergal locked up tight in one of the cells on the lower level of *The Blood Hunter*.

He'd be safe there.

Or would he?

Fergal had told her that if he didn't find this man he was dead. What did he mean?

She wished he would open up to her. All the same, she wouldn't have him locked up. He'd saved her life. She couldn't repay him by maybe causing his death. But she could keep a close eye on him. And maybe mention her concerns to Rico.

"Is it okay if I go get some more food?" Fergal asked rising to his feet.

Rico shook his head. "Amazing."

"I'll come with you," Tannis said. "I want to talk about… your brain."

"Me too," Callum said.

Fergal looked at her and raised a brow.

"I'm going to go shower." Daisy answered the unasked question. "Get a change of clothes." *Have a chat with Rico.* "I'll see you there."

He gave her a long look, but shrugged. "Okay."

She waited until they had gone.

"So what's up?" Rico asked.

Daisy tried for a casual shrug. She was going to have to be careful here. She didn't want Rico going overboard and maybe locking Fergal up anyway. Or worse. "Why do you think anything is up?"

"Come on, spit it out. What do you think I should know?"

"Nothing, really. Fergal saved my life back at the prison. He could have left me, and they would have caught me and…"

"So, he's a good guy."

She tried for another casual shrug. "Maybe. Maybe not. I like him."

"I noticed."

"But I think he has another agenda. One he's not sharing with us."

"And you think whatever his agenda is—it's going to be an issue?" He shook his head. "Stupid question. You wouldn't have brought it up if you didn't think there was some issue."

"I'd just feel happier if I knew what it was."

"Have you asked?"

"Yes. He needs to find someone. I know that much but no more, and he won't open up. He doesn't trust us."

"So what do you want me to do? Beat it out of him?"

She smirked. "Didn't he nearly thrash you last time you fought? I doubt you could."

"Maybe not. So what? We could lock him up for his own safety."

"No. I don't want to do that. I just wanted to let you know. So you can keep an eye on him."

Rico studied her for a moment and gave a nod. "Okay. But if you find out anything, you come and tell me. If he's a danger to us, I want to know. Up until then, it's your call."

"Thanks."

"So how are you doing?"

"Good." She bit her lip. "I killed a man back at the prison. That's when Fergal saved me. I lost it. Again."

"It had to happen. So how do you feel about it?"

"It was…" She was going to say *the best feeling in the world*, and then she remembered the feeling of Fergal deep inside her. Warmth washed over her.

"It was…?" Rico prompted.

"It was amazing. But for the first time, I really got that I was different. I came face-to-face with the darkness and it was part of me. And I hated it. The man was a stranger. I killed him, and I enjoyed it. He didn't deserve that."

"Well, maybe we can find you a few people who deserve to die. There are always plenty about."

She hadn't thought of it like that. There was a lot of killing to be done in the near future. Some people needed to die, but she'd always considered it wrong to actually get pleasure from their deaths. But things were different now. She was different.

She was a vampire.

A bloodsucking monster.

A creature of the darkness.

She'd been rejecting the idea, clinging to the remnants of her humanity, trying to hold on to the nice girl she had been. And she had been nice.

Could there be a middle ground?

"Do I have to lose myself completely?" she asked.

Rico shook his head. "No. The old you is part of the new. We have a bad reputation, but the truth is, in the past, only those drawn to the darkness were changed, so vampires tended to be on the dark side. But we don't have to be totally evil. You know what it feels like now to take a life. It's good. But don't kill pointlessly."

"You're not evil," she said.

"Perhaps not now. But when I was first changed, I killed indiscriminately. And frequently. I fucking loved it."

"Were you drawn to the darkness?" she asked.

"I was never a good man, but I didn't consider myself evil. Then the Church took my wife, burned her at the stake as a witch. After that, I went hunting the darkness. They offered me a chance of revenge, and I grasped it."

Revenge. She wanted revenge. For Janey and Tris. For her family. And it was so close now. She couldn't let Fergal mess that up. "I'm going to find Fergal." She'd ask him nicely and see if he wouldn't open up, let her help him.

"Well, tell me if you find out anything."

"I will." Maybe.

"And perhaps it might be a good idea not to let your boyfriend tie you up again until you're sure of exactly what he's after."

Chapter Twelve

Fergal kept his eye on the door, but Daisy didn't appear.

He'd eaten two more bowls of food while answering Tannis's questions about how he'd accessed the computer systems. He'd told her the truth. He saw no point in lying. And she was impressed.

"You know," she said, "we need a tech person on *The Blood Hunter.* We've struggled since Janey…left. But once this Church business is finished we'll be open for business again, and a source of good intel is always useful."

He wasn't quite sure what she was saying. "Are you offering me a job?"

"Why not? Daisy likes you, and I trust her judgment."

For a minute, he contemplated the idea. Truth was, it made him feel all sort of warm and fuzzy, not something he'd ever felt before. If he'd been the type of guy who wanted to belong, he might have even shed a tear. What would it be like being part of *The Blood Hunter*? They were a motley bunch of space pirates. A motley bunch who happened to include the ex-leader of the known universe and the leader of the

Rebel Coalition. Somehow, they attracted powerful people.

He glanced at Callum Meridian where he sat at the table. "You okay with this?"

"Yeah," Callum said. "And there's no reason why you can't keep up with the reporting at the same time. *The Blood Hunter* has the most up-to-date information delivery systems available."

Again, he felt that little jab of curiosity. What would it be like to be part of this? And with Daisy thrown in. If she still wanted him. Where the hell was she?

But perhaps it was better she wasn't here. She clouded his judgment. This was a fucking fantasy. No way could he join *The Blood Hunter* and go have fun in space with them.

First they had to deal with the Church. And if they did that, likely Fergal was a dead man.

The knowledge was like a bucket of ice water poured right on top of his warm fuzzy feeling.

"I'll think about it," he lied, pushing back his chair and getting to his feet. "You mind if I have a look around?"

"No problem," Callum said. "The ship responds to voice control and will ignore you if you try and go somewhere you're not supposed to be."

That was exactly what Fergal intended to try. He needed to find a way to delay the attack on the Church, and he was pretty sure he could get past any security system they had in place. Of course, he hadn't mentioned that when Tannis was questioning him, and she obviously hadn't thought it through.

No, what he needed now was a good bit of sabotage, and then he could climb into his shuttle and fly away. Go to Trakis Five, find Stefan, get his antidote. And somewhere along the way decide whether he wanted Temperance Hatcher to die. After that, he'd disappear because there would be a whole load of people unhappy with him.

Including Daisy.

A pang of something nasty stabbed him in the gut.

He ignored it.

"We leave in six hours," Tannis said. "If you don't want to tag along, you need to be off the ship by then."

"I'll remember."

He stepped out of the galley and stood for a moment undecided. Should he go find Daisy first, say his good-byes? Though she wouldn't realize it was good-bye.

There was that something again, prodding him in the stomach, as though he had a choice. For the first time, he actually considered letting things take their course. He stopped in his tracks and leaned against the curved wall of the corridor while he tried to come to terms with the idea.

His whole adult life had been driven by one goal—to be able to say, "fuck you" to his father. To tell the bastard that he wasn't going to die. Ever.

It was weird. He'd never been particularly keen on the idea of living forever. He just didn't want to die. There was a difference. And he still didn't want to die. More so than ever.

Trouble was, what he needed to do in order *not* to die would ruin his chances of what might be his only go at a meaningful existence.

With Daisy.

On *The Blood Hunter*.

But who knew? They would both be immortal. Perhaps given enough years she might forgive him. A few centuries, perhaps.

No, he wouldn't say good-bye.

He pushed himself away from the wall and continued down toward the next transporter bubble. The place was quiet. He half hoped he would bang into Daisy, now that he'd decided he wasn't going to seek her out, but he saw no one.

"Engine room," he murmured. The bubble drifted downward.

The engine room was empty and as pristine as the rest of the ship, gleaming white and silver. He wandered around, his hands stroking the sleek metal. He'd never been interested in engines. How did you stop one working?

He'd maybe need to consult the ship's computer. There was a console in the far corner; he could no doubt hook into that. But he didn't hurry.

The truth was, he didn't want to do this. But what he planned wouldn't hurt them. It would only delay them.

Wimp. He shook himself, headed to the console, was reaching out toward it—

"Looking for something?" Rico said from behind him, and he whirled around.

The vampire stood, leaning against the door to the engine room, arms folded across his chest. As Fergal studied him, Rico straightened, his arms unfolded, and he rested one hand on the laser pistol at his thigh.

The action wasn't threatening, but all the same Fergal knew there was a warning there if he was willing to accept it. He wasn't. He could take the vampire. Even armed.

"Nothing in particular. The captain said it was okay for me to look around."

"You should get Devlin to show you in here. This place is his baby."

"I'll do that." He took a step closer.

A lazy smile curled Rico's lips. "So has Tannis offered you a job?"

"You knew she was going to?"

"I guessed. She was positively salivating at the intel you pulled."

"You think I should take it?"

"Up to you, but you'll make Daisy happy."

Fergal took a step closer. He concentrated on his right hand; he'd form a blaster shield that would protect him from the laser and propel the shots back to Rico. Should give him enough of a chance to knock the guy out.

Rico's eyes narrowed, tension radiating from him, but the smile never faltered, as if he was urging Fergal on.

He shifted onto the balls of his feet, readying himself, just as the room filled with the shrill of an alarm and a red light flashed on the wall.

Rico cast him a quick look but raised his wrist and spoke into the comm unit. "What the fuck is going on?"

The tension oozed out of Fergal's muscles. Mission screwed. Were they under attack?

"Dragons?" Rico snapped. "You're fucking kidding me. Or not." He shut off the comm and looked at Fergal.

"Dragons?" Fergal asked.

"It's a long story. Looks like we're leaving a little earlier than anticipated. So you need to decide now. Staying or going?

And once again, he didn't have a lot of choice. "Staying."

"Good. Let's go see about these dragons." They took the transporter bubble up to the bridge. "Were you really going to try and take me back there?" Rico asked.

Shock flashed through him. "Of course not."

Rico chuckled, but at that moment they arrived at the bridge, so there was no opportunity to say anything further. He glanced around but couldn't see Daisy.

"Okay. What the fuck is going on?" Rico snapped as he stalked onto the bridge.

"There are a whole load of dragons breathing fire at the compound," Tannis said.

"Your friends, I presume?" Rico asked.

Fergal realized he was speaking to Saffira, who was pacing the floor, rubbing her forehead.

"They can sense me. I think I've worked it out. It's hard for them to get a lock when I'm moving, but we've been in one place too long and they found me."

"Then it's time to get moving again." Rico threw himself into the pilot's seat. "Ready for takeoff." He turned to survey the room. "Is everyone on board who needs to be?"

"We've lost Candy," Tannis said. "Again."

"Fucking little bitch is more trouble that she's worth."

"She had a reunion with Jon and Alex, then promptly vanished. Thorne went after her."

"Well, they'll have to catch a ride on one of the other ships. They'll be safe here once we're gone." He turned to Saffira. "I'm presuming your friends will follow us."

Saffira nodded. "I think so. You want me to—"

The rest of the room turned on her as one. "No!" they said in unison.

"I'm getting better," she said.

"I don't think we'll risk it just yet," Rico said.

Risk what? Fergal had no clue. But he was more interested in something else. "Dragons?" he said to the room in general. He was presuming they didn't mean real dragons. "And if anyone mentions long stories I might explode."

At that moment, Daisy hurried onto the bridge. She'd obviously showered. Her hair hung damp around her shoulders, and she'd changed her clothes. More black pants, but a red shirt this time, which showed off her white skin. He couldn't believe how pleased he was to see her when he hadn't expected to again. His plans had gone to shit, but he couldn't keep the smile off his face. He walked across, wrapped his hand around the back of her neck, and kissed her.

She looked slightly bemused when he released his hold. He glanced up to find everyone watching them. Daisy shook herself awake. "What's happening?"

"Dragons," Fergal said, watching closely for a reaction.

"Crap. Not again."

Not the reaction he was expecting.

"Okay, everyone," Rico said. "Strap yourselves in. The ride might get a little bumpy."

Fergal followed Daisy to the seats at the edge of the room and sat in the one next to her.

The ship was rising now, the monitors showing the walls of the cavern and the ceiling. He expected it to part so they could get out of there, but it remained stubbornly closed.

"Are we going to crash?" he asked.

"Rico is waiting for the last minute to open the doors. Less chance of them burning us."

"Burning?"

"The dragons. You know, breathing fire…"

"Yeah, right."

He sat back in his seat and tried to relax, but failed.

They were going to hit the roof. He was going to die here. And he wanted to know about dragons first. He reached across and took Daisy's hand and squeezed then risked a glance at her face. Her eyes sparkled with excitement, and a grin stretched her lips. Fucking crazy.

At the last minute, the roof parted and *The Blood Hunter* was free. At the same time, the screens filled with fire— crimson and orange flames—and he swore the temperature rose inside the cabin. Sweat beaded on his forehead.

For a second the monitors cleared, and he saw a…dragon.

"Fuck me. Dragons."

"Hold on," Rico said, and they were away.

As *The Blood Hunter* shot from the planet, the acceleration pushed him back into his seat. Within seconds, the flames cleared from the screens.

Below them, the planet was vanishing into the distance. But a whole horde of winged creatures were on their tail.

"Go to stealth," Rico said.

Now, while the screens still showed the dragons, they were no longer following, but milling around aimlessly. And finally, like the planet, they vanished.

"Well, that was fun," Rico said. "Next time could you give us a bit more warning?"

"I'll try," Saffira said.

"Okay, we're on our way to Trakis Five, people. Let's go blow the Church to pieces."

Not part of Fergal's plans. But right now his nosiness was hands-down beating any concern for the future. "So tell me about dragons," he said to Daisy.

"They followed us back from the other universe."

"Right. Of course they did."

"No. Really. They are the source of Meridian. It's their secondary form of reproduction—they produce this…stuff that combines with human DNA and forms a sort of hybrid. Hence the wings."

"So will he"—he nodded toward where Callum stood, wings folded neatly at his back—"eventually turn into a dragon?"

"We don't think so," Daisy said. "Thorne is already ten thousand years old, and he hasn't changed any more. Breathing fire would be cool, though."

"I'm not sure 'cool' is the word."

A slight headache nagged at his mind. Time for his medication. He reached into his pocket for the bottle, shook the last pill out onto his palm. A bitter reminder that time was running out. He needed to find Stefan. Even then, what were the chances that he would have the antidote handy? Not high, especially if he'd been incarcerated somewhere all this time. This was the end. But instead of being pissed off that he wouldn't get to stand in front of his father, he had an image of Daisy all warm and sweet beneath him. Or on top of him.

"Are you okay?" she asked.

He gave her a sideways glance, and she nodded toward the pill still lying on his palm. "Yeah," he said. "Just a headache."

It was weird. Before he hadn't wanted to die. Now he wanted to live. The difference in perspective from those two similar outcomes was huge.

He threw the pill to the back of his throat and swallowed. It stuck on the way down, and he swallowed again.

So he wanted to live. But at what price?

How much time did he have? This would either be fast or it would be not at all. He needed to beat *The Blood Hunter* to Trakis Five, find Stefan, and get him out.

But he needed help. He looked over to where Rico huddled in a little group with Tannis, Callum, and Devlin. They all raised their heads to stare in his direction. Without a doubt, they were discussing him. Tannis frowned.

The thing was—why would they trust him? He knew their plans, and they had no reason to believe he wouldn't betray them. They owed him nothing. Well, except maybe for Daisy. He had saved her life back at the prison.

Could he confide in her? Would she trust him enough to help him?

He really wanted her to, and not only because it might be his one small chance to live, but because he…well, the sad fact was he wanted her to like him.

His muscles locked up tight, and a tic jumped in his cheek. Sweat still beaded his forehead, and he wiped it away with his sleeve. He hadn't cared whether someone liked him since his mother, and look how well that had turned out. In the end, she had seen killing herself as the only way to free him. As long as she was alive, his father had had complete power over Fergal. Only alone, with no one to worry about but himself, would he have a chance to get away, be free.

That's all freedom was. Another way of saying you had fuck all else to lose and no one left to care about.

God, he was bitter and twisted. He wouldn't wish his godforsaken character on anyone. So his plan was…

Keep his distance. Especially from Daisy.

Use her, but don't let her mean anything to him. Or not more than she already did. He was still safe. Could still walk away.

Well, if he was alive and capable of walking anywhere.

On with the plan.

He turned to her, and she blinked those huge green eyes at him. She seemed at peace. Her skin flushed with the blood she had taken.

"What is it, Fergal? Tell me. You can trust me—I'll help if I can—whatever it is."

It was what he needed to hear, but a little pang of guilt prodded him in the middle. "Do you think I could have a shower?" he asked. "I sweated a little back there—you know, the whole dragon thing." He took a deep breath. "And maybe we can talk."

She smiled brightly, her face lighting up. "Come on, we'll go to my room."

"Sounds like a plan."

They both got to their feet and headed to the door. Fergal couldn't miss the meaningful look Rico cast Daisy as they left the room, and it occurred to him that maybe, if Rico didn't trust him, that was because Daisy had said something.

They took the bubble to Daisy's room. "You want clean clothes," she asked.

"Yeah."

"I'll go find you something."

She left him alone, and he stood looking around, searching for anything that might help. In a drawer, he found a set of silver cuffs. Kinky. But he slipped them in his pocket, together with the key, and headed for the shower.

When he came out, wrapped in a towel, Daisy was sitting on the bed with a pile of clothes in front of her. He realized he didn't want to get dressed. He wanted to lose himself in her.

He strode across, hunkered down in front of her, and kissed her. For a minute, she seemed to abandon herself in the kiss before pulling back.

"No?" he asked.

"I can't," she said. "Not without…" She raised her wrists, and he knew she meant without tying her up.

"I'm game if you are."

She shook her head. "Maybe not a good idea right now."

"You don't trust me?"

"No."

"Well, that's fucking honest anyway." And it hurt. He'd wanted her trust.

"How can I when you won't talk to me? Won't tell me what's going on? All I know is that you need to find a man, but how or where…?" She gave a helpless shrug.

He stood looking down at her, considering his options. He couldn't think of a way to do this without Daisy's help, and he doubted she would do that without him revealing more of what was going on. "Give me a second to dress and we'll talk."

After grabbing the bundle of clothes, he headed back into the small bathroom. He dressed quickly, in black pants and a black shirt—Rico's, from the size and style—then transferred the cuffs into the pants pocket and pulled on his boots.

Daisy was still seated on the bed, and he crossed the room and sank down next to her, leaning his back against the wall and stretching his legs out in front of him. Now he was here, he didn't know how to begin, and he stared straight ahead until her small hand edged into his and she squeezed his fingers.

"Tell me," she said.

Maybe he needed to go back to the beginning. Perhaps not the very beginning, but the start of this particular episode.

"I didn't go undercover in Cybercom because I wanted a

story," he began. "I went because I'd heard they'd discovered an alternative to Meridian. A way to be immortal."

"And you wanted that?"

He shrugged. "Who wants to die? Anyway, as you know, I chopped off my arm, got in there on the pretext of getting another, and once on the inside, I signed up for their alternative program. It was still very much in the experimental stages, and a lot of the volunteers never made it. When you picked me up the first time, twenty years ago, I'd only been in the program a couple of months. I was responding well but still on the antirejection drugs."

"Is that the pills you're taking now?" Daisy asked.

"No. They're something else, but we're getting ahead of ourselves. Things weren't too bad back then. We were confined to the space station, but I never felt like a total prisoner. That changed after the Church took power. Again, at first it wasn't so bad. There was a lockdown on all personnel, but the research went on and we were allowed access to the comms so we knew what was happening in the world."

"And that changed?"

"Yeah. The last five years we were virtual prisoners. My room was nice enough, but it was really no more than a cell. They still went on with the research, but we were no longer told what the procedures were and what the expected outcomes would be. We were in effect lab rats with no say. I got the impression that the research wasn't going well. A lot of people vanished."

"Dead?"

"Some. Others... Six months ago, I woke one night to find a man in my room—a friend, or the closest thing I had in that place. His name is Stefan Wolfe, and he was the top scientist at Cybercom. He told me that the company was about to be taken over by the Church. He was convinced they wouldn't allow him to continue with the research and there was something he needed to do. Something had gone drastically wrong with the last phase of the process. He showed me all the others. They'd been turned into mindless drones, unable to think for themselves, only able to do what they were programmed to do."

"And will that happen to you?"

"I hope not. Stefan had been working on a suppressant that should solve the problem, but the last stage needed six months to mature—time to combine with human DNA and become active. Normally, that would have been done in vitro, but Stefan was scared he wouldn't be allowed to finish."

"So what did that have to do with you?"

"Everything."

Chapter Thirteen

Daisy held her breath. Where he was going with this? Fergal had the sharpest brain of anyone she knew—the idea of him as a mindless drone was inconceivable.

But he was opening up to her. This was what she'd wanted. Except she hadn't wanted to hear anything *really* bad.

"Stefan told me the attack was imminent," Fergal said. "They didn't have time to get everyone out and besides, if they tried the Church would come after them. But he believed he could get me out."

"He wanted to help you. Why?"

"I told you we were friends. And it wasn't help, exactly. He injected me with the suppressant he was working on. The idea was, I stayed alive for the six months it would take for the drug to develop, then I would go find him."

"But that's good, isn't it? So you're going to be all right?"

She'd been sitting beside him, but now she shifted around so she could look into his face as they spoke, try to discern the answer in his eyes. They were blank—he'd gotten too used to hiding his emotions.

"Maybe," he said.

She swallowed. She could do this. "So tell me the rest."

"While he was my friend, he knew me too well, didn't trust me. So he decided not to leave it to my altruistic urges to go back."

"What does that mean?"

"It means, he made sure I had to go find him after the six months was up. He didn't only give me the suppressant. He gave me a poison at the same time."

"But why? Why try to kill you?"

"He wasn't trying to kill me. Stefan was playing it safe. He knew there was a good chance that given the drug I would fuck off and he would never see me again."

"And would you have?"

"Maybe. I don't know, but he didn't give me the option. He injected a lethal poison into my system and gave me enough antidote to last six months."

"The pills you've been taking. They weren't for headaches?"

"In a way. The first sign the poison is affecting my system is a headache, so I know when to take the pills. I've been trying to spread them out, but I wasn't sure how far I could go."

Something occurred to her. "You took the last one just now."

"Yes."

"How long have you got?"

"Twenty-four standard Earth hours."

"Shit. We have to go find this man. I'll help. We'll find him."

"I already have."

There was that bad feeling again. She swallowed. "Where is he?"

"On Trakis Five."

"Shit." She studied him but could still tell nothing from his expression. "How long have you known?"

"Since before your first attempt on the prison break. I had a transfer all set up to Trakis Five. As a prison guard, I could have gotten access to Stefan easily."

"And we messed that up."

"A little. It might still have worked if—"

"If you hadn't broken your cover when you saved me." She jumped to her feet, unable to sit still any longer, and paced the room, her mind whirling. "Is this guy in the prison on Trakis Five? Is that who you were looking for?"

He shook his head. "No and yes. I was looking for him, and he was definitely transferred there, but he's not registered at the prison. My guess is, he's being held at the Church's headquarters."

"So if you had gone through with the transfer, you might have been there when we attack, and you'd be dead."

"I'll be dead anyway."

"There has to be a way around this." She paced some more. "Maybe you could go in with the advance party. Find this Stefan guy while the others are dealing with Hatcher."

He ran a hand through his short hair. "Can you say, with 100 percent certainty, that your friends will help me?"

She chewed on her lip, and her fang nicked her flesh. The taste of her own blood flooded in her mouth. Would they help him? Tannis would do anything for her crew. But Fergal wasn't crew. When Saffira had asked for help, they'd refused her. But that had been different. It would have put them all in danger.

Would this?

She didn't know. She believed Fergal, but did she believe him enough to put her friends in harm's way? Could she help him without involving them?

Because if she went to Tannis and she refused to help,

that would be the end. And Tannis might very well assess the risk as too high, even if she believed Fergal. Daisy hoped not, but she was in no way sure. Tannis had become driven. She blamed herself for Janey's death, and maybe it had been her fault. But it meant that Tannis was focused on two things: keeping the rest of the crew safe and killing Temperance Hatcher. Until those tasks were done, she wouldn't be deviated. And she might well see allowing Fergal in, when he knew of their attack, as too big a risk.

"I don't know. But there has to be a way."

"I was going to take a shuttle and head down there on my own. I thought I had a bit of time before the attack. I could get in, find Stefan, and get out again without anyone knowing."

"If Tannis won't allow you to go in with them, she's not going to allow you to go on your own."

He held her gaze. "I know. And I think they're watching me, so no chance to sneak away."

That was her fault. If she hadn't told Rico she didn't trust Fergal, maybe he would have had a chance to get away. But perhaps Rico wouldn't bother while Fergal was with her. He would presume she was watching him. She couldn't believe she was actually considering going against her own people, putting them at risk. They'd understand—wouldn't they?

And she didn't really believe she would be putting them at too much risk. Because she did trust Fergal. Sort of. And she owed him her life. If it hadn't been for her losing it back on Trakis Four, maybe his plan would have worked. Maybe not, but they couldn't know that. So she was responsible.

He'd told her and that meant so much. Perhaps not everything; she sensed there was still something he was holding back, but he would tell her one day.

"I'll help you," she said.

His eyes widened, and she realized while he'd been

willing to try this, he hadn't expected her help. That made her sad. She was guessing Fergal hadn't had many people on his side over the years, though she also guessed that was mainly his fault.

"We'll take one of the shuttles," she said.

"We?"

"I'm coming with you."

His eyes narrowed. "I don't think that's a good idea. I work alone."

"But this time you might need a fast getaway. I can either go in with you and help, or I could stay on the shuttle, be ready to come get you or just get away fast."

"No."

"Then I'm not helping you. It's not safe to go in there without backup. Besides, there's another thing."

"And that is?"

"I can contact the crew once we're gone. If I'm on board, they're not likely to blow you out of the sky if they catch up with us." At least she hoped they wouldn't. But maybe they would see it as betrayal and decide to terminate her as well. And there would be the added advantage of ridding the ship of the bloodsucking problem she'd become.

Fergal pursed his lips as he thought about it, but gave an abrupt nod. "Okay, but you do what I tell you."

"I'm really good at taking orders."

"I noticed," he said dryly.

"When do we go?"

"It depends. Do you have any long-range shuttles on board?"

"We have every type of shuttle you can think of."

"Then I think we should go now."

All of a sudden, she was scared. Scared of where this was going. That the crew *would* see her helping Fergal as a betrayal. They'd been so good to her. But it wasn't really a betrayal. If Fergal did anything at all she didn't like, she'd rip his throat out. And she'd contact them as soon as they were away. Explain.

What was the alternative? That she watched Fergal die when she could help him?

Not going to happen.

Her comm unit buzzed. She glanced down. Rico. She pressed to open the link.

"Just checking in," Rico said. "Is our friend behaving himself?"

Now was the moment to decide. She looked across at Fergal. His face remained expressionless. Could he see her doubts? Was he letting her make her own decision?

She chewed on her lip.

"Daisy?" Rico prompted. Did he sound suspicious?

Taking a deep breath, she nodded to Fergal, and relief flared in his eyes. "He's fine," she said into her comm unit. "Fast asleep, actually."

Rico was silent for a moment. "Okay. Well, inform me if you need any backup. You know, we could lock him up until this is over."

"I don't think that's necessary. He's told me he needs to find someone, but that it will wait until after the attack."

"Good. But don't take any risks."

"I won't." Guilt gnawed at her insides, but she ended the call and looked around the room. Did she need to take anything with her? She would be back. Wouldn't she? "Let's go."

Fergal nodded and got to his feet. "Thank you. I know that was hard."

She didn't try to deny it. "Rico has been so good to me. He saved my life. He's kept me vaguely sane over the last six months…"

"And you feel like you're betraying him?"

"Yeah. But I'm not. Not really. Because I trust you, and I know you better than they do. You won't betray the attack."

"No, I won't."

They walked down to the docking bay rather than take the transporter bubble, in case anyone was monitoring them. In the bay, she stood for a minute searching the huge, cavernous room.

"Wow," Fergal said. "You weren't kidding."

"Callum had this ship built, and he spared no expense. She's a beauty."

Around twenty shuttles were parked in the area, from small two-seater models to bigger vehicles that would carry up to ten in comfort. The bigger shuttles also had the greater range, and she headed to one standing at the end of the row.

Fergal followed her up the ramp.

"Open," she murmured, and the doors slid apart.

"You can fly all these?" he asked.

"Yeah, they're easy. Easier than yours, anyway."

"Good."

She gave him a sharp glance, but his face remained bland.

The door led straight into the single circular room. Eight seats in four rows of two. The pilot's and copilot's were directly in front of the consoles. She sat in the pilot's seat, flicked a few switches, and the ship came to life beneath them.

"That's us ready to go," she said.

Fergal was still standing, and she swiveled her chair to look at him.

"Come here," he said.

"Why?"

"Because I need to kiss you."

Need—she liked that word. Was she pathetic that she wanted to be needed? She pushed herself slowly to her feet and took the single step to eliminate the space between them. This close she could smell his now familiar scent, warm man overlaid with something slightly metallic. She breathed him in deeply, resting one hand on his chest over the rapid thud of his heart.

He threaded his fingers through her hair and tipped back her head. As she stared up into his silver eyes, she saw the regret there. Regret for what, she wasn't sure. Then his mouth lowered to hers, and he kissed her. His tongue pushed inside, and she sensed the darkness stir sleepily. Instead of fighting, she welcomed it, and it sank back down into her subconscious. She gave herself up to the kiss, pressing her breasts against his chest, her hips against his groin, feeling the hard length of his arousal.

Now was so not the time for this, but she couldn't pull away. He intoxicated her. She breathed him, tasted him, heard his ragged breath in her ears. His hands stroked down her arms, pulling her tighter against him.

The first indication that something was wrong was the cold touch of metal against her right wrist. She went motionless, his mouth still against hers, but before she could react, he'd twisted her left wrist behind her and fastened it to the right so her hands were secured behind her back.

She took a step away from him, and he didn't try to hold her. Staring up into his face, she could see the determination in his eyes. She rattled the cuffs, but she was held tight.

Fergal reached across and pulled the laser pistol from the holster at her waist. "Sorry, sweetheart, but I need a little time to get out of blaster range." He flicked the switch to stun and stepped back. "This will hurt, but it also means you can tell them I overpowered you. Don't mention you wanted to come along. Just go back to your life. Your friends."

"I don't want to tell them that. And you're my friend. Please, Fergal, don't do this."

"I have to. I can't take you in there. There's a 99 percent chance that this is a suicide mission. And I don't want you to die for me. I've had that once in my life, and never again."

Who? She hated that person for turning Fergal into the cold, lonely man he was now. "Who was it?"

He shook his head. "It doesn't matter. I like you, Daisy, but I won't let myself care for you, and I won't let you be used against me. Besides, there are things you don't know about me, and believe me, if you knew, you wouldn't want to come along."

"There's nothing—"

He cut off the words by kissing her. In that moment, she knew he was going to do this. Anger rose up inside her, stirring the darkness, but anything was better than the despair that threatened to swamp her.

This time it was Fergal who stepped back. She stared into his eyes, saw the moment of resolve, the flash of light, and all was pain and darkness.

He'd known when she spoke to Rico that there was no way he was taking her with him. Christ, for a moment he'd actually considered it. With Daisy at his side, anything seemed possible. But it wouldn't work. And Daisy was a vampire. No way could he take her anywhere near the Church.

She appeared so small and helpless lying on the floor of the shuttle, her long pale hair covering her face. Crouching down beside her, he smoothed aside the silky strands, stroked a finger down her cheek.

Hopefully, she'd hate him for this.

He had no clue how long she would be out—vampires didn't exactly react as expected to these things. Scooping her up in his arms, he straightened and headed out the door. At the top of the ramp, he searched the docking bay for somewhere he could leave her safely, finally settling on one of the smaller shuttles.

He carried her across. "Open," he murmured, and the doors parted. Inside, he put her down on the floor beside the pilot's seat, unlocked the cuff from her right wrist, wrapped it around the metal chair leg, and refastened it so she was tied to the seat. There was nothing she could reach that would help her. At the last moment, he removed the comm unit from her wrist and tossed it across the room. Apart from killing her, there was nothing else he could do. And that really wasn't an option.

He leaned across and kissed her on the forehead. She'd be okay. Her friends would look after her. She wasn't alone.

It took a force of will to step away. After closing the doors behind him, he headed back to the shuttle. He stood for a moment staring down at the console, then drew his pistol and shot out the comm unit. He had an idea Daisy would try to talk him out of this once she awoke. And he didn't want to give in to temptation.

Two minutes later, he was in the air. He half expected the docking bay doors to remain shut, keeping him prisoner, but as he approached, the internal doors opened. He hovered for a second while they closed and the external doors parted, and he was out in space, flying away from *The Blood Hunter.*

Chapter Fourteen

Her chest ached. Daisy raised her hand to rub it. And found she couldn't. She was somehow unable to move.

She shifted so she was sitting upright, blinked a couple of times. Directly in front of her was a pair of long black boots.

"What did I tell you about not letting him tie you up?" Rico sounded resigned more than anything else.

"I didn't exactly let him," she mumbled. Fuzziness filled her head, and she shook it, trying to bring back what had happened.

Fergal had shot her. The bastard. And then he'd run off to die alone.

She gritted her teeth. He was allowed to save her, but he wasn't allowing her the opportunity to save him in return. Or so he thought. She had to go after him. "Could you untie me?" she asked.

"I don't have a key. I'll have to shoot it out." But he was already drawing his laser pistol. "Scoot back as far as you can."

She slid back on her bottom until her arms were

outstretched and closed her eyes. The laser seared the skin of her wrists, but the cuffs snapped and she sat for a moment, thinking about what to do next.

"How long have I been out?" she asked.

"How the hell would I know?" He didn't offer her a hand up. Despite his calm words, he was pissed.

Hard luck. "How long since you called me?"

"Just over an hour. I decided to check in at hourly intervals. When you didn't answer, I came looking. So tell me, exactly how fucked are we?"

She pushed herself to her feet and swayed, then rested a hand on the back of the seat in front of her while her legs steadied. "We're not fucked at all."

He raised an eyebrow. "No?"

She needed to get to the bridge, see if Fergal was out of contact distance. She hurried off the shuttle and into the transporter bubble. Rico was right behind her.

"Bridge," he said.

Everyone was waiting as the doors slid open. Even Alex and Jon had managed to get out of bed.

Tannis frowned as she gave Daisy a once-over. "What's with the cuffs and where's our friend Fergal?"

"Gone," Rico said.

"Shit. How screwed are we?"

"We're not screwed," Daisy ground out.

"And how do you work that out?" Tannis snarled. "Did you actually let him go? Knowing he knows our plans?" She ran a hand through her short hair. "I can't believe you freaking let him go."

They were all looking at her, and she couldn't meet their eyes. Did they hate her? Think she'd betrayed them after all they'd done for her? But still she couldn't lie. "I didn't let him go. I was going to go with him, help him. But he shot me instead. He didn't want to take me into danger. He's a good man."

Rubbing her forehead to ease the pressure, she hurried across and sat down at one of the consoles. She flicked a few switches, and Fergal's shuttle came up on the screen. She pressed the comm unit, but nothing happened. He must have disabled the communication system.

"He's still within blaster range," Tannis said as she peered over her shoulder. "We can shoot him out of the sky."

"No!" Daisy's hand reached for her pistol, but at the last moment she dropped it to her side.

Tannis narrowed her eyes at the movement. "You'd fight me over this?"

Daisy shook her head. "No. But please don't do it."

"Give us one good reason why not. Looking at where he is now, he's heading straight for Trakis Five. Which to my mind means he's about to betray us."

"He's not." Daisy swiveled her chair around to face the room. "He's not going to betray us. He just needs to contact a friend of his on Trakis Five."

"And who would that be?"

"A man called Stefan Wolfe."

"Why?"

"Because Fergal will die if he doesn't."

Alex moved from Jon's side to stand next to Tannis. "Stefan Wolfe?"

Daisy nodded. "Yes. He was head scientist at Cybercom, and now he's in prison on Trakis Five."

"I know," Alex said. "I met him, but he's not a prisoner. He's a guest, and he's working with Hatcher."

Her brows drew together. "You're sure?"

"Yes. Absolutely. I don't know what they're up to—Hatcher didn't exactly confide in me—but they were working with someone else. That guy who appeared out of the black hole at Trakis One. The old leader of Earth."

"Great, just great," Tannis muttered. "Max freaking Beauchamp. That was the worst day's work we ever did saving that bastard."

Max Beauchamp had been the last president of the Federation of Nations back on Earth. He'd led the exodus, but his ship had disappeared through the black hole five hundred years ago when the fleet had first come across the Trakis system. *The Blood Hunter* had found the ship damaged and lifeless on the other side of the hole. They'd woken them up from cryo, fixed the ship, and helped Beauchamp and his people get back here.

Big mistake.

"I never met him," Alex said. "I don't think Hatcher and him get along too well, so he's not around much."

Tannis pursed her lips. "Pity, we could have added him to the to-do list." She turned to Daisy. "So, it looks like your friend is double-crossing us after all. Let's take him out."

"No. Wait. Fergal doesn't know. I'd swear it. He thinks this guy is a prisoner."

"And you're 100 percent sure of that?"

She chewed on her lip. Was she? She remembered something. "Yes. He was searching the prison records looking for him."

Tannis frowned. "Yeah. When he got us the intel we needed on Trakis Five, the prison records came out as well."

Daisy's mind worked furiously. "That's why Fergal couldn't find him. That's why he wasn't on any prison records—because he's a guest."

So what was Stefan Wolfe doing? Had he turned sides? Cybercom had always been an independent company, their aim purely profits. Maybe this was just them working for the highest bidder.

"Do you know what this Wolfe guy is working on with Hatcher and Beauchamp?" Tannis asked Alex.

"No. Hatcher didn't trust me—he never spoke of anything important while I was near, but it was big. Hatcher is planning an offensive that will take out the last of the opposition. And something from Cybercom is going to help him."

"Fergal said that the test cases had all turned into drones that could be controlled by computer input."

"So maybe he's offered his army of drones to Hatcher."

Daisy pressed her fingertips to her forehead, trying to ease the ache of so many thoughts going round and round. She was sure that Fergal had no clue his friend was working with Hatcher. Which meant he was walking into a trap. If he did manage to find Wolfe and reveal himself, Wolfe would hand him over to Hatcher.

"So do we zap him?" Tannis asked, interrupting her thoughts.

"No."

Everyone else remained silent. She glanced at Rico where he slouched in a chair opposite, but his face was noncommittal. No help there.

"Give me one good reason," Tannis said.

"He saved my life."

Tannis sighed. "Pretty good."

"He didn't have to," Daisy said, pushing her advantage. "And if he hadn't, he would be on Trakis Five now."

"And he'd probably be in prison or dead."

"Yes, but the point is—he didn't know that."

"No." Tannis sighed again. "So what do we do?"

"I say ignore him," Rico said. "I think there's a good chance he'll be taken prisoner. But I don't think he'll betray us. Or he'll grab this friend and get away. He knows we're not far behind him."

At least Rico trusted Fergal. All the same, Daisy wasn't sure she liked his take on things. In fact, she hated it. "I have to warn him," she said. "He's walking into a trap."

"And how do you plan to do that?" Tannis asked. "He's obviously destroyed the comm unit."

"I'll take a shuttle. Go after him."

"No way. You won't reach him before he hits the planet."

She opened her mouth to say she'd go down and find him, but snapped it shut again. She'd go after Fergal alone if she had to, but perhaps it was better to keep that to herself. Tannis wasn't above locking her up until it was too late if she thought it was the right thing to do for the crew.

Tannis studied her for long minutes, her head cocked on one side, analyzing her, and Daisy held herself very still to prevent herself from squirming.

"You care about him?"

She swallowed. It wasn't something she'd even allowed herself to think about. She was a vampire. Vampires didn't do love. Well, at least not new ones. They were coldhearted killers. And she'd been using Fergal for sex. Nothing more. Except she didn't feel like a coldhearted killer. And the memory of his lovemaking started a warm glow inside her, melting the coldness.

She bit her lip, tasted blood, nodded. "Yes."

"Great. Just great." Tannis turned away and paced the bridge, her movements jerky. Daisy held her breath.

"Okay," Tannis said at last. "We won't blow him up, but we'll keep to the plan. We can't afford to go in before the other teams are in place. And we don't have the manpower to send anyone in ahead of us. Besides, that might just alert them. So we presume your judgment is sound and he won't betray us. When we go in, you come along, find your boyfriend, and we take him out with us. But you'd better be right, because if we lose Hatcher now, I'm going to be so pissed."

"But—"

Tannis held up her hand to forestall any further comments. "That's it and as far as I'm willing to go. And it's a long way. If you're wrong about him, we're fucked. So start praying that you're not."

"Praying to whom, exactly?" Rico drawled. "We're about to attack the Church. I doubt God is going to be on our side."

"I doubt he's on Hatcher's side, either. In the meantime, do we revise our going-in strategy just in case? Start thinking, everybody."

Daisy sat back in her chair and let the conversation flow over her. She was itching to move. She knew Tannis had been generous; her first instinct would have been to protect the crew of *The Blood Hunter* and blow Fergal out of the sky.

But however generous, it wasn't enough.

What did this Stefan guy want with Fergal? Was he nothing more than a giant petri dish for growing God knows what in Fergal's brain? Maybe they didn't even need him alive. Maybe they would kill him as soon as he showed his face and just harvest whatever it was he'd been harboring in his head.

And what if she messed up going in? What if she caused them all to die? What if Fergal did betray them? How could she be sure? Her brain was about to explode.

All the same, she had to reach him before he contacted his friend. She had to warn him.

And if he really was their enemy, she had to kill him.

She'd brought this on them.

Now it was her job to clean it up.

She glanced across to find Rico watching her, his eyes narrowed, and she managed a weak smile. She was trying to work out the numbers in her head. No way could she overtake Fergal now—she'd given him one of the fastest shuttles. But if she left straightaway, she might be able to intercept him as he reached the planet, or maybe he'd pick her up on the surveillance monitors and he'd know someone was following. He might even guess it was her.

So she needed to go. And hope that they wouldn't blast *her* out of the sky. She didn't think they would, but you never knew what Rico would do if you pissed him off enough.

She lifted a hand to rub her head, and the cuffs rattled. "I'm going to go see if I can get these things off," she said, raising her arms and shaking the cuffs. "I'll be right back." Of course, they would know as soon as she was gone, but she couldn't help that.

A whole lot of eyes followed her as she left the bridge. She walked rather than taking the bubble—she needed to think. Plan.

Once in her cabin, she sat on the edge of her bed and tried to pick the lock, but her hand was shaking. "Fuck," she muttered and threw the pick across the room.

"You need some help?"

She glanced up to see Rico lounging in the open doorway, arms folded. He straightened and crossed the room, picked up the pick and crouched down beside her. "So you're going after him alone?"

She jerked out of his hold and stared into his face. "How did you know?"

"Fucking crew has never been able to take orders. Why should anything change now?"

"Does Tannis know?"

"Probably. You never were any good at hiding your feelings." The first cuff clicked and fell free, and he started work on the second.

"And are you going to try and stop me?"

"Honey, there's no try about it. If I wanted to stop you, you're stopped."

She sniffed but had no doubt he was telling the truth.

He unlocked the second cuff, and it dropped to the floor. "And no. I'll let you go."

"Why?" she asked, rubbing her wrists.

"Because there are some things you don't recover from."

"And you're not going to suggest I take someone with me?"

"No. Alone, you might slip in unnoticed. Security isn't one of the Church's strong points. A single person might succeed where a team of us would be picked up."

"And I've got something that might help," a voice said from the doorway. Alex stood there, a bundle in her hands. "Here." She thrust it toward Daisy, who grabbed the bundle and shook it out. It was Alex's high priestess's robes, the ones she'd been wearing when Tannis pulled her out of Trakis Five.

"There are a lot of the sisters at the headquarters right now. These might help you get in there unnoticed. And here," she said, handing her a small wrist unit. "I've programmed this with the floor plan of the inner area where Stefan Wolfe was staying."

Daisy blinked. "Thank you."

"I want you out of there safely. Just try not to smile too much—the teeth sort of give you away."

"I don't think I'll be doing a lot of smiling."

"And keep your eyes down—try and look demure. And hold your hands like this." Alex clasped her wrists in front of her body.

"I will."

Daisy didn't bother stripping off her pants and shirt, just pulled the heavy robes on over the top, and an immediate sensation of suffocation swept over her. The robes were tight and a little short. Alex was smaller than she was, but she managed to do up the row of tiny buttons even if she couldn't breathe afterward.

"And the finishing touch..." Alex held out the black headdress, and Daisy took it from her.

"I'll add this later." She stood for a moment gazing at the two of them. "Don't look so serious," she said. "I'm coming back."

Alex patted her arm. "Of course you are."

It was weird; she'd always thought of Alex as the same age as her and even less mature. Now Alex was twenty years older, and while that wasn't immediately obvious, if you looked into her eyes, you could see the maturity reflected there, and the pain. She'd been a prisoner for the last ten years, separated from the man she loved and from her children. The Church hadn't known about Angel or Candy, which was just as well, as they would have had more hostages for Alex's good behavior.

"How's the hunger?" Rico asked.

"Fine. I haven't even thought about it since..." Since she'd woken after Fergal knocked her out. She didn't think she'd ever gone that long without thinking about blood.

"Good. You're getting it under control. Very impressive."

She couldn't put this off any longer. "Okay, well, this is it."

They took the transporter bubble down to the docking bay. As the door slid open, she found Tannis and Devlin standing beside one of the shuttles, talking together. Were they going to try to stop her? But Tannis just raised an eyebrow as she approached. "Nice outfit. You make a great priestess."

Daisy flashed a fang.

"Very unholy. You're going after him?"

"I have to."

"I think we all realized that." She waved a hand at Devlin. "Devlin has been working on one of the shuttles, fitting the stealth device."

"It's still not 100 percent, but should hold out. And she's already set to your voice control."

"Thank you." It would make getting in unnoticed much easier. She'd been planning to land a distance away from the Church's headquarters so as not to be spotted, but with this she could land on the roof and they wouldn't pick her up.

Devlin shifted from foot to foot. "You want company and I'll come with you. You might need backup. Or get hungry."

"I couldn't…" She broke off.

"Hey, don't go all mushy. But I talked to Saffira, and she's in agreement. You all came back for us when it meant almost certain death."

"We lived."

"It could have gone either way, but you still came. How can we do less for you?"

Daisy swallowed and blinked back a tear. Looked like she was getting mushy after all. Then she took a deep breath and shook her head. "No," she said. "I think my best chance is to try and stay unnoticed, and that will be easier alone. If it comes down to a fight, one more person won't help."

"I think you're right," Tannis said. "But remember, we're behind you." She glanced at her wrist. "We attack in twenty-three hours. If you're caught, try and stay alive that long, and we'll get you out. And try not to bite anyone."

"I'll try."

Tannis reached for her and took her in a hug. For a moment it felt tentative—Tannis wasn't one for hugging—then her arms tightened around her. Finally, she released her and stepped back. "You've been with us so long. Try and stay alive."

"I will."

Her footsteps were heavy as she climbed the ramp. She couldn't help but wonder if this was the last time she would see her friends. More than friends—her family. At the top she turned around.

They all looked so solemn.

"Tell Fergal the job offer is still open," Tannis called out.

They'd offered him a job? He hadn't told her that. But it was too late to discuss now. She had to go. She gave a waggle of her fingers and turned her back on them.

The shuttle woke around her as she strapped herself into the pilot's seat. She kept herself from thinking as she went through the preflight checks.

Five minutes later, she was flying away from *The Blood Hunter*. Only when the ship was far behind her did she let the tears fall. They dripped crimson onto the white skin of her hand.

She allowed herself thirty seconds to wallow, and then she wiped her face, checked her coordinates, and set the shuttle to maximum speed. For the first time, she didn't feel the thrill of exhilaration as she headed into the vastness of space.

Chapter Fifteen

"Fuck."

Fergal slammed his fist down on the console. Stefan wasn't here. Or at least Fergal was as sure as he could be without going and checking out the cells himself. But something told him he wouldn't find the scientist. There was no one listed who matched any of the information he had on Stefan's last transfer.

And he needed to get the hell out of there. The place was crawling with security. Much higher than he'd expected from the intel he'd pulled while on *The Blood Hunter*.

Something must be going down.

He needed to warn them. But he'd risk exposing himself if he contacted the ship.

For a second, he stood indecisive, then slammed his fist into the console a second time. He so did not need this right now. This had to be the absolute worst time to develop a conscience. Though it was more than conscience. The thought of Daisy walking into this mess unaware gave him palpitations.

He wondered if she hated him right now. Had she forgiven him? Had she understood? Maybe she'd be up and awake and if he commed the ship, he would get to talk to her one last time.

Without taking any longer to talk himself out of it, he slumped down in front of the console, opened the comm unit, and entered the codes for *The Blood Hunter.*

"Well, well, if it isn't our friend Fergal."

Not Daisy, but Tannis. And strangely, she didn't sound too pissed.

"Where are you?" she asked.

"Church's headquarters. In the prison section."

"And I'm guessing you haven't found your friend."

So obviously, Daisy had told them about Stefan. But how did Tannis know that he hadn't managed to locate Stefan? "How do you know that?"

"Because he's not in the prison."

"And do you know where he is?"

"Currently an honored guest of everybody's favorite priest, Temperance Hatcher."

Shock punched him in the gut. "What?"

"According to Alex, he's staying in the main building, he's not a prisoner, and he's working on something with Hatcher."

"I don't believe it."

"You'd better."

He scrubbed his hand through his short hair, trying to make sense of what she was saying. Could Stefan be working with the Church? He really didn't believe it.

Did he?

Maybe they'd offered him a chance to finish his research. To Stefan, his work was everything. But in exchange for what?

An army of mindless drones, perhaps?

But the Church was totally opposed to the idea of what Cybercom had been trying to achieve. Even if Hatcher was aware there was an army coming after him, Fergal doubted that would sway the priest from the righteous path.

"So, nice as it is to hear your voice, why did you call?" Tannis interrupted his thoughts. "I take it you have a reason."

He shook his head, trying to get his mind back on the present. "I wanted to let you know that the security here is much higher than you thought."

Tannis was silent for a moment. "How much higher?"

"A lot. You'd be walking into a bloodbath."

"And you didn't want that. How sweet."

There wasn't a lot he could say to that. "I'm sending you an uplink with the revised security details."

"Thank you."

"You still coming in?"

"Hell, yes. You have about ten hours to get your friend—if he's still your friend—and get the hell out of there. Or you can stick around and mooch a lift with us. After we've dealt with Hatcher." She was silent for a moment. "There's still a job for you here if you want it."

There was that warm fuzzy feeling again. "Is Daisy around?" He tried to make the question casual but was quite aware he failed totally.

"I was going to get to that. No, she's not around."

Why did he get a bad feeling? "Can you get her?"

"Not going to happen, because right around now, Daisy is somewhere above your head, wandering the Church headquarters, looking for you."

For a second, the words didn't make sense. "You have got to be fucking kidding me."

"No. When we found out your friend was working with Hatcher, she had to come and warn you. Of course, if you hadn't destroyed the comm unit on your shuttle, we could have called. But you did. So off she went."

"Well, fucking comm her and tell her to get back."

"No can do. She's already landed and left her ship. We might break her cover if we comm now."

"Cover?"

"She's dressed as a nun. But I've got to be honest, she makes a totally crap sister, so you might want to go and intercept her."

A vise tightened around his chest. He sat and stared straight ahead, trying to get the panic under control, slow his breathing. "Couldn't you have stopped her?"

"We tried."

"Don't you have any fucking control over your crew?"

"It's what she wanted."

"Fuck." He gritted his teeth together. Stupid fucking imbecile.

"I hear you saved her life," Tannis said.

"So?"

"That makes her your responsibility. Make sure she gets out of there."

"Yeah, right. A fucking vampire in the middle of a whole bunch of fucking priests. Shit. She won't spontaneously combust or anything...will she?"

"I don't know. Wait a sec." There was a minute's silence. Fergal was itching to go, but he needed to understand what he was up against. What he was facing.

"No, she should be okay," Rico answered.

"What about crosses?" God, they were everywhere. There was even one on the wall above his head right now.

"Should be all right as long as the person wielding it isn't an actual believer, and there are fewer of them about than you'd think."

"Holy water?"

"The same."

Why hadn't he found out all this while he was on *The Blood Hunter*? Because he hadn't thought he would need it. He scrambled his brains for anything he knew about vampires. After his first meeting with Rico all those years ago, he'd looked up everything he could on the subject, but most had been conjecture. "Garlic?"

"Love the stuff. Look, just keep her from direct sunlight. Avoid crosses if you can. If you get caught, try and keep quiet about the whole vamp thing. We'll spring the pair of you when we get there. But if they discover what she is, chances are they'll stake her."

"Jesus."

"You'll do okay," Rico said. "Go find her."

The comm light flashed off. They were gone. Fergal stared straight ahead at the console, still trying—and failing—to slow his breathing. His hands were shaking. Shit, even now she could be walking into trouble. What if she lost it like she had back on Trakis Four? Why the hell had they let her come? And come alone.

Breathe.

He just had to find her. Get her somewhere safe or preferably back on her ship and heading away from here. From him. Hell, didn't she know he was nothing but trouble?

But beneath his panic was something else. She cared. Cared enough to fight her friends for him. To come after him and try to save him. No one had ever done that for him before.

Well, not since his mother.

The thought was like slamming headfirst into an ice asteroid.

No way was he going through that again. He refused to let someone matter to him, and he ignored the little nagging voice that told him it was already too late.

He wouldn't let her matter.

He'd go find her, and he'd carry her back to her ship if he had to.

He'd tie her to the seat, set the autopilot, and send her

back where she belonged. Then he'd go find Stefan, and he'd do what he came here to do. But now, he'd be aware that maybe Stefan wasn't his friend after all. He was still trying to wrap his brain around that one.

First he had to find Daisy.

Take a deep breath.

Make a plan.

Glancing around the room, his gaze settled on the prison guard he'd knocked out. Now he crouched down beside the man and felt for a pulse. Nothing. Fergal undressed him quickly, pulled the uniform on over his own clothes, and strapped the laser pistol around his waist. It might give him a little cover.

Next, he pulled up the building plans on the console. He needed to be methodical. He couldn't afford not to think straight right now. After imprinting them in his memory, he shut down the console and set off.

He eliminated two more guards on his way out of the prison, hiding their bodies as best he could. The next rotations weren't for two hours, and with a little luck, he should have that much time. But since when had he been lucky?

Five minutes later, he left the prison and reached ground level. It was the middle of the night, so at least he didn't have to worry about the sunlight thing for a little while. Hopefully, by the time the suns rose, Daisy would be well on her way away from here.

He passed a group of priests, but no one gave him a second look. Then a couple of sisters. He looked at them carefully, but they definitely weren't Daisy.

Where would she be?

Tannis had said that Stefan was a personal guest of Temperance Hatcher. Which meant he'd be staying in the private residence on the upper floor. It would make sense for Daisy to go there. Or would it? She wasn't aware that he'd contacted Tannis and knew about Stefan. So she'd expect him to be in the prison searching.

He did an about turn and hurried back the way he had come.

He was pretty sure she wasn't already in the prison. He'd have spotted her. So if he loitered around the entrance, he'd intercept her. But what if he was wrong?

Shit. His head was going to explode, and not only because he was six hours late with the antidote. How long did he have?

Everything was falling apart. Not that it had ever been particularly together, but at least before he'd had simple goals: live forever and go boast to his dad that the devil was never going to get him.

Now everything was so much more complicated.

Why couldn't she have stayed on *The Blood Hunter*?

Because she cared for him.

He stopped his pacing and banged his head against the wall.

"Fergal?"

He'd been so wrapped up in his thoughts, he hadn't even seen her. Which just went to prove that she was no damn good for him. All the same, when he looked at her in that ridiculous outfit, a wave of warmth flooded him and a smile tugged at his lips. She was dressed in black from the top of her head down to her feet. The black headdress hid her hair and framed her face, her white skin a stark contrast.

He stalked toward her, meaning to bawl her out for being a stupid, incompetent bitch. But somehow his arms went around her and he dragged her to him and kissed her like he'd never let her go. He lost himself in the taste of her, that musky cold flavor he'd come to love.

"What...?"

His arms dropped from her, and he whirled around, drew his laser pistol, and blasted the priest who stood staring at the two of them, eyes wide. Probably didn't come across a lot of nuns snogging in the corridors. The man crumpled to the floor. And Fergal came back to himself with a crash.

"Don't move," he snarled at Daisy.

She raised an arched brow but very sensibly moved nothing else.

He kicked open the door, which led underground and into the prison, grabbed the priest by the shoulders, and dragged him through. He looked around for somewhere to hide the body and eventually dumped it in an empty cell, where it was hidden by the darkness.

When he turned, Daisy stood directly behind him.

"I said don't move."

She flashed him a smile. "And has anything about me suggested I'm good at taking orders?"

Anger washed over him at her words. Irrational anger, but he couldn't control it. She was going to die here. Because of him. The anger spiraled in his head, all mixed with fear and panic so he couldn't see straight.

He slammed his fist into the wall, and the pain broke through the other emotions. Taking a deep breath, he turned to look at her.

How had he come to this? He hadn't considered he had a heart—now he could feel it thudding, racing, threatening to explode out of his chest. He was no good to her like this. He needed to get himself under control, get her out of here.

"What the fuck do you think you are doing?" he growled.

"I came to warn you about—"

"I know about Stefan. I just talked to Tannis."

Her brows drew together. "You did. So you knew I was here?"

"Why the fuck do you think I was wasting my time hanging around looking for you when I should have been searching for Stefan?"

"Oh." Her shoulders sagged, and he longed to wrap his arms around them, pull her to him and tell her how it made him feel that she'd come for him. But that sort of crap would not get her out of here alive.

"I don't want you here. I work alone. I always have and I always will."

"Hard luck," she snapped. "I'm here now, so get over it."

"Not for long. Straighten your dress—you're leaving."

A determined expression settled on her features. "Not without you."

"How about I don't give you a choice?"

"How about you do? And don't think you can try that tying me up crap. I won't fall for it again."

"You reckon?"

She stood with her hands on her hips, the position totally incongruous in the nun's outfit. "Yeah, I reckon."

He shook his head. And decided maybe a little truth would help. "I need to keep focused, and you're a distraction."

"I am?" Her expression softened.

"Yes. So, I'll see you safe back to your shuttle, and afterward, I'll find Stefan, and we'll be right after you."

"What if he doesn't want to come? What if he really is working with Hatcher?"

"He isn't."

"You don't know that. And if he doesn't cooperate, you might need some help getting him out of here. Besides, my shuttle is on the roof. If—"

"On the roof? Are you crazy? I'm betting it will have been found by now. Hardly inconspicuous up there." He was going to have to take her to his, which was parked a mile away from here and would waste valuable time. But what choice did he have?

"No. It's safe. I left it in stealth mode—Devlin set it up. It won't be found unless someone bumps into it. What I was saying was, even if you take me back to my shuttle, we're going to have to go back through the main building. We might as well look for your friend at the same time."

What she said made sense, but he wasn't convinced. It would take longer, and he wanted...*needed* her away from here. This place was tainted. The scent of incense hung heavy in the air. It reminded him of his childhood, raising all the old feelings of hopelessness and despair. Being with Daisy, here in this place, felt so wrong. As if everything was falling apart, leaving him helpless to save her as he'd been helpless all those years ago.

"And," she continued, dragging him from his less than happy thoughts, "I did a quick survey of the place on the way down. I'm pretty sure I know where he is. We can go back that way, slip in, pick him up, and be out of here."

It sounded way too easy.

Daisy studied him surreptitiously. He was close to capitulation, and he wasn't happy about it. Part of her was pissed off that he was so against her being here, that he didn't believe she could help him. But beneath that, she knew the real reason he was so shocked to see her here was because he was scared. Absolutely terrified that she was going to get caught.

That could only mean he cared.

Cared for *her*, and suddenly she was glad she was here, with Fergal. Whatever happened, he cared for her, and that filled her with a warmth and a sense of belonging she'd never experienced in her entire life before.

Six months ago, she'd cheated death, and ever since, the feeling that she should have died, that maybe there was nothing left for her here, had lingered in her mind. While she'd been grateful to Rico, at times it had been so hard she had wondered if it wouldn't have been better…

Her friends had turned into food, and she knew they feared her. Plus, they all had someone, and she'd felt like an interloper in the only home she had ever had since her parents died. Before that, really. Her parents had been in love, which was nice but had meant that even back then she had felt like an outsider.

For a little while, as part of the crew of *The Blood Hunter*, she'd experienced a growing sense of belonging, but then everything had changed, her world had fallen apart. She'd sat and watched from the sidelines as everyone had found someone. Or died. Everyone but her. She'd even failed at dying.

She'd seen them fall in love—even the cynical Devlin— and she'd wanted that. Dreamed of finding someone of her own. Then Rico had changed her, and she'd tried to put the hopes and dreams behind her. Who would possibly want her now?

Fergal did.

She could see it in the tense lines of his body, the little frown line between his brows, the way his eyes darted from her to the door and back again. There was real fear in his eyes. Not for himself. For her.

She'd been waiting for him to speak, but now she closed the space between them, reached up, slid her hands around the back of his neck, and pulled him down to her. She kissed him lightly at first, feeling the resistance in the strain of his body away from hers. Something seemed to snap inside him, and he was kissing her back, his mouth slanting over hers, his tongue pushing inside. She wanted to melt into him, but she held herself a little apart. They couldn't afford to lose it, not here; she just needed a token to give her strength. Finally, his lips pulled free, but his arms came around her and he gathered her close.

For a minute they stood, touching along the lines of their bodies, so she could feel the hammer of his heart through the thick layers of clothing.

He took a deep breath and pushed her away, stood looking down at her, his face free of expression except for a little telltale tic in his cheek just above his mouth. "Let's go find Stefan," he said.

Daisy wisely restrained herself from punching the air, but she couldn't bite back her grin.

Fergal's eyes narrowed, then he scowled. "Don't think this means we're a couple or anything. I still work—"

"Alone," she finished for him. Once they got out of here was time enough to show him how wrong he was about that. Her blood fizzed in her veins, excitement bubbling inside her.

"And you do what I tell you," he said. "I say 'run' and you run. I say 'hide' and you—"

"Hide," she said. And she would…if she thought it was a good idea.

They could do this. The place was crawling with security, but no one had questioned her on the way down through the building. Obviously, the whole nun thing rendered her just about invisible. Fergal in his security uniform would hopefully be the same.

"I'll go first," she said. "I think the nun's cover is the better one."

"I don't agree," he said. "*I* go in front."

She tightened her lips. "But I know the way."

He looked at her for a second and gave an abrupt nod. "Okay, but the first sign of trouble and you get behind me."

"Of course," she said demurely.

Fergal opened the door and peered out into the main corridor. He glanced back, nodded, and stood aside for her to pass. She grasped her wrists together as Alex had shown her and lowered her head in an attempt to look demure.

How hard could demure be?

Fergal walked a couple of steps behind her.

Trouble with acting demure was she couldn't see where she was going—perhaps she'd save it for if they met someone. The first five minutes they saw no one. She kept her walk slow as befitted a woman of God, though her feet itched to break into a run.

She didn't like this place. It reeked of something sweet and sickly.

As she turned a corner, a sister approached them. Daisy looked down and kept her eyes firmly on the smooth, shiny floor until the woman passed. Then a group of security officers, but again they didn't slow. There were so many about, she'd noticed on the way down, far more than expected, which in some ways worked in their favor. With so many new people here, it would be unsurprising if they didn't recognize everyone, so Fergal could pass unnoticed.

Finally, after two flights of stairs, she came to a halt and peered back at Fergal. Ten feet down the corridor was a set of double doors, white, inlaid with gilt, and a huge cross painted on them. A guard stood at attention in front of the doors.

"This is the entrance to the private residence," she murmured to Fergal, who had come to a halt behind her. "We need to get in there."

Fergal pursed his lips. "Walk up and say you're here to see Hatcher. I'll be right behind you.

She nodded. Clasped her wrists, looked down, and did her best to glide the last ten feet. "I have a message for High Priest Hatcher," she said.

"Yes, Sister. I'll clear it with His Eminence."

That didn't sound good. But before he had a chance to speak into his comm unit, Fergal stepped forward. His right arm reached out, except it was no longer an arm but a long silver knife, which sliced into the guard's throat. The man collapsed as blood erupted from his jugular, filling the air with the sweet intoxicating scent. All of a sudden the hunger, which had been sleeping, roared into life. Daisy swayed toward the body but knew instantly the life was gone and there was no food for her there.

She sniffed the air, searching for another source.

Food—she needed to feed the darkness. It rose, choking her, blinding her to everything but need.

"Daisy!"

The sound of Fergal's voice pulled her back to herself. Just enough to remember where she was. She licked her lips, turned her head to stare at Fergal. But she could scent the wrongness of his blood. No food there, either.

But there were others close by.

"Daisy," he said again. This time he grabbed her by the shoulders and shook her slightly. "Come on, sweetheart, get a grip. You can do this. Pull it together."

It wasn't the words but the fear in his voice that broke through the raging hunger. She swallowed, gritted her teeth, searched inside herself, and pushed the darkness back down. She was breathing hard, but she'd done it. She grinned. She'd done it!

Beside her, Fergal's face had a gray tinge.

"Sorry," she said.

He glanced from her to the body that lay crumpled at her feet.

"Shit. I didn't think. I wanted a quick way to silence him, but I should have…"

"It's okay. Come on, we need to get the body out of sight before anyone comes. Drag it into that room over there."

While she waited for Fergal to dispose of the body, she rubbed at the blood that stained the floor until it wasn't too noticeable.

When he got back, he searched her face.

"I'm fine," she said. "Really, I am. Now, let's get through this door."

"I pulled the codes from the system," Fergal said. "They're pretty simple for the internal doors. Stand back." She stepped away and watched as he punched a code into the door panel.

The doors slid open.

So far, so good. She was starting to believe that they would do this. Maybe they'd find Hatcher as well and they could kill him now, save *The Blood Hunter* the trouble of coming down here before the attack.

That feeling of excitement bubbled up inside her.

Through the doors, they stepped into luxury, thick carpets under her feet and beautiful furniture lining the walls of the corridor. She stood for a moment, glancing around her. A number of doors led off from the corridor, and she counted them off in her head. According to Alex, the fourth door should lead into the apartment where Stefan Wolfe was staying. She took a step toward it when the door opened and at the same time, the shrill of an alarm shrieked through the building.

"Shit," Fergal said from behind her.

Chapter Sixteen

Things seemed to move in slow motion.

Daisy couldn't wrench her eyes away as the door opened. A figure appeared, framed in the opening. Her breath hitched in her throat.

Fucking hell.

Hatcher. In the flesh. A wave of darkness surged up inside her. Without thinking, she slipped her hand inside the slit she'd cut in her robes, her fingers closing around the hilt of the laser pistol strapped at her waist.

Fergal came up beside her and rested a warning hand on her other arm. "No," he said very quietly.

She breathed slowly, forcing the darkness down, concentrating her mind. The alarm rang in her ears, but there was no reason for the man in front of her to have any idea she was not what she appeared to be. Clutching her wrists together so hard her nails dug into her skin, she kept her eyes down, peering up through her lashes. A second figure appeared behind Hatcher, and Fergal's hand tightened on her arm.

Close by, the sound of running feet was getting closer, boots slamming against the marble.

The footsteps slowed, and her nostrils filled with the scent of warm bodies, sweat overlaid with the hot sweetness of blood. Had they found the dead priest? Maybe it was protocol to head for the private residence when the alarms went off. Head up here to protect the big boss.

Keep it together and they could still get out.

"What's going on?" Hatcher said.

Daisy gave him a quick peek. He had cold, silver-gray eyes, with a hint of madness lurking in their depths. The last time she had seen him had been the day he captured *The Blood Hunter*, held them all prisoner, and forced Callum to destroy Trakis Seven. That day, he had killed Janey and Tris. A rush of hatred froze her blood, but she couldn't allow that free rein. Not here. Not now.

Beside her, Fergal had gone still as if frozen in place. She risked a sideways glance and found his gaze fixed on Hatcher.

"Well?" Hatcher snapped.

There were people directly behind them now. A lot of people. But Fergal appeared impervious. All his attention on the man in front of them.

"Cain?" The man behind Hatcher spoke, and Fergal seemed to shake himself out of his daze.

Stefan Wolfe, she presumed. Daisy glanced at him as he came up beside the priest.

Friend or foe?

They were about to find out.

But before he could speak again, a third figure appeared behind Hatcher. Someone she knew. More to the point, someone who knew her. Max Beauchamp, the last president of Earth.

Shit.

Icy coldness engulfed her core.

The crew of *The Blood Hunter* had saved this man's life. From the expression on Beauchamp's face, it didn't look like he was going to be all that grateful.

She held her breath, waiting to see what he would do. But she knew at a glance that he'd recognized her. His eyes narrowed. She found herself shifting closer to Fergal, though there was nothing he could do. The numbers against them were too great. All the same, she tried to catch his eye. Were they going to make a fight for it? While their chances weren't good, fighting still had to be better than giving in. Although maybe they would just be locked up, and in a few hours, *The Blood Hunter* would be here to rescue them.

But Fergal appeared dazed. He'd glanced briefly at Stefan, but his attention was back on Hatcher. He didn't even seem to notice Beauchamp. Or her, for that matter. What the hell was the matter with him?

Max Beauchamp stretched out a bony finger. "That woman is a"—he hesitated, obviously not quite able to get the word "vampire" past his lips—"a monster."

She resisted the urge to flash her fangs. He'd obviously never forgiven her for wanting to eat his daughter, back when she was newly changed and had almost no control over her urges.

She tugged at Fergal's arm as the guards moved up behind them, glaring into his face, willing him to give some indication of what he wanted them to do. He appeared to snap out of it as the guards grabbed them both from behind. Her hand was still on the pistol—she could still take that bastard Hatcher, or Fergal's friend who was obviously no friend at all, but Fergal gave a small shake of his head.

She unclenched her fingers from around the pistol.

"Who is she?" Hatcher asked, his cold gaze sliding over her. At least *he* was unlikely to recognize her. The last time they'd met, she'd been green.

Fergal gave a shrug. "Just one of the sisters I picked up as cover."

"She's a member of the crew that discovered my ship," Max supplied for them. *Bastard.* So much for gratitude. "She's a bloodsucking spawn of Satan."

Hatcher glanced at the guard who held her and gave a small nod. The headdress was wrenched from her head, and her hair tumbled halfway down her back.

"Well, she's no nun, that's for sure." Hatcher's cold eyes slid down over her, leaving her feeling like she was covered in a layer of slime.

"I've read up on them since I was on their devil ship," Max said, and Daisy only narrowly resisted rolling her eyes. Who was he trying to impress? He stepped closer and pulled something out of his pocket. A large cross on a silver chain dangled from his fingers. Fear pricked her, but as the cross grew closer, she felt nothing. He pressed it against the skin of her forehead, and she waited for the sizzle of flesh, but the metal was cool against her skin. Looked like Max Beauchamp wasn't a true believer after all. How surprising.

His gaze narrowed on her as he stepped back. "She must have some protection." But a frown formed between his eyes. Either he was totally deluded or he didn't know the cross thing would only work if wielded by a true believer. She suspected a little of both.

Daisy kept her expression serene, tried not to hope.

Fergal said nothing. He still didn't appear quite with it, and she wanted to scream at him. Once in the cells, they would have a hard time escaping. If they were going to make a break, it had to be now.

"Take her away," Hatcher said. "We'll test her properly later."

"No!" She didn't want to be parted from Fergal, but they were already dragging her away. She had to stop them.

She glanced at Fergal, but he looked away. The hands tightened on her arms. Something shattered inside her, and the darkness, so close to the surface, roared into life. Her vision hazed with crimson.

"Daisy, no!" At last, Fergal seemed to come back to life. Too late.

Her gums ached with the need to feed, her fangs extended. With ease, she twisted free of the hands that held her, lunging for the man closest. A small part of her brain screamed at her to stop, but the scent of blood was in her nostrils, filling her mind, and the darkness took control.

A moment of sublime pleasure as her fangs sank into the flesh of the man's throat. Warm blood filled her mouth, and she swallowed convulsively.

"Vampire." She heard the word as though from a distance. Something hard pressed up against her side. A flash of pain, and she went under.

Fergal stared at the lifeless body crumpled on the floor. His mind was numb, and it was as though he'd rolled back the years. He was eight again, and his mother was dead. Dead to make sure he would live. Seeing Hatcher brought everything back, and he felt useless and powerless. Shit scared.

A wave of panic rose up inside him. He squeezed his eyes shut and pushed it down by force of will.

When he opened them, nothing had changed. He held himself still, fighting the urge to run to Daisy. He couldn't help her. Not right now. And he couldn't afford to let them see how much she meant to him. She wouldn't be dead. Rico had said they could be injured but not killed by a laser blast. Somehow, he would save her. He just needed to keep his head and remember he had something Stefan wanted. At least, he hoped he did.

But what was to stop Stefan from taking it?

Simply knock Fergal out and drain him dry.

He still didn't know whether his friend was working with the bad guys. Stefan had never been interested in religion, considered it a load of bollocks, but he certainly seemed on friendly terms with Hatcher. Maybe the priest had offered him the means to carry on with his research. Stefan was single-minded—he wouldn't care where the funding came from.

Though Fergal would have sworn he would care what was done with his research at the end of it all. So what did the Church want with Cybercom? As soon as the question flashed up, an image of that army of drones rose up in his mind.

"Is she dead?" Stefan's voice broke into his thoughts.

"She was already dead. A walking corpse," Hatcher sneered. "But it would take more than a laser to finish the monster off. Fire or sunlight." He nodded to the guards. None of them appeared keen to go near Daisy, though she looked small and helpless lying unconscious on the floor.

"Move," Hatcher snarled, and the nearest guard stepped forward. He crouched down and picked her up gingerly, slinging her over his shoulder so her silver fall of hair reached nearly to the ground.

Fergal said a silent vow as she disappeared from view. He would save her. Whatever the cost. He glanced to the priest. Whatever price he had to pay.

The guards let go of his arms, but he was surrounded. Now with Daisy gone, the attention of the three men turned to him. Fergal glanced away quickly as he encountered Hatcher's gaze. The priest couldn't know him. It had been too long. A different lifetime.

Instead, Fergal concentrated on Stefan but could read

nothing in his expression.

Max Beauchamp looked merely irritated. Fergal pulled up what he knew of the man. He'd been the leader of Earth, the one who had helped them escape whatever disaster had destroyed the planet. His ship, the *Trakis One*, had disappeared into a black hole over five hundred years ago, shortly after the fleet had reached the Trakis system.

Then twenty-one years ago, the *Trakis One* had reappeared through the same black hole. Max had made an attempt to claim leadership of the new world, but by that time, the Church was already taking control. Maybe Hatcher had realized that a secular leader was also needed, and Beauchamp was given the title of president, though it was rumored that he had no real power.

He was tall, thin, ascetic-looking in his dark suit, with pale blond hair and pale eyes. The hair on Fergal's neck rose, and a shiver ran through him. The man was seriously creepy.

How long did he have?

He peered back the way they had taken Daisy. What was his best course of action? What was Stefan planning?

Shit.

The panic was starting to rise again. He gulped some deep breaths and swallowed it down.

"So who is he?" Hatcher asked, waving a hand in his direction.

The moment of truth.

"His name is Fergal Cain," Stefan said. "He's a reporter."

"A reporter?" Hatcher's tone made it sound like something on a level with a bloodsucking monster. Obviously, he had no high opinion of reporters. What a surprise.

"He's been after a story on me and Cybercom for years."

Well, that was good news. Whatever Stefan's plans, they didn't involve telling the truth as far as Fergal was concerned, and that had to be a positive. At least he thought it did. He rubbed his scalp; the headache was getting worse. Stefan caught the movement, and Fergal saw the first emotion flit across his face. Amusement? The bastard was finding this amusing? Which meant it had to be really funny—Stefan had never had much of a sense of humor.

He tried not to let the hope rise too high. Whatever Stefan's plan, Fergal doubted it involved saving Daisy. No, he was on his own with that. Daylight wasn't far off, and Rico's warning rang in his head.

He glanced up to find Hatcher watching him, considering him, and the focus made him want to squirm. It always had.

"Maybe we can use a reporter right now," Hatcher said. "Show the world what we have in store for the nonbelievers."

Presumably, he had tripped an alarm at some point, but they couldn't have found the bodies of the priest or the guards he'd killed. They wouldn't believe a reporter would go that far to get a story. Hopefully, the bodies would stay hidden long enough to play this through.

"Maybe." Beauchamp studied him as well. "But I don't trust him. What was he doing with the girl? What's his connection with *The Blood Hunter*? The ship hasn't been seen in years. Now your little priestess and her...husband escape, and this girl turns up. I don't like it."

Fergal thought fast. What might keep Daisy alive a little bit longer?

"I employed them," he said. "*The Blood Hunter*—they're mercenaries for hire to the highest bidder. I needed to get in here, and someone sent me to them. After all—one of them did used to live here."

"Callum Meridian. So he is still alive?" Hatcher asked.

"I told you he was," Beauchamp snapped.

Fergal got the impression there was no love lost between the two men. No doubt they both wanted the ultimate power, and Beauchamp wouldn't be satisfied with second place for long. Maybe he could use that in some way.

"That was twenty years ago and you admitted—in another universe. They haven't been seen since."

"They're still around," Fergal said. "Doing jobs for hire. They gave me the plans to this place, told me where to find Stefan, and the girl came along as extra cover and firepower if I needed it. It should have been easy."

Hatcher pursed his lips but nodded. "Okay. We'll consider the situation and decide if you can be of use."

"You know," Stefan said, "perhaps I could give him the real inside story on Cybercom."

Hatcher looked at him sharply and smiled. "Why not? For now, take him away and lock him up."

Fergal threw Stefan a meaningful look—at least, he hoped it had meaning—then allowed himself to be hustled away. They were taking him in the same direction as Daisy. She'd be nearby. They half led, half pushed him along the corridor, down the flights of stairs and unsurprisingly back to the prison section, underground.

They tossed him into a cell and slammed the door shut behind them.

Fergal lay where he'd landed. Closing his eyes, he took a few deep breaths and tried to calm his brain. There was still a good chance they could get out of this. It was unlikely they'd kill Daisy straightaway. She only had to last a few more hours, and *The Blood Hunter* would be here to save her. If not him.

He pushed himself to his feet and studied his surroundings. Hardly impressive, but he'd also seen worse. The cell was about nine feet by nine feet with a cot built into the wall and a toilet and tap in a small alcove. The walls were white and the floor was gray, but overall it wasn't too bad. He went and splashed cold water on his face, trying to ease the ache behind his eyes. How much longer did he have? Where the hell was that bastard Stefan?

He sank onto the thin mattress and put his head in his hands.

Hatcher had to be at least a hundred and twenty years old by now. He looked almost the same, but then he'd always appeared old to Fergal. He'd only been twelve when he'd last laid eyes on him, but he would have recognized him anywhere. Obviously, the opposite wasn't true. But then Fergal had changed somewhat more drastically.

What did he feel about him?

The truth was, he didn't know.

Hatred, definitely, but it was far more complex than that. Otherwise he would have come back and killed him and thought nothing of it.

So why hadn't he?

It was doing his head in, and the sharp little stabs of pain weren't helping.

He knew the crew of *The Blood Hunter* meant to kill Hatcher. Was he going to let them? They had good reason. Maybe not as good as his, but good.

Or could he use that information to save Daisy?

Of course, he could always go to Hatcher and appeal to his better nature, but he wasn't sure the man had one. Actually, that was a lie. He was certain he didn't have one.

All the same, he was Fergal's—

The cell door opened, cutting off his thoughts, and Stefan stood in the opening.

"About fucking time," Fergal muttered.

"Nice to see you as well." Stefan strolled into the room, and the door clicked shut behind him. He pulled his hand out of his pocket and tossed a small brown bottle to Fergal.

As he caught it, relief flooded his system. At least this gave him some time and would get rid of the pain, which was making thinking increasingly difficult. He unscrewed the lid, expecting pills similar to those he had been taking for the last six months, then frowned and glanced up to where Stefan leaned against the wall of the cell. "Is this the antidote?" he asked.

"No, it's painkillers. I'm guessing you've got a whopper of a headache right now."

Fergal could feel his eyes narrowing on the other man, but he tossed two of the pills into his mouth and swallowed them dry.

"So are you going to finish what you started and poison me?" he asked.

"You were never in danger of dying."

"I wasn't?"

"The poison wasn't enough to kill you. If you hadn't taken the antidote you would have gotten a really bad headache, but you would have been fine." Stefan grinned. "You're my friend. Would I poison my friend?"

Fergal rose slowly to his feet. He put the bottle of painkillers down carefully—he was betting he was going to need them all—then he flew at Stefan. He changed his arm as he dived through the air so by the time he crashed into the other man, it was a sharp stabbing blade.

Stefan slammed into the wall, and Fergal laid the blade across his throat so a thin line of blood welled up.

"You fucking bastard. You made me believe I was going to die."

Stefan choked, opening his mouth, but no words came out. Fergal growled but released the pressure on his throat, and Stefan swallowed. "I needed to be sure you would come back and find me."

"You could have fucking asked."

Stefan's eyes narrowed. "Tell me the truth, Fergal, have you ever done anything in your entire life that wasn't in the best interests of Fergal Cain? Would *you* have trusted you to come back?"

He wanted to deny the accusation. Unfortunately, he couldn't. His whole life had been about getting himself where he needed—or rather wanted—to be. But that was no longer true. He'd saved Daisy from the prison on Trakis Four. He hadn't needed to, and it had fucked up his plans, but he had done it anyway. His first-ever altruistic action.

"I would have come back." He lowered his arm and stepped back. "Maybe."

Stefan shook his head. "At least you're honest. You'd have come if you thought there was anything in it for you. So don't get in my face about something I believed I had to do."

"Yeah, you had to get me back to finish your research. That's all you've ever cared about. You're hardly Mr. Altruistic yourself, you know."

Stefan pursed his lips. "Actually, in this case I am."

"Of course you are." Fergal ran a hand through his hair, pressing his fingers into his scalp, though the pain was already receding. He took a couple of steps back and sank down onto the cot.

"So how have you been?" Stefan asked. "Anything weird happening?"

A whole load, but he wasn't opening up to Stefan until he found out how Daisy was. "The girl I came in with. Where is she?"

Irritation flashed across the other man's eyes; Stefan hated to be deflected from what he considered the important stuff. He frowned. "Does it matter? You said you paid her to help you get in here."

"I lied."

The frown deepened. "About which part?"

"The paid bit. She's a friend. Actually, she came after me to warn me that you had turned traitor and were working for the bad guys." He watched Stefan closely, trying to gauge the man's response. Amusement, maybe? Stefan was really turning into a happy guy.

"I think it's a little harsh to refer to the Church as the bad guys. All they want is to get the worthy among us into Heaven."

"Yeah, right. The worthy. Unfortunately, I suspect that neither you, nor I, come into that category."

"And neither does your little bloodsucking friend. Jesus. A vampire? Is she for real, or is it some sort of genetic modification gone wrong?"

"No, she's real. Apparently, vampires came from Earth along with the humans and a few other things."

"Well, that's bad news for her."

"Why's that?"

"Hatcher gave orders for her to be tied up in the courtyard outside at dawn. If the legends are true, when the suns come up…"

"She'll burn." Shit, there was that panic again. But he could do this. This wasn't about him anymore. It was about saving Daisy. Who, despite being the undead, was one of the most alive people he had ever met. And one of the best. She was good. Truly good. "Where is she now?" he asked.

"Does it matter? Forget her, Fergal. She's going to die, and there's nothing you can do about it. And we have work to do. I have to get you to the labs, take some blood samples—"

Fergal lunged for a second time. This time he pinned Stefan with an arm across his chest so he could still talk. What threat would work best with Stefan?

"You've told the guards to stay away?" he said.

Stefan gave a wary nod.

"So let me tell you how it's going to be. I swear if you don't help me save my friend, I will tie you up and make you watch while I slit my wrists and every damn drop of my precious blood goes down the fucking drain."

Chapter Seventeen

Stefan stared at him, his brows drawn together. "You'd do that? For a girl?"

"Did I mention the word 'friend'?"

"You once told me you don't have friends, you have contacts and acquaintances."

"Well, I've got one now."

Stefan was silent for a minute. Fergal gave him the time to think but didn't release his hold.

"Actually, you have two," Stefan said. "If we can still be friends."

Fergal took a deep breath, gave a curt nod, and released his grip on the other man. Stefan got to his feet, rubbing his chest. "Is it my imagination or are you even stronger?"

"Stronger, faster. My cognitive function is through the roof."

Stefan's eyes lit up with a zeal Fergal recognized. "We need to get you to the lab, do some tests—"

"First we need to save my friend. How many hours until dawn?"

"Just under three. There's time to get this thing moving and still try and do something for your little bloodsucker."

"No. We go see Daisy, then the lab."

For the first time, he saw a flash of anger in the other man's face. Stefan paced the room and then whirled around to face him. "Have you any fucking idea what's been going on here?"

Fergal studied him. Yes, there was definite anger, but beneath that was a very real fear—he didn't think he had ever heard Stefan swear before. "Why don't you tell me? Just make it quick."

Stefan slumped slightly. He hadn't been sure Fergal would cooperate, and the idea had terrified him. Stefan didn't do terror—he was usually so immersed in his research he didn't have a clue what was going on around him. The last few months had obviously made him take notice.

"They came into Cybercom the day after I got you out. Beauchamp was in charge. He took the drones first, loaded them up, and brought them straight here. The rest of us were dragged off to prison on some trumped-up charge, crimes against the Church, making monsters or some such rubbish. Most of the executive board I never saw again. I think they were executed—"

"They were," Fergal said. "I found the records when I was looking for you."

"Shit. Beauchamp told me the others were being held in a safe place. But he probably thinks the fewer people who know where his new army came from the better."

"So the Church is creating an army? I did wonder."

"Yeah, they plan to strike first, wipe out any possible opposition. Get some stability. And then…"

"And then what?"

"Beauchamp has been keeping things close to himself. But from what I've gathered, he plans an expedition."

"An expedition where?"

"Back through the black hole at Trakis One. God knows why, though."

"Actually, I can guess."

Stefan raised a brow. "And are you going to tell me?"

Was he? He wondered for a moment whether he should reveal what Daisy had told him about the other side of the hole. But hey, Stefan was his friend—there had to come a point where you trusted people. "Meridian. Beauchamp is going after immortality. The source of Meridian is on the other side of the black hole."

"And you know this how?"

Fergal tapped his nose. "A good reporter never reveals his sources."

"Humph. Actually, it doesn't take a lot of working out. The girl you were with was part of the crew that woke up Beauchamp on the other side of the hole. And by the way, if you ever get the chance, feel free to point out what a huge mistake that was. She's obviously your source. I would one day like to know the story behind that, but right now we have more important things to discuss."

"Yeah."

"Anyway," Stefan continued, "they had their own scientists, but they kept me alive as insurance. Then a couple of months ago they obviously came to the conclusion that their people were never going to get the drones working—"

"You had something to do with that?"

"I did. After I'd gotten you out, I set the rest up on a continuous biofeedback loop that ensured they wouldn't respond to any uploads. They couldn't get them to do more than blink."

"Shit. These were once fucking people. And you've turned them into robots."

"Don't you think I know that? And don't you think I

want a chance to put it right?"

"You know what—I have no fucking clue. It's always been about results for you, Stefan. You never saw us as people. Just successful experiments."

"And failures. Maybe. But let's say that the last few months have been a wake-up call. I *will* solve this. I *will* give them back their minds, and after that, they can all tell Beauchamp and the Church to go take a hike."

"You still think you can do it—give them back their free will?"

"Well, you're still alive and still functioning. I've been holding them off, telling them the units—"

"Units?"

Stefan looked away. "The other volunteers, the ones who survived the last phase—you saw them—Beauchamp prefers to refer to them as units rather than people, as that way he can persuade everyone he isn't using some sort of monsters, just machines."

"The man's an asshole."

"Yes. Anyway, I told him the units were damaged from the crap his crappy scientists had done, but it would clear the system in time."

"And will it?"

"No. Without the altered DNA that's been evolving in your body for the last six months, they'll stay as they are, probably forever. And inside, somewhere deep inside, they are still living, thinking human beings."

"Shit. Look, let's go get Daisy out and then—"

"I know you're worried about your friend, but we should do this first. Right now, I can get you out of here. They don't see you as a huge threat. But if you try and save the girl and fail, I won't get another chance. They'll probably kill you along with her. And you'll be consigning a whole load of people, people you knew well, to a living death."

"Yeah, and maybe giving Beauchamp his fucking army." He ran a hand through his hair. His headache was gone. All this time, he'd thought he was dying, and all he'd needed was a fucking painkiller. And he'd thought he was dying because Stefan had told him so, and he'd done that because he didn't trust Fergal. Could *he* trust Stefan now? What if he did his part and Stefan refused to help, just locked him up in here while they put Daisy out in the sun to fry?

"I will help you," Stefan said as though reading his thoughts.

Fergal sighed, suddenly weary. And hungry. "How long will it take?"

Stefan grinned. "An hour, tops."

"Then you'll help me see Daisy."

"I'll do whatever I can."

"That's got to be good enough. Let's go. But I need food as well—my metabolism has rocketed."

"Interesting. You can tell me about any other changes on the way to the lab."

Fergal sat munching on a plate of stew while Stefan hooked him up to an IV line. They were in a laboratory across the building from the prison section. It was situated on the first floor and one wall was made of glass and looked down on a huge cavernous room filled with Max's army.

"There are more here than you had at Cybercom," he said.

"I had to do the treatment on a few more subjects." He must have caught something in Fergal's expression, because his own became defensive. "I had no choice. I had to get them to trust me long enough for you to get here."

"Did you really believe I'd make it?"

"I believed you would if you were capable of it. You're one of the most tenacious people I know. Once you decide on something, you don't let go. I knew you'd find me. And you've been undercover most of your adult life—you're good at hiding. So yes, I hoped."

Most of his adult life? Longer than that, if only Stefan knew the truth. He'd assumed his first alter ego at the age of twelve.

"Who were they?" he asked, nodding down into the room below.

"Prisoners scheduled for execution, so you could say I saved their lives. They even had a couple of Collective members, though they didn't make it through the initial conversion. You know they've been experimenting on some of the Collective they've captured—trying to work out what makes them tick."

"Bastards. But the Collective has been researching that for hundreds of years and gotten nowhere."

"Well, that didn't stop Beauchamp's lot trying."

He drummed his fingers on the metal of the chair while the blood drained from his arm and into the console in front of him. Dawn must be only two hours away now. Daisy would be alone, frightened. Had the bastards told her what they intended?

"So how will you know if it's worked?" he asked when he could no longer contain his impatience.

Stefan glanced up from the screen he was watching. "It's worked."

"You can tell already?"

"I told you—the proof is that you're alive and still functioning."

"Oh, great. So there was a chance I wouldn't be."

"Would you have said no and risked ending up like them?" He waved a hand toward the drones.

Fergal shook his head. "How much longer?"

"Fifteen minutes."

"Then what happens?"

"The system will filter out the processed DNA from your blood and feed it straight into the main line that links into them."

"How long until they start to think again?"

"An hour, maybe two. I don't know exactly."

"And what do you think is going to happen? You think the guys in charge here are going to stand aside and let them walk away?"

From the confused expression on Stefan's face, he hadn't quite considered what happened next. "Why wouldn't they?"

Jesus, the guy was naive. "Er, because they have this army of super-strong, almost indestructible cyborgs that they require for their devious master plan."

"But…" Stefan shook his head.

"Maybe you'd better start thinking about what happens next, Stefan." That might work well for Tannis and her people. If the cyborgs all tried to escape, the place would be in chaos. It would be much easier for Tannis to slip in and kill Hatcher. But was that really what he wanted? He pushed thoughts of Hatcher away—they complicated matters.

"Okay," Stefan said, pulling the needle from his arm. "That's done."

Fergal pushed himself to his feet.

Stefan had brought him past the guards at the prison entrance with no problem. No one seemed to question him— they were obviously used to the doctor coming and going. Had he visited the prison to select suitable subjects for the conversion? Was that what they thought he was doing with Fergal? It occurred to him, not for the first time, that Stefan was not a moral man. On the other hand, he wasn't evil, merely single-minded. If something was shoved in his face hard enough, he would take a look and decide it was wrong.

If he was truly untrustworthy, he would have told Beauchamp what he had done to Fergal, and he would have been imprisoned and helpless. He hadn't, so Fergal could only hope he would keep his word and help him now.

He couldn't wait for *The Blood Hunter* to save them. They weren't due to turn up for another six hours. By that time, Daisy would be ashes. He had to get her out of that cell and either back to her shuttle or hidden somewhere until they arrived.

"So have you an idea how we can do this?" he asked as they made their way through the prison.

"I've been thinking," Stefan said. "I'll take you to her, then I'm going to see Beauchamp, tell him I want to try her for the conversion. If nothing else, it will give us some more time. Once the others come around, there's a good chance the place will descend into chaos and you can get her out."

"Okay, but don't leave it too long."

Stefan stopped him with a hand on his arm. "Problem," he said.

"What?"

"They've stationed a guard outside her cell. They won't let me through. We have to go back—you can wait somewhere else while I go see Beauchamp."

"No way." He thought furiously for a moment—he wasn't leaving her in that cell alone a second longer. "Come on, walk past with me as though nothing's wrong."

For a second it looked like Stefan was going to argue, but he must have realized how determined Fergal was, and he nodded and led the way around the corner. Fergal kept his eyes averted but shifted his right arm into a stabbing weapon. As they passed the guard, he lunged to the side, grabbed the man by the shoulder, and plunged the blade through his throat, piercing the spinal column. The man died in a second.

Fergal picked him up before he hit the ground and threw him over his shoulder.

He took a few steps and peered into a cell next to the one the man had been guarding. The room was empty, and he kicked open the door and dropped the body on the small cot. The guard wore a utility belt with a laser pistol and a whole load of keys. Fergal stripped them and fastened the belt around his own waist. When he turned back, Stefan stood in the doorway, shock stamped on his face. He'd killed countless with his experiments, but had probably never seen a man die violently before.

He stepped aside to let Fergal pass, and he hurried back to the cell and peered through the glass window in the door. His heart hitched; they'd shackled Daisy to the wall, her arms stretched high above her. Her head hung on her chest, and her hair covered her face. Maybe she hadn't come around from the laser blast. But something in the way she held herself, a tenseness in her body, showed she was awake.

She raised her head and stared straight at him with eyes tinged with crimson. Blood still stained her chin, and her lips curled in a snarl, showing one sharp white fang. There was nothing human left in her expression.

A shiver of primordial fear ran through him. He pushed the emotion down and unlocked the door.

The bastards were going to burn her.

The thought pierced through the haze of darkness. They'd gloated as they had chained her up in here.

At dawn, they planned to stake her in the open and let the sunlight do their dirty work. At least she'd get to see the sunrise one last time.

The air was tinged with the scent of singed flesh and

material where they'd blasted her with the laser pistol, all mixed in with the sweet, sickly scent of the blood of the man she had bitten. For once, the smell didn't raise her hunger; instead her stomach churned.

The guards were gone now, although she knew there was one outside her cell. He kept his distance, maybe afraid she would infect him with something. She tried to force down the rage and fear and think rationally. But her whole body shook with terror. Back on Earth, she had seen a woman burned alive, heard her screams. The memory still haunted her dreams.

And she didn't want to die.

Where was Fergal? Had his scientist friend betrayed him? He'd been with Hatcher—he must have changed sides.

Was Fergal somewhere in the prison? Would they make him watch as they burned her? At least there was a good chance he would still be alive when *The Blood Hunter* got here. They would save him. But it would be too late for her—she'd be reduced to a little pile of greasy ashes.

A sound at the door made her jump. She raised her head and snarled, but the face in the glass was familiar, and a wave of warmth washed over her, calming her tremors.

She blinked, and her vision cleared as Fergal pushed open the cell door. He stepped inside, and her mouth tugged up into a broad smile that she couldn't seem to stop.

She'd believed she would never see him again, and it was enough that he was here. She forced her gaze beyond him to where a second man loitered in the doorway. Stefan Wolfe. So was he a true friend after all, though he didn't look happy. Unlike Fergal, who was grinning at her like an idiot. Like she was no doubt grinning at him.

"I missed you," he said.

"Me too."

He crossed the few steps between them, took her face

between his palms, and kissed her on the forehead. She closed her eyes and relaxed. This was enough. He'd come for her. Even if she died now, she would be content.

Then she snapped back.

No, she fucking wouldn't.

She wanted out of here. She wanted them both out of here. Time to discover what was really going on. Whether there was a plan, a chance. She peered past Fergal to the man who still hovered in the doorway.

"So is he a friend after all, or did you bring me a snack?" she asked.

The man blanched, but Fergal chuckled. "He's a friend." He released her and turned back to his friend. "Don't you have something you need to do?"

The man nodded. "I'll go to Hatcher, see what I can arrange."

"We've less than two hours. You fail and I'm making a break for it. So be quick."

Daisy waited until the door closed behind him. "What's he going to do?"

"See if they will let him use you for research. It will give us more time."

"You know what they plan?"

He nodded curtly.

"I lost it again. I'm sorry. If I hadn't they might not have been so sure, might have waited. But I was so angry. That man killed Janey. I hate him. Hate feeds the darkness. I've found out that much."

"It doesn't matter," he said. "We'll get out of here." He pulled a small key from the belt he wore and unlocked the shackles that held her arms above her head. She rubbed at the red marks on her wrists. Then she ripped the black robes down the front, spraying the room with tiny buttons, dragged the dress over her arms and hips, and kicked it into the corner. The release was enormous. She could breathe again. She went to the small alcove and splashed her face with cold water, washing away the dried blood. When she turned back, Fergal was at the door, peering through the window.

"Should we make a run for it?" she asked.

"We will if we have to, but the place is swarming with guards. We'll wait and see if Stefan is successful first."

She slumped down on the cot behind her and studied him. Lines were etched between his eyes—he was worried. Obviously in no way sure of his friend.

"Did he give you more antidote?"

He let out a short bitter laugh. "He didn't need to. He never really poisoned me, just told me he had as insurance so that I would come back."

"He didn't trust you."

"Why would he? He's known me for a long time."

"Why did you stay so long at Cybercom?" she asked. "I know in the end you were prisoners, but before that you must have had a chance to leave."

"For the first few years, I needed the antirejection drugs. After that, I waited because Stefan hadn't completed the process. He was still working on the final phase of his little project."

"Immortality?"

"Yes."

"You're scared of dying?"

"Strangely, no. Though if you'd asked me that when I was growing up, I would have given you a different answer. My father was very into the whole fire-and-brimstone thing. You know—follow the Lord's path or you'll roast in Hell's fires." He rubbed at his arm as he spoke. "Well, I very rarely managed to follow the Lord's path, so for a lot of years I fully expected to end up in Hell's fires."

"You actually believe that? That's why you don't want to

die? You're scared you'll go to Hell?"

He grinned, the seriousness lifting from his expression. "Fuck, no. I gave up believing in Hell or Heaven years ago."

"Why don't you want to die then?"

"I sort of made a promise to someone—that no way was the devil going to get me."

"To your dad? You still see him."

He was quiet for a moment. "Shit, I've never told anyone this crap before. But no, I haven't spoken directly to my father since I was twelve years old."

"You still hate him? After all this time?"

"Yeah. I guess so—some things you never get over. But it's complicated when it's your dad. I've come to see that. Otherwise I might have gone back and killed the bastard before now."

"Seems a little excessive."

He took a deep breath, and for a moment, she thought the conversation was over. And she didn't want it to be. She knew she was getting to the heart of what made Fergal tick, what had made him into the man he was.

"My mother killed herself when I was eight. He drove her to it."

"Couldn't she have taken you away?"

"She tried. We ran away twice, and both times, he had us brought back. She was genetically modified, though she had no outward signs and didn't know it when she married my father. Neither did he." He gave her a grim smile. "At the time, my father was head of the Church's program for the abolition of abominations."

"How did he find out—I'm presuming he did?"

"Yeah, he found out. I had a sister. She was born when I was five, so I remember her…just. She had webbed fingers and toes."

"What happened to her?"

"She died. Smothered in her cot."

Her hand went to her mouth, and she stared at him. "Your father did that? Killed his own daughter?"

"It was never spoken outright, but yes. Things weren't the same afterward. My mother never really recovered from the death, but even before that, she was always a little unstable. And afterward he started the beatings—driving the devil out, he called it."

She had a flashback to the pale lines on Fergal's back, and a wave of rage rose up inside her, making the blood pound in her veins. She quashed it down. "He beat you as well?"

"Yeah, well, I definitely had the devil in me. Anyway, after the second time we ran, he made sure we wouldn't try it again. He kept us separated so we'd have had to leave the other behind. She killed herself to give me a chance to be free."

"Oh, Fergal. I'm sorry." She blinked back her tears for the little boy he had been and the man he had become.

"It's weird, but in his own twisted way, he did love her, and me as well. He was doing what he thought was right." He shook his head. "Crazy asshole."

"Did you love him?"

He looked away again. "Growing up, all I wanted was for him to say something good. The few times he did—I lived for. Yeah, I loved him and hated him. Now—enough. We have a little time. Let's not waste it talking about history."

"Okay, one last question."

"One."

"Are you immortal?"

"Let's hope we get to find out." He came across and sank down on the cot beside her, took her hand in his and tugged her up close. "No more questions." He gave her a long look out of half-closed lashes, and her breath hitched. "You know," he murmured, "there's something about imminent death that makes me horny as hell."

Chapter Eighteen

Did they have time for this?

Daisy glanced at the door, half expecting to see a whole load of the bad guys ready to bear down on them. But the door was closed, and she could see no one through the small window.

They weren't going anywhere until Fergal's friend got back. So why not?

Maybe this wasn't the best time to make love. They were surrounded by enemies. But it also might be their last chance. She needed him to hold her. To wipe out the fear and push back the darkness. They weren't out of here yet, and they still might die. Couldn't they take a little time-out, just to forget the bad things and maybe to remember that there were definitely things worth living for?

She looked at Fergal, so close beside her. Lines of pain, or fear, etched his long, lean face, but his silver eyes were as clear as she had ever seen them, as though he had been through some sort of catharsis. And maybe he had—after all, he'd said he'd never told anyone about his father before.

He returned her gaze with one that was hot and heavy, and her nipples tightened, heat pooling in her sex.

Yeah, they deserved this.

Staring into his eyes, she crossed her arms in front of her and held them out to him. "You want to tie me up?"

He studied her for a long minute, and in the silence a slow beat started between her thighs, a fire sparking into life in her belly.

"No."

"No?" He didn't want to make love after all?

"I'm not kidding myself that we're definitely getting out of this, and if not, just once, I want to feel your arms around me when we make love."

"You do?"

"Oh, yeah. And your legs."

"What about my teeth—you want to feel them?" She really didn't want to lose it and bite him. Not now.

"I'm willing to take the risk. Are you?"

She peered inside herself and realized that the fear had left her for now and the darkness was once again sleeping. She wanted him so much, but she wanted to relax, and could she do that while she worried that she might rip out his throat? Hardly an image she wanted him to take to the grave.

Though hopefully, there wasn't going to be a grave anytime soon, if ever. In all likelihood they were both immortal now. Eternity with Fergal. What would that be like? She didn't know and wasn't sure any relationship could survive eternity, but she desperately wanted the chance to find out.

She nodded, and the tension in his body smoothed out as he relaxed.

Without waiting, she dragged her shirt over her head, kicked off her boots, jumped up and tugged off her pants. In seconds, she was naked.

Fergal sat, a slightly bemused expression on his face, but only for a moment. He reached out, his hard hands on her hips, and dragged her to him. She toppled onto his lap, and he slanted his mouth over hers.

The kiss held an edge of desperation. Daisy opened to him, and his tongue pushed inside, filling her with the unique taste of him. She was used to it now and no longer found the hint of cold metal off-putting. Instead, it woke the sleeping darkness.

But this time she didn't fight or try to push it back down into its corner. Instead, she welcomed it as it stretched and reached out along her nerves, through her blood. She kissed Fergal back, her tongue stroking his, slow and gentle, and she felt him respond. Cupping her face in his hands, he kissed her deeply and warmth stole through her, mingling with the rising darkness.

His hands slipped down her body to slide around her rib cage just beneath her breasts, and he picked her up and laid her on the bed. Shifting so he lay half by her side, half over her, he rested on his elbow and stared down into her face.

"I want to kiss you for hours, but..."

"But we might not have hours," she finished for him.

He gave a wry smile. "You know one of the things I love about you is you always tell the truth."

"Yeah, it's a bad habit. Now we are on a time limit here, so..." She slid her hand around the back of his neck and pulled him down to her. She loved the feel of him, the heavy weight of his big body against hers. The hardness of his erection pushed against her hip, and she squirmed so she lay directly beneath him, then opened her legs and wrapped them around his waist. Now she could feel him pressed against her core, and she wriggled, sending shivers of pleasure pulsating through her.

Fergal lowered his head and licked across one taut nipple,

sucked it into his mouth. Heat flooded her, sinking down through her belly to her sex, leaving her drenched with need.

He moved to the other breast, nipped it with his teeth, and a sharp jolt shot through her, lifting her hips from the bed, tightening the grip of her legs wrapped around him.

One of his hands pushed between them to unfasten his pants, so she could feel the scalding heat of him against her skin. His other hand shifted lower, to ruffle through the curls at her sex, and one long finger slid inside.

"Fuck, you're wet," he murmured. He pulled the finger out, rubbing the moisture up over her clit so she gasped at the sensation. Closing her eyes, she gave herself up to it as he massaged the swollen nub, bringing her to the brink. He stopped moving, and she blinked open her eyes.

"Are you okay?" he asked.

His gaze searched her face, and she knew what he was asking. She gave a jerky nod, and his lips curved up in a smile. "Good."

As he parted her with his fingers, the tip of his cock pushed inside, and he flexed his hips, filled her.

Her spine arched, and she came in a flood of pleasure. He held himself motionless as her body spasmed, only withdrawing when she went still beneath him. The drag of his shaft against the sensitized skin almost brought her again, but she relaxed into the rhythm. He moved slowly, but with purpose, each long slow stroke filling her completely, pushing at her womb. She closed her eyes, concentrated on that place where they joined so all she knew was the ebb and flow of his body on her, in her.

The pleasure was a heavy weight building inside her, spreading, suffusing her whole body with warmth, embracing the darkness so the coldness at her center entwined with the heat of his lovemaking.

"You ready?" She vaguely heard the whispered question

but had no power to speak, to break the spell holding her. Instead, she bucked her hips against him.

He must have understood, because the tempo changed and he was pumping into her, faster now, harder, and at the end of each stroke, he ground against the swollen mass of nerves at her core. Everything inside her tightened, she was flying without a ship as she'd always dreamed of. Then he pushed again, and she shattered into a thousand pieces and she was falling, hurtling to the ground. She snapped open her eyes, and Fergal was there to catch her. As her back arched, he lowered his head, kissed her, thrust into her one last time, found his own release, and they were flying together.

When she opened her eyes, the air was tinged with crimson. But she blinked, and it was gone. And the darkness slept.

Fergal smoothed the hair from her face and dropped a kiss on to her forehead, then gripped her hips and turned her so she was lying sprawled across his body.

"No biting."

She smiled. "Not even the urge to nibble."

"Should I be offended?"

"No. My darkness likes you."

As she spoke the words, she realized they weren't the whole truth. She loved him. She could see that now. And as she acknowledged the fact, warmth stole through her, easing the inner cold. That's why the darkness hadn't fought for control; it recognized Fergal, was content to share her. Love would always conquer the darkness.

But even as she gave a name to her feelings, she knew she couldn't say the words out loud. Not yet. They would have to wait until later. She suspected there were decisions ahead, hard decisions, and she didn't want to burden Fergal with her love and make those decisions harder.

Maybe she deserved to die. Rico had never said to her

outright, *we are evil*. Maybe he'd known she wasn't ready to accept that truth. But he had hinted, told her there would come a time when she would have to face up to what she was and either accept or reject it. If she rejected it, she would fail. He'd told her there were vampires who courted destruction, unable to continue with the knowledge of what they had become. Even if you were immortal, it was easy enough to end it all if you wanted death enough.

Now she could look inside herself, stare into the darkness, and accept it as part of her. She'd faced it clearly now, and she didn't think she was evil. The darkness lacked a conscience, an understanding of the morals that governed most people's lives. All it understood was hunger and need. But it was also willing to work with her if she allowed it, and together they could become something more. The outcome was really down to her. She could be anything she wanted. Well, if she got the chance and they didn't fry her to a crisp at the first opportunity.

Maybe there was a place in this world for such as her. And she'd rather be a bloodsucking monster than a hypocritical asshole like Hatcher, who killed in the name of some god who would probably strike Hatcher down with a bolt of lightning if he could be bothered.

She lay with Fergal's arms around her, listening to the thud of his heart while he stroked her hair. She should move. She really didn't want to be naked when Stefan returned, but it felt so good to be held. Finally, she pushed herself up and pulled free. "Thank you," she said.

A lazy smile flickered across his face. "My pleasure, but for what, exactly?"

"For trusting me. For giving me the courage and opportunity to trust myself."

"Anytime. But it worked, didn't it? You were different this time. You weren't fighting."

"No. It felt right. There was no conflict. As though at last I'm one person again. Not him and me. He likes you."

"He?"

"Maybe she, maybe it."

She rolled off him. For a second, he held on to her hand and then let her go. After straightening his own clothes, he watched as she pulled on hers, ran her fingers through her hair, plaiting it loosely so it was out of the way. Sitting on the floor, she pulled on her boots.

Time to get back to the real world.

She got to her feet, strolled to the cot, and sat cross-legged beside Fergal. "So what do we do if your friend's idea fails?"

"It won't fail."

She rested a hand on his knee. "Come on, Fergal, we need to discuss this."

"I won't let you burn."

She shuddered. No, she didn't want to burn. But if there was a way to save Fergal, they should take it. She should have died all those months ago. Everything else had been extra. At least now she could never be sorry that Rico had changed her.

She wouldn't have missed meeting Fergal again, not for anything.

Even living forever.

She opened her mouth to tell him that, but he hushed her with a finger to his lips.

"Stefan's coming back."

Fergal watched the fear blossom on her face. No doubt, like him, for a little while she'd managed to forget their dire circumstances. His body felt sated from making love, and he wanted nothing more than to drag her into his arms, close his eyes, lie with her, and pretend the world didn't exist.

But Stefan's footsteps were getting closer—he was almost running, and that wasn't a good sign.

But though his body was satisfied, his mind was jumping. Maybe it was another side effect from Stefan's non-poison wearing off completely, but he didn't think so. It was nothing like the headaches he'd gotten when he'd put off taking the antidote—the headaches that had persuaded him he really was poisoned. This was like a computer screen that refused to be switched off. A humming… He shook his head, trying to clear it, but it remained a constant drone in the background.

He pushed himself to his feet and went to stand beside Daisy. He hadn't meant to touch her again, but at the last second, he pulled her into his arms and held her hard against him. Was still holding her when Stefan banged on the cell door and pushed it open without waiting for a response.

Fergal raised his head, looked into his friend's face, and knew the answer.

"Shit," he said.

Daisy pulled free and turned to Stefan but didn't speak.

"What happened?" Fergal asked.

Stefan shook his head. "No go. While Beauchamp would have gone for it—the whole deal is his baby—Hatcher wouldn't even consider the idea."

"There must have been something you could say to persuade him."

"I tried. He was totally closed to even waiting, something about her friend getting away from him and it wasn't going to happen again. He hates her and this ship she belongs to, blames them for everything that's gone wrong. Callum Meridian going missing, his priestess making a dash for it… that hit him hard."

"It did?" Daisy asked her brows drawing together.

"Hatcher isn't popular. He's not exactly a people person."

"No." Fergal certainly couldn't argue with that.

"But the priestess was always a favorite, and everyone loved her. Otherwise, he would have gotten rid of her long ago. Don't know why, but the way he talked about her, they didn't get on." Stefan had never kept up with current affairs, too wrapped up in his own world. "Anyway, he blames her lot"—he waved a hand toward Daisy—"for the high priestess doing her vanishing act. He wants her dead and soon."

"When?"

"They're coming for her now. He gave the order as I was leaving."

Fergal glanced at the unit on his wrist—still thirty minutes until dawn. But time was running out. The first flickers of real panic licked through his body.

"And they've tripled security," Stefan continued. "He's not taking any chances."

"There must be a way for you to get us out."

"There isn't. I've tried. There's no way out of this area except by the front door, and no one's getting through that who shouldn't. We're underground, the walls are solid—no breaking through them. You have to accept it, Fergal, she's not getting out."

"No. I won't fucking accept it."

"Just leave her. I can get you back to your cell. When the fuss has all died down, I'll get you out of here."

"You really expect me to go and leave her? Let them take her out there and—" He broke off and gave a sideways glance at Daisy. She was pale, but composed. He could see no fear in her eyes, just acceptance. Well, he wasn't going to accept it. No fucking way.

He smashed his fist into the wall but felt nothing. There had to be a way.

"Maybe you should do as he says, Fergal."

Her voice was soft, and he turned to face her full on and snarled, "Shut the fuck up. I won't let them—"

"Then kill me now. You know how to do it. You said you'd researched vampires."

"You've got to be fucking joking." Yeah, he knew how to do it—stake through the heart, fire, sunlight, or decapitation. He could slice her head off, and it would be all over. No way.

Shit, there had to be a way out. But he couldn't concentrate. The humming in his brain was growing, rising to a crescendo, clamoring at his skull until it finally broke through and a red-hot shaft of pain sliced into his brain.

He crashed down to his knees. Was vaguely aware of Daisy dropping beside him, reaching for him. His mind filled with words, screaming at him, senseless noise, rising and filling his head. His fingers dug into his skull as the pain swelled, until finally something snapped, and everything went black.

When he came to, his mind was blank. He lay on the floor, his head on Daisy's lap as she stroked his hair. Stefan was pacing the room; he could see his boots, backward and forward in the small space.

"He's awake," Daisy murmured.

The boots came to a halt beside his head. Fergal pushed himself up so he was sitting and then to his feet. He swayed but found he was stable enough. "What the hell just happened?"

"The others are regaining consciousness."

"The others? You mean the drones?" He shook his head. Found it didn't hurt. "What the fuck are they doing in my head?"

"Look, before you start ripping into something, let me tell you one thing."

Fergal's eyes narrowed, but he nodded.

"You remember the biofeedback loop I taught you before we started on the final phase?"

"Yeah."

"If you feel anything coming on again, start that. It

should keep you in control."

"Well, that's a fucking relief. Now, what's happening to me?"

Stefan took a deep breath—what he was about to say obviously wasn't good—and Fergal only narrowly resisted the urge to snap, *hurry up*.

"The drug I gave you should really be given to everyone in the same way, so each individual develops the suppressant over a period of time, as you did."

"Instead, you gave them it from me—that's what's happening now?"

"Yes."

"And that's what's causing this?" He waved his hand at his head.

"There's a connection. Given time and training, you can feed information to them all. Like the computer inputs we use now."

"And they'd have to follow my instructions."

"That's the theory, but right now your only chance is to use the loop and keep them out."

"Otherwise?"

"They'll explode your brain."

"You knew this would happen."

"Not *knew*, but I suspected."

"And you still went ahead?" *Some fucking friend.*

"Hey, it's not an ideal world, and I worked with what I had."

"Me." Shit, what was the point in getting angry now? Besides, he would have agreed anyway, he was just pissed off that Stefan hadn't thought to mention the side effects before he'd started the transfer.

It was a pity it wasn't complete, and that it would explode his brain if he tried to use it, because right now, an army of cyborgs on his side would be very useful. "That last one wasn't too bad. I feel okay now."

"They're only just awakening. You got a flicker from maybe one or two individuals. Once they are all online, imagine what you felt magnified a thousand times."

That didn't sound good. No point in having an army to command if he didn't have a brain. "Okay. The loop it is." His brain was back to the low hum, and he started the feedback loop—the last thing he needed right now was his brain exploding. Or him blacking out. After a minute's concentration, the loop was operating in the background. "Done. Do you know how long until they're all aware and able to function again?"

"At the current rate, four hours and twenty minutes."

After *The Blood Hunter* was scheduled to arrive. "And after that—what? You release them and they get out of here and live happily ever after? You think they'll let you?"

"They won't have a choice. Their ordinary army won't stand a chance."

"What if they want to stay?" Fergal asked.

"We'll worry about that later."

If there was a later. He turned to Daisy.

"Are you okay?" she asked.

"Yeah, fucking brilliant." He shook his head. "Sorry."

"For what?"

"Getting you into this."

"I think I managed that all on my own." She bit her lower lip, and a bead of blood formed. She licked it clean. "I think you should go with him."

"Yeah, I thought you might. Not going to happen, babe."

"Babe? I like that." She swallowed. "I'm going to die. They won't let me go, and I don't want to burn."

"I won't let you."

"The only way we can be sure is if you kill me now. That way you might have a chance to get away."

He'd known what she was going to say, but still the words sent a shaft of pain through him. This was like his mother all over again. Dying to save him. Well, it wasn't fucking happening. He'd brought her to this. But what could he have done differently? He'd had no choice but to come here, or at least he'd thought he had no choice. What he should have done was made sure that Daisy hated him. He'd always been good at making people dislike him—why hadn't he managed with her?

His gaze lingered on the purity of her features, the line of her cheek, the curve of her lips. Maybe because he didn't want her to hate him. He wanted someone in the world who thought well of him. He wanted *Daisy* to think well of him.

"I'm not ready to kill you yet," he said.

"There's no other way."

"We fight," he said.

Stefan took a step forward. "You can't, there are too many."

"No such thing," Fergal said. The truth was he'd rather die than kill Daisy just to save his own pathetic life. As he accepted that, a weight dropped from him. For the first time, he'd found something more important than proving his father wrong. Than saying *up yours* to the old bastard.

He held out a hand to Daisy, and she slid her palm against his. "You ready for a good fight, sweetheart?"

"I'm ready." She leaned forward and placed a kiss on his lips. "Just promise me, if it looks like we're beaten, kill me."

He reached out his free hand and stroked a finger across the smooth white skin of her throat. "One cut right here and you're gone."

She took a deep breath and nodded. "Thank you."

"I'll fight with you," Stefan said.

Fergal grinned. "And share the fun? I don't think so. Besides you can't fight—you can't even aim a laser pistol straight, and you have responsibilities. In fact, get out of here now and go see what's happening to my army."

"They can't save you, Fergal."

"I know. But Daisy can. Give her your pistol and get the hell out of here."

Stefan nodded, unbuckled the weapons belt at his waist and handed it to Daisy. She strapped it on, checked the pistol, and slipped it back in the holster.

"Go," he said to Stefan.

He opened his mouth, snapped it closed, turned, and left the room.

Fergal took a deep breath. "You ready?"

"No. You know, I never wanted to be immortal. I had the chance at the Meridian treatment, but…I wasn't ready. Now I'd give anything for more time."

"Don't give up yet," he said. "I never wanted to live forever, either. I just didn't want to die. Now I want to stay with you." He cupped her face in his palms and kissed her gently. "I love you," he said. "And I never expected to say that to any woman—never wanted to."

"You know, before all this started, I was feeling pretty sorry for myself. It seemed like everyone else had found someone. They were all so goddamn smug and happy and I was alone and would always be alone. Who was ever going to care for me now? It was hard enough when I was green."

"I liked you green."

"Yeah, I know. But I was sure that I'd never have anyone, and deep down, I believed that I was a monster and I didn't deserve anyone." She stroked a finger down his cheek. "I'm just saying—it was worth it, whatever happens."

"And?"

She grinned. "And I love you."

He kissed her again, held her close for a long minute, but if he concentrated, he could hear the sound of booted feet coming along the corridor. "We have to go," he murmured into her hair.

"I know."

She stepped back and drew her weapon. She was so small and looked so young and helpless even with the pistol in her hand. Then she raised her head and snarled, showing one sharp white fang, and he realized she wasn't helpless at all.

Fergal drew his own weapon, transferred it to his left hand, and shifted his right into a long sharp blade. His gaze strayed to the line of her throat—if the time came, could he do it?

Chapter Nineteen

Fergal opened the door and peered down the corridor.

"It's clear," he murmured. "But they're not far away. Come on, let's go."

Daisy tightened her grip on the pistol and followed him out from the cell and into the white-walled corridor. The artificial light was bright after the dimness of the cell, and she blinked. The *thump* of booted feet was growing louder. It sounded like a whole lot of men to take one little vampire.

As Stefan had said—Hatcher was taking no chances. He wanted her dead. Well, maybe she was going to die, but not at Hatcher's bidding. Not if she could help it.

There were only two directions to go: one led farther down underground and no way out, the other led directly into the path of the oncoming guards. There was really no choice.

"Ready?" Fergal asked.

"Yes."

She followed him along the corridor to a sharp bend, and he halted. "I'm guessing they're about twenty feet away."

She nodded.

"We go on three. One, two, three."

As one, they stepped around the corner. Fergal's pistol was already blazing as they moved. Daisy held her finger down on the trigger as a group of about ten men came into view. They scattered to the walls as the lasers hit their midst, leaving two bodies on the floor. Daisy adjusted her aim and went for the group on the right, as Fergal shot to the left. Two more went down, but they were drawing their weapons now. A laser blast headed her way, and she dove to the side. It missed her by an inch, and the heat seared past her. More blasts were coming at her now, one scorching the skin of her shoulder. Fergal took a hit in the side, but it didn't slow him down, and she realized he'd used his right arm as a shield.

"Back," Fergal yelled, and she leaped back behind the corner and stood pressed against the wall, her breath coming short and sharp.

"We have to go again. We have to finish them before they get reinforcements," Fergal said. "You okay?"

"Yeah."

"Go then."

She ran, zigzagging to avoid the laser blasts. When she gave up trying and let her new increased senses take over, she evaded them with ease, keeping her finger clamped down tight on the trigger as she sprinted. Fergal was ahead of her, running straight, his flattened arm held in front of him to deflect the blasts.

The guards were dropping; only three were left standing when they suddenly turned and ran. Fergal didn't slow, and she raced after him. They were almost at the entrance now. Of course, even if they escaped the prison area, they still had to get through the headquarters. But one thing at a time.

A sense of euphoria filled her, and she threw back her head and laughed. Fergal glanced quickly back, a frown on his face. Maybe he was worried she was losing it again. But she wasn't, she just felt alive. Which was ironic.

They were closing in on the three running guards. Her gums ached, and her fangs grew longer. She could almost hear the blood thundering in their veins. Their hearts pumping. Without slowing her pace, she stretched out her arm and pressed the trigger. The man at the rear fell to the floor. Fergal shot another, and she took the last. They leaped over the bodies and kept going.

Ahead of her Fergal skidded to a halt. "Stay behind me."

She didn't want to stay behind, but she did as she was told. Peering around Fergal, she spotted a group of guards up ahead. So far, they were just looking at them—maybe Fergal's uniform was enough to slow them down, make them hesitate.

Fergal shot into the group. As they spread apart, she realized they were guarding the main entrance—they'd almost made it. Staying behind Fergal, she shot around him, and one of the men crumpled to the floor.

Fergal shot another. They were returning fire now, but Fergal deflected the blasts.

They were going to make it.

In front of her, Fergal went rigid. The gun dropped from his hand, and he crashed to the floor. The same as he had in the cell.

She was exposed now, though most of the blasts were going wild. Her laser pistol was blown out of her hand, and she searched around frantically for another weapon. A downed guard sprawled about ten feet away, and she dived for him, wrenched the pistol from his hand, and shot from the floor. She rolled onto her hands and knees and crawled back to Fergal, still firing.

Something slammed into her arm, but she ignored the pain, kept going.

Was he dead? Icy cold locked her muscles as a haze of crimson veiled her vision, and she made a conscious effort to push back the darkness.

He couldn't be dead.

He groaned, his eyes blinked, and the tightness eased from her limbs.

Someone grabbed her from behind. She fought, pulled free, and whirled around. Then lunged for the man's throat. His blood filled her mouth, and she swallowed. No time for feeding, she ripped out his jugular and pushed the body away. Lunged for another as a blast caught her in the center of her chest, and she crashed into a man directly behind her.

The blast didn't knock her out, but she was stunned and hung loosely from the man's grip, unable to make her arms and legs obey her. A second man pulled her hands behind her back, and she felt the coolness of metal as he snapped the cuffs around her wrists.

Fergal pushed himself to his feet so he stood only a foot away—close enough. A circle of men surrounded them. They'd stopped shooting now that they were both unarmed, but they watched him warily.

This was it.

Fergal looked into her eyes. Her gaze slid down his body to his right arm. It was a silver, razor-sharp blade. She raised her gaze to his face and stared into his eyes.

I love you.

The words whispered through her mind. Had she said them or Fergal?

She raised her chin, baring the line of her throat.

This was the end, and still she couldn't regret what had happened, only regret what they would never have.

She waited, very still. It was only seconds, but they seemed to go on forever, and still he didn't move. A scream rose in her throat, but she swallowed it down. That would give her away.

Her eyes dropped to his side. The blade was gone, and

once again his arm was just an arm. Her gaze flashed back to his face, and she saw her own hopelessness reflected there.

"I can't," he whispered.

He'd failed her.

He'd stood there ready to do what was needed. But at the last minute, he couldn't do it. He couldn't kill her. Was physically incapable of slicing her head from her body.

He loved her.

Despair flashed in her dark eyes. Then fear that now she would burn.

He wouldn't, *couldn't* let that happen.

Hard hands grabbed him from behind and cuffed his wrists, but he didn't try to fight them. The fight was over. They'd lost. *He'd* lost.

His stomach roiled with nausea, and his head ached viciously. He was frantically trying to rebuild the feedback loop. The surge had been too strong and unexpected—it had shattered the loop, opened him up to the others in his head. Now he closed his eyes and forced himself to concentrate. Within seconds, the pain receded and the roar subsided to a hum.

When he opened his eyes, nothing had changed. A man gripped each of Daisy's arms. Her hair had come loose at some point in the fight so it hung down her back. She was so beautiful, his chest ached.

Her eyes were filled with resignation and forgiveness.

She'd given up, accepted what was to happen, and she didn't blame him. She was closing herself down, shutting herself off from the outside world. Her eyes glazed over as she turned inward.

"Daisy!"

She blinked as he shouted her name. Shaking her head, a frown formed between her eyes.

Off to the side, what was obviously the leader of the guards was talking into his comm unit. He looked up at them and spoke to the men holding Daisy.

"Take the girl to the courtyard as planned."

Daisy stiffened in the grip of the two men but showed no other response to the words.

Dawn was only minutes away.

"And take him back to his cell."

"No," Fergal said.

A frown flickered across the man's face, but he didn't respond, just nodded to the guards holding him.

Fergal thought furiously, trying to reason through the pain and humming in his head. Every cell in his body rejected the idea of what he was about to do, but they were already trying to drag Daisy away. Her gaze locked onto his, and she fought then.

"No, wait. Listen to me," Fergal shouted.

The man turned back slowly and took a step toward him. He stood looking at Fergal for moment, then he drew back his fist and punched him hard in the belly. Fergal doubled over as pain flooded his body. He forced himself to straighten, and the guard hit him again. The man didn't like him too much—hardly surprising since at least ten of his people were dead or seriously wounded.

Fergal gritted his teeth. "Tell Hatcher"—he took a deep breath and avoided looking at Daisy—"tell High Priest Hatcher that I have news about his son."

The man's eyes narrowed.

"If you don't tell him, I'm guessing you'll be in trouble, so I suggest you comm him right now. And tell him I'll only speak if the woman comes with me."

For a moment, he thought it wasn't going to work. The

man frowned and stepped away, turning his back on Fergal while he spoke quietly into the comm unit. Fergal risked a glance at Daisy. Her brows were drawn together in a frown, as if she couldn't work out what he was doing.

That wouldn't last. Soon she would know who he was. How would she look at him then? Certainly not with love.

The guard glanced back. His eyes weren't friendly, but he gave a curt nod. "We're to take them to the high priest."

There was a lot of grumbling among the guards, but they hustled him toward Daisy and marched them side by side out of the prison complex and along the same route they had taken earlier.

Fergal cast her a sideways glance. She must have sensed it, because she'd been staring straight ahead, but now she turned slightly so she could look into his face. Her eyes were clear, no tinge of crimson, and he relaxed the tiniest bit.

He was trying to think through what he needed to do while maintaining the feedback loop in the background and all the time wondering how Daisy would react to what he was about to say.

Not yet.

She'd hear it soon enough.

"Are you okay?" he asked. He noticed a ragged burn through her shirt where she must have taken a laser shot.

"I'm fine. Maybe a little…confused. What's happening, Fergal? Why aren't I outside tied to a stake? Not that I'm complaining. I just don't understand."

"I'm sorry. I couldn't do it. I couldn't kill you. Not if there's a chance."

Her brows drew together. "And is there? A chance, I mean."

He was about to answer, but the guard behind him rammed a laser pistol between his shoulder blades. "Quiet."

He gave a small nod and turned back to face the front.

They were climbing the staircase that led to the private residence now.

Shit, he was so not ready for this.

He'd loved his father once, and that never really went away, however much he might want it to. The need for his father's approval had lingered inside him.

He was going to test that to the limit.

What if he revealed the truth, asked his father for Daisy's life, and the old bastard went ahead and killed her anyway? It would be over—that last little hope that his father wasn't part monster.

And what would he do next? He had an idea, but if he went ahead, Daisy definitely would hate him for eternity. Actually, he'd hate himself.

But she would be alive.

And maybe there was a way he could redeem the situation. He could still feel the hum in his brain, filtering through the loop. A thousand minds waking, aligning with his. His to command. And at the small price of blowing up his brain.

They halted before the double doors. The head guard spoke into his comm unit, and the door opened from the inside. Someone shoved Fergal from behind, and he stumbled, awkward with his hands still tied behind his back.

They were in a conference room, empty but for a table and chairs. Taking a step closer to Daisy, he waited. Maybe Hatcher had no interest in the son he hadn't seen for nearly forty years.

But after five minutes a door in the far wall opened, and Hatcher stepped through.

Fergal had avoided looking too closely at the last meeting, scared of what he might see or feel.

Hatcher was tall, on a level with Fergal. He had the same gray eyes, but the older man was thinner, his body skinny beneath the long black robes, his face hollowed with shadows beneath eyes that still gleamed with a true believer's zeal.

He was alone this time. Maybe he didn't want any witnesses to what he was about to hear. Did he suspect? From the expression in his eyes, Fergal guessed not.

They ran over Fergal with a detached curiosity.

"Chain the girl to the wall," he told the guards.

They dragged Daisy to the edge of the room. One kept her covered with his pistol while the other unlocked her right wrist, slid the cuff through a ring on the wall at waist height, and snapped it back on her wrist.

She stood up straight, her head rose, and she glanced between the two of them. Was she seeing the similarities that were so obvious to him now? He didn't think so. There was still a little frown between her brows.

"Now, leave but stay outside," Hatcher told the guards. "If either of them tries to escape, kill them—and do it properly this time."

"What about the man?" the head guard asked, clearly not happy with Fergal on the loose.

"The cuffs will be sufficient."

Obviously, they didn't know about the cyborg thing, hadn't seen his hand shift back in the prison. That might work for him. The guards didn't look happy, but they gave him a warning look and left the room, closing the door behind them.

Fergal opened his mouth to speak, but Hatcher waved a hand to quiet him. His other hand went to the cross he wore around his neck, big but plain silver. Holding it out in front of him, he glided toward where Daisy hung from the wall. She watched him warily, a pulse fluttering in her throat. Her gaze flashed to him then back to Hatcher, but she didn't speak.

Fergal stepped forward to protest, but Daisy stopped him with a small shake of her head. When Beauchamp had pressed his cross to her skin there had been no effect. Beauchamp was obviously not a true believer. He suspected, however much he hated the idea, that wasn't the case with Hatcher. He had always believed in what he did.

The priest stopped, still an arm's length from Daisy. He studied her for a moment and pressed the cross against the white skin beneath her collarbone. Daisy flinched but didn't make a sound as the air filled with the stench of singed flesh.

Finally, he pulled the cross free, leaving the perfect brand on her pale skin.

"Interesting," Hatcher murmured almost to himself.

Daisy curled her lip, revealing the tip of one fang, and Fergal shot her a warning look. The less she appeared to be any sort of threat, the more likely he could talk them out of this. It didn't help that crimson sparks flickered in her dark eyes.

"Daisy!"

She licked her lips and nodded. "I'm good. Say what you need to say. I don't like the company."

He'd forgotten that she had almost as much reason to hate Hatcher as he did. And none of the other conflicting emotions. He turned to Hatcher. "She doesn't like you. I'm guessing the feeling is mutual."

"I have no feelings for this creature. Just a job to eradicate evil where I find it."

Daisy growled. "Slit your own throat then, old man."

Fergal ran a hand through his short hair. This was not helping. "Shut up, Daisy."

She flashed him a look. "No. He killed Janey and Tris. He's the evil one here."

Fergal sighed. He wasn't going to argue with her. Obviously, she hadn't figured out who Hatcher was to him yet. Time to get all the sordid details out in the open.

Maybe Hatcher thought it was time to move things along

as well. He turned from Daisy and waved Fergal to one of the seats at the table. Fergal took the seat. The truth was he was feeling a little shaky. He could do with some of Rico's whiskey right now.

Hatcher took the seat opposite him. The silence seemed to draw out. He could hear Daisy's slow steady breaths, feel the focus of her gaze on them.

"You told the guards you had information about my son," Hatcher said. "Well?"

Fergal stared into his father's face as he spoke. "If I give you the information, will you promise not to kill her?"

Hatcher cast a glance at Daisy. "How can I kill her when she's already dead?"

Fergal gritted his teeth. "Well, promise not to make her any more dead than she is right now."

Hatcher pursed his thin lips. "If you know of my son, you must know that we aren't exactly…close."

And there was the understatement of the millennium. "I know you haven't set eyes on him since he was twelve."

He ignored Daisy's indrawn breath and kept his focus on Hatcher. The priest was studying him, something flickering behind his cold eyes. "Tell me."

The moment of fucking truth. "Don't you recognize me…Father?"

For a minute, the room seemed to freeze in time. No one moved. Fergal held himself very still.

Hatcher pushed himself slowly to his feet. He paced the room, his fingers rubbing at the silver cross as he kept his gaze averted from Fergal. Finally, he came back to stand across from him and stare down.

"How do I know you're telling the truth?" Hatcher said. "It's been nearly forty years. Maybe you met my son, he told you his sordid story, and you hope to use it for your gain. To save a monster." He nodded to Daisy.

"Take a good look at me. I have your eyes." Fergal rose to his feet. They were identical in height, and he stared into silver eyes so like his own. "Or would you like me to show you the scars on my back from the last beating you gave me? Or tell you about the time we stood over my mother's dead body after she killed herself because of you."

"Enough!" Hatcher turned away, his whole body rigid.

Fergal waited but couldn't resist a quick glance at Daisy, needing to see what was in her face.

Pity.

She pitied him.

Well, that wasn't hate, at least. Then again, it wasn't love, either.

"She was an abomination. You both were. I needed to beat the evil out of you."

Fergal allowed himself a small smile that he knew wouldn't be reflected in his eyes. They were so close now. His right arm tingled. He knew he could shift, pierce Hatcher through the eye before he could shout out and alert the guards. But he couldn't do it—something held him back. He tried to tell himself that it was because they would never get out alive, but there was more to it than that.

All the same, he was filled with the need to make this man suffer as his mother had suffered. Also, there was one thing he could do, one lie he could tell, that might make his father value him more—see him less of an abomination—and piss off the old man at the same time.

"Actually," he said, "she wasn't an abomination. Neither of us were. What a lot of wasted effort on your part."

Hatcher's knuckles whitened where he gripped the silver cross against his chest. "What are you talking about? I saw the evidence."

"You smothered the fucking evidence, you murdering bastard. But in fact, it might have been evidence of something, but certainly not that my mother was genetically modified."

"I saw your sister. She was an abomination."

"My half sister," Fergal said gently and waited while Hatcher tossed that comment over in his mind.

"What are you saying?"

"Wasn't I clear enough for you? My baby sister wasn't your child. Any genetically altered DNA was not from my mother. Your wife."

"You can't know that. You were only eight when she died. She would never have revealed such things to you."

"But I was a somewhat precocious eight-year-old. Having your sister smothered by your father can have the effect of making you grow up fast."

"I don't believe you."

But Fergal knew that he did. "What—that she would be unfaithful to you? You think you gave her everything she needed? You were a cold-blooded bastard who was hardly ever there for her."

"I was doing God's work."

"Slaughtering innocents? My mother told me the truth the day before she killed herself. She expected me to tell you. She said once you knew, you'd be good to me again—you'd stop trying to beat the evil out of me."

Hatcher still clutched the cross, but there was a fine tremor in his fingers now. "She would have told me."

"Maybe she believed you wouldn't have been too happy with her being unfaithful. Maybe she didn't dare risk revealing it even to me until she'd decided to kill herself. Until you drove her to it."

"So you are pure?"

Fergal let out a short, bitter laugh. "Hardly. But my DNA is 100 percent human." That was a total lie—who knew how much of him was human now? Not a lot, he was guessing.

Hatcher seemed almost in a daze. He took a step toward

Fergal, who backed away instinctively—he didn't want the old bastard touching him. The thought made his skin crawl.

Hatcher shook his head. "I need…" Without another word, he swung around and strode to the door at the back of the room. Fergal caught a brief glimpse of more guards before the door swung shut behind his father.

He turned to Daisy. She was watching him, her expression wary.

"So?" he asked.

Chapter Twenty

Daisy's mind was numb. So were her hands. She wiggled her fingers, trying to get the blood flowing, then took stock of her injuries. The laser burn on her arm was almost healed, but the place where Hatcher had pressed the cross to her flesh still stung. She glanced down; the cross was a red brand on her white skin. Quite pretty, really.

"So?" Fergal urged her again.

"Um…er…" She couldn't think of what to say. Poor Fergal. Growing up with that monster. How must he have felt, knowing his mother killed herself to set him free? At least Daisy could see now why he tried so hard to keep his distance.

But Temperance Hatcher was his *father*.

Ugh!

In some ways, she could understand why he hadn't told her. For Christ's sake, who would want to admit to that? All the same, she wished he'd prepared her.

Had he thought she'd look at him differently if she had known? Would she have? It wasn't as though he got along with his dad. Or even had anything to do with him.

But *Temperance Hatcher*.

Probably the person she hated most in the world. The person her friends were on their way to kill. Right now.

"Speechless?" he asked when she remained…speechless.

She swallowed. Then again. Cleared her throat. "Why didn't you tell me?"

He cast her a disbelieving glance. "Is that supposed to be a rhetorical question?" He shrugged. "Maybe because I didn't want you to know. I'm not exactly proud of my old man."

"No. I can understand that. But you're also not responsible for him."

"You wouldn't have looked at me differently if you'd known?"

"I don't know. But I wouldn't have blamed you. We can't choose our families."

Well, in a way he had—by choosing to put Hatcher behind him. He'd left when he was twelve, and they'd obviously had no contact in the years since. And he'd only revealed his identity now to save her life. After all, they'd met Hatcher earlier, and Fergal had said nothing.

There was something else.

Fergal had mentioned his father had used him and his mother as hostages for the other's good behavior. And hadn't Fergal just handed his father someone else to use against him?

Her.

Damn.

"Was that true about your mother?" she asked. "Being unfaithful?"

He peered at the door where Hatcher had disappeared. "No, I made it up. She was never unfaithful—she loved the bastard too much. But I knew it would hurt him. Plus, he's more likely to value me if he considers me 'pure.'"

"Good. Come here," she said.

He'd been keeping his distance as though he was scared to come close. Scared that maybe she would reject him. Now he stepped closer, but his expression remained wary.

"Kiss me," she murmured.

"Why?"

"Jesus, Fergal. Because I want you to. Because you just saved me from a very unpleasant end at great personal cost to yourself."

"I haven't saved you yet," he said. "There's no guarantee that he'll do anything for me. You might have noticed we're not exactly close."

"No, and I'm glad. Did you ever plan to tell him? To see him again?"

He moved closer, halted in front of her, so close his chest brushed against her breasts. "Yeah, I had a plan. Once I got my immortality, I would come back and tell him he could shove his religion up his ass and that I wouldn't be meeting his devil anytime soon."

She smiled. "That would have been good. You can still tell him that."

"I don't think I'll antagonize him any more than I have to right now." He nodded toward the cross-shaped scar beneath her collarbone. "Does this hurt?"

She shook her head. The sting had faded to a dull ache. "You think he'll do what you ask and not...?"

He took a step back. "Kill the woman I love? Who knows? He's done it before, if only indirectly. But I hope so, and at least it's giving us some time."

"Yeah." But was it enough? *The Blood Hunter* wouldn't turn up for a few hours, and the place was crawling with soldiers. But still, with the element of surprise, they had a good chance of getting to Hatcher.

Would Fergal stand by and let them kill his father? He claimed to hate him as much as they did. But it wasn't so simple.

Fergal winced. His hands were still cuffed behind him, but while she watched, his right hand turned silver, elongated until it slipped through the cuff before returning to normal. He rubbed at his head.

"Are you okay?"

"I'm not sure 'okay' covers it. It feels like a thousand people are trying to crawl into my head with me." He gave a weak grin. "Hey, guess what, a thousand people *are* trying to crawl into my head. I wish I could talk to Stefan. Find out what's happening."

"You think he's on our side?"

"Hell, no. Stefan is on Stefan's side, but right now, he's leaning more to us than the Church. Hatcher is unstable. So far, he's let Beauchamp run with this, but that could change at any time. To him, we're just as much monsters as all his other abominations. Well, all we can do for now is wait." He gave her another grin. "And maybe pray."

"Yeah. Or maybe you could kiss me like I asked."

He looped her hair behind her ears, caressed the skin of her cheek, sending tingles running through her. Then he lowered his head and kissed her. Her arms moved instinctively, trying to come around him, and were brought up short by the chain shackling her to the wall. Instead, she pushed her body against him while her lips parted beneath his. His hands rested on the wall on either side of her shoulders, and he leaned in even closer, thrusting his tongue into her mouth, the kiss taking on the hard, bitter edge of desperation. She kept her eyes open and stared into his eyes, so close. Her nostrils filled with the metallic scent now so familiar, her mouth with the taste of him. She could hear the harsh rasp of his breath.

Finally, he drew back, resting his forehead against hers as

both their breathing returned to normal. Lowering his head, he pressed his lips to the mark of the cross. As he straightened and stepped back, she held his gaze. "Whatever happens," she said, "whoever your father is—it doesn't matter. I love you."

"Well, hold on to that thought, because it might be tested."

She didn't like the sound of that, and she shifted as unease rippled through her. "Why? What are you planning?"

"Nothing. I hope we won't need to do anything. I'm hoping Hatcher stays away for the next two hours and your friends pop up and save the day."

"But you don't think that's going to happen?"

"I don't know. Let's just say that I usually don't expect the best. Now, let's see if we can't make you a little more comfortable while we wait." He raised his right arm, and one finger extended into a long, thin blade. Crouching down beside her, he fiddled with the cuffs at her wrists. One snapped open, and she pulled free of the loop on the wall.

"Thank you."

He sank down to sit on the floor beside her, his back against the wall. Daisy followed him down, and he wrapped an arm around her and pulled her close. She rested her head against his shoulder and let out a long sigh. "Tell me how you managed when you were twelve. How did you survive, stay hidden?"

"It's not so hard when you're on your own and don't have anyone else to look out for."

"Ouch," she said.

"I didn't mean..."

"Yes, you did. If I hadn't come after you, maybe you would have found Stefan and gotten away and none of this would have happened."

"Maybe." He was silent for a minute, and she didn't push him. "I don't want to be on my own anymore," he said eventually. "I survived—existed. Nothing more. You've shown me how much more there can be, and I don't want to go back."

Her chest ached, and despair flooded her mind. It wasn't goddamn fair. Rico would have laughed at that—life wasn't fair, he would have said. *Don't plan on it being fair.* "Damn. I wish…"

"Don't." Fergal squeezed her shoulder. "Wishes don't change anything." He took a deep breath. "Tell me one of your long stories. You must have loads of them. Tell me about finding the *Trakis One.*"

Was he crazy? How could she concentrate at a time like this?

"Come on, Daisy. Take my mind off the fact that my father is a crazy madman priest and my girlfriend is a bloodsucking monster."

She almost smiled but shook her head instead. "Okay." She gathered her thoughts. "It was over twenty years ago for you, only six months for us. We had to break into the old Church headquarters to rescue Alex and Rico, and they were after us. So were the Collective, and the captain was dying of the Meridian poison—"

"She'd been to Trakis Seven?"

"Yes. Callum was giving her the treatment in exchange for helping him, but then he had to blow up the planet before she got it and…" She shook her head. Those had been dark times. "Anyway, Callum claimed Meridian actually came from the other side of the black hole that guards the system, and so we thought—why not?"

He chuckled. "Why not indeed. Not many people would consider diving into a black hole. Go on."

"Well, Rico got us through, and there on the other side was the *Trakis One*, pretty much lifeless, but orbiting the hole and in one piece."

"So you boarded her and found Beauchamp and…"

"Not quite—there was a whole lot that happened before that. First, we had to go find some Meridian for Tannis. We landed on the planet and—"

"Shh," Fergal interrupted her. "They're coming."

When she concentrated, she could hear the footsteps. Hatcher wasn't alone.

Fergal got to his feet. He held out a hand to her, and she slid her palm in his. He pulled her up and refastened her cuffs behind her to the loop on the wall. Then he did the clever thing with his hand and recuffed himself. He winced again, and something flickered behind his eyes—a flash of metal—but he blinked and it was gone.

Sitting on the chair opposite her, he cast her a last glance and focused on the door.

It opened a minute later, and Hatcher came back in, followed by three guards. Without acknowledging Fergal, he came to stand in front of her. Now she knew to look, she could see the similarities. His eyes were so like Fergal's, pale gray, but cold. His gaze ran over her, and his lips turned down. Obviously, he didn't like what he saw.

"Take her into the sunlight," he said to the guards.

Daisy's mind went blank at the words. Some part of her noticed that Fergal had jumped to his feet. One of the guards turned and aimed his pistol at him, and he stopped abruptly.

"Don't do this." Fergal's voice was hoarse. "If you ever cared anything for me, or my mother, then don't do this."

Hatcher nodded at the guards, and they stepped toward her. One of them produced a key and unlocked the cuffs, refastening them behind her back.

Would it hurt? She'd never asked Rico that one. Would it be quick? Would she be able to stop herself from screaming? She didn't want to give them the satisfaction, but she really wasn't sure she'd be able to hold back. She had a flashback to the woman they'd burned back on Earth. She had screamed, even before the flames touched her flesh.

"Father!"

Hatcher turned to Fergal. "Don't you understand? I'm doing this for you. I was nearly destroyed by loving a woman I thought was an abomination. I'm saving you from the same fate, saving you before this goes too far." He nodded to the guards. "Take her. And my son. He must watch, see her for the creature she really is."

"It's already gone too far. I love her. And if you murder her as you did my mother—"

"Your mother chose to take her own life."

"You drove her to it."

"I was helping her. As I am helping you now. To find God." He smiled, and it was far scarier than any expression she had seen on his face so far. "You are pure, my son. There is no reason why you can't seek the Lord's forgiveness and come back to the fold."

"You're fucking crazy. That's what you are." Fergal swallowed, brought himself under control. "Look, if you keep her alive, you'll have leverage over me. I'll do anything you want to keep her safe."

"I have faith you will come back to me of your own free will. God has brought you to me for a reason."

They were dragging her across the room now. She didn't fight—they still held a pistol aimed at Fergal—but she didn't help them, either. She kept her gaze locked on him. He cast her a despairing look, and a new, unrecognized fear unfurled inside her.

"Wait," he said. "Just give us some more time. Just a couple of hours. Just…"

"Take her," Hatcher said.

"No! Wait." He licked his lips, swallowed. This time when he looked at her, his eyes held an apology and maybe a good-bye. "I have information. Important information."

"Tell me."

Daisy suddenly had an idea where he was going with this. She shook her head, frantically. "No, Fergal, don't. Please don't." She couldn't bear that he would buy her life with the lives of her friends. She'd rather burn now than live for an eternity with that knowledge.

"I have to," Fergal said.

Hatcher's gaze flicked between the two of them. "What is this information?"

"I want her life in exchange for what I tell you."

The priest pursed his lips. "Perhaps. If the information is important enough."

"Believe me, it's important enough."

"No, Fergal. Please don't do this." She fought them now, twisting in their arms. One of the guards drew back his fist and clipped her on the side of the cheek. She sagged between them, and the room went black.

Fergal stared at the limp body hanging between the two guards. Her pulse fluttered at her throat, but she was out cold. It was better that way. He wouldn't have to look at the hatred in her eyes as he betrayed her friends.

But he could see no other way.

He needed more time. How could he go from having eternity to having less than a few hours? That was all he needed.

"Okay," Hatcher said. "You have her life. Though she will be imprisoned. Now tell me."

"Goddamn it, swear it on your God. On your cross. I want to hear the words."

Hatcher raised the cross to his lips, kissed it. "I swear on my God and my cross that the girl will not be harmed."

Fergal nodded. He took a deep breath. "Her people, the crew of *The Blood Hunter*, are on their way here now to assassinate you."

Hatcher's eyes widened. "They mean to break into the building and take me here. Are they crazy?"

"They hate you."

"When?"

"In less than two hours." Maybe he should mention the attack to take place afterward. And maybe he shouldn't.

"Give me the details."

Fergal glanced sideways at Daisy. But he'd done this now—he was too far in to back out. His head was killing him. Waves of pain washing over him, sucking him under. He reinforced the feedback loop, but it was hardly keeping the others at bay.

If he let go, how long would he have?

He pushed the thought aside and tried to concentrate on the now. Hatcher—he still couldn't think of him as Father—was still unaware of Fergal's involvement with Cybercom, and he wanted to keep it that way. He didn't think Hatcher would be able to stop what was happening to his brain, but maybe he would kill him rather than have an abomination for a son. And he needed to stay alive, needed to keep Daisy alive. It was all that mattered now.

"Three of them."

"Who?"

He'd forgotten that Hatcher knew the crew. "The captain, the pilot, and Devlin Starke."

"Starke is still with them?"

"Yes."

"Good, the last of the rebels. We'll make a spectacle of their execution—let the people see the rebellion is dead."

Not quite. Fergal had seen an army readying itself on

Trakis Two. But again, Hatcher didn't need to know that. At least it sounded like they would try to take them alive. While there was life, there was still hope.

Except for him.

He'd accepted that when he'd made this decision.

"Where and when."

"I told you, less than two hours." He glanced at the unit on Hatcher's wrist. "One hour, forty-five minutes, to be exact. And they have access to your schedule. So it will take place wherever you're supposed to be at that time."

"Good. Thank you, my son. You won't regret this."

He already did. But how could he have acted differently? He couldn't stand by and see her burn.

Hatcher turned to the guard. "Take them to the holding cells."

"I want to talk to her."

He pursed his lips. Then nodded. "Why not. You can persuade her to recant her sins. Maybe there is forgiveness even for such as she. But it will be the last time you'll see her. I won't have my son consorting with evil."

Fergal glanced toward Daisy and found her awake. He willed her to look at him, but she kept her gaze firmly on the floor.

He truly hated his father at that moment.

But not as much as he hated himself.

Chapter Twenty-One

Daisy lay on the cot in the small cell, staring up at the white ceiling.

She was totally aware of Fergal in the cell next to her, only separated by a set of bars, but she couldn't bring herself to look at him, talk to him.

They hadn't been taken back to the prison, but to the holding cells on the first floor. There were bars on three sides. And guards all around.

She wasn't getting out of here, and her mind searched for a way to warn her friends.

Hatcher was going to kill them. And it was all her fault. She'd rather be dead than live with that. But she hadn't been given the choice.

What right did Fergal have to make that sort of decision on her behalf? He should have understood her well enough to know she would never have asked for her life at that price.

She wished she hadn't passed out. She wanted to know what else Fergal had told his father. Had he revealed anything about the attack? Would it even go ahead if Tannis and the others failed in their mission and were taken? Skylar and Callum would get their revenge, but it would be too late for the others. Hatcher would have killed them, and it was all her fault.

They had left her wrists cuffed behind her back, but she hadn't been restrained in any other way. Why would they, when there was a whole squad of armed guards outside, ready to zap her if she so much as looked at them funny?

Maybe Skylar and Callum would rescue her, and she'd have to tell them why their loved ones had died, and they would kill her anyway. They would certainly kill Fergal for his part in this.

And weirdly, she found she didn't want Fergal to die.

At the thought, her anger rose. She should want him to fucking die. She should want to kill him herself. But she didn't.

He'd done this for her. But he shouldn't have. He had no fucking right.

At the thought, her anger flared hotter.

She fed that anger, because it was much better than the pity and despair she'd been feeling up until that point. Peering inside herself, she poked a stick at the place where the darkness slumbered. She needed it right now, needed its coldness wrapped around her, isolating her from her feelings, which were so painful and raw. It flexed and uncoiled inside her. But it felt different; always before it was as though the darkness controlled her, but now she could sense it waiting for her bidding. Except she had nothing to bid it. She was powerless.

And it was all Fergal's fault.

That was better than it being all her fault.

She rolled onto her side so she could look through the bars and into the cell next door.

Fergal had told his father he wanted to talk to her, but

so far, he hadn't said a word. Which was good. Because she would have ignored him.

He was sitting on the floor, his back against the wall, his side against the bars between their cells. They'd uncuffed him, and his hands rested on his bent knees. She left his face until last and went still as she examined him.

Sweat beaded his forehead, lines of pain etched around his mouth, though when he saw her looking at him, they smoothed away, leaving his face clean of expression.

"I don't expect you to forgive me," he said.

"Good."

"I couldn't watch you burn." He turned to face her, and his hands rested on the bars.

"You should have killed me earlier. You promised."

"I don't want you dead."

She glared at him. "I'd rather be dead than have my life at this price."

"Maybe. Maybe the price won't be too high."

She caught her breath as hope fluttered to life inside her, batting feeble wings against her stomach. Did he have a plan? Had he found a way to warn Tannis? "Why? What do you mean?"

He cast a meaningful glance at the guards outside, who could hear every word they said. "Nothing. I meant nothing. Just that you'll get over it."

She wriggled into a sitting position so she could study him better. He really didn't look well. "Are you okay?"

"I'm fine."

"You look—"

She broke off as there was a commotion among the guards. Peering through the bars, she saw Fergal's friend Stefan arguing with them. Fergal pulled himself to his feet and strode across the small cell to stand at the front on the side farthest from her.

Finally, the guards let Stefan through, but they watched him closely as he approached where Fergal stood, his big hands wrapped around the bars. Stefan stepped up close, and the two men talked quietly. Daisy strained to hear, but Fergal had his back to her and their voices were too low. She didn't know whether it was the guards or her they didn't want to overhear them. She suspected both.

Stefan appeared to get heated about something, his voice rising.

"You can't, Fergal, it will destroy you."

Fergal obviously persuaded him, because the other man gave a curt nod, whirled around and stalked back through the guards.

He did not look happy.

But neither did Fergal.

Something extremely unpleasant was going on in his head. That much she was certain of. She'd wanted him to feel bad, to feel guilt. Now the grim expression on his face caused her a stab of pain.

When he went back to his corner and slid down to sit on the floor, she only hesitated a second. She struggled to her feet, crossed her cell, and sank to the floor next to him. Now only the bars separated them. And when Fergal's hand slid through to rest on her knee, she didn't move away.

The sun must be fully up by now. She didn't need to sleep during the day, but she could feel it tugging at her mind. Leaning her back against the wall, she closed her eyes and waited for what would come next. The destruction of everyone she held dear.

The guards came for them an hour later. Daisy blinked open her eyes as they unlocked the cell door. Her arms ached from being held behind her, and she scrambled to her feet and rolled her shoulders to ease the tension. Fergal was already up and heading toward where the guards waited.

She glanced to her own guards, and they returned her look warily. Obviously, news had spread of what she was, and they were taking no chances.

One gestured for her to turn around. When she did, they tied some sort of gag over her mouth. No doubt so she couldn't call out to warn her friends.

They didn't bother to gag Fergal, but why would they? He'd given them this information, and he was hardly likely to warn the crew of *The Blood Hunter* now. No doubt if he did, his dear dad would toss her out into the sunlight without a moment's thought.

A ring of guards surrounded them as they made their way to the main audience room on the first floor. She remembered the route from the information Alex had given her. And this was where they'd planned to attack Hatcher.

He obviously knew the details.

The room was huge. And windowless. A raised dais stood at one end, and a screen had been set up behind it. Chairs lined the side walls. There was a lot of activity, mostly soldiers milling about. She spotted Hatcher on the dais in his long black robes. His gaze flickered to her, then away as though he found even looking at her distasteful. He was talking to a soldier, an officer by the looks of the man, but he waved their guards to a halt as they came up level with him, then took a step toward Fergal.

"I'm told the scientist came to see you. Why?"

"Apparently, you'd told him he could have me for his experiments. He was a little pissed off that I'd been moved without his knowing."

"That was before I knew who you were. He won't touch you. And he won't be around much longer. Once he's done his purpose, he and his work will be destroyed."

"His purpose?"

"God's work," Hatcher replied.

"Yeah, right."

So Hatcher meant to destroy the rest of Cybercom. How would Beauchamp feel at being deprived of his army? Did he even know what Hatcher planned? Somehow, she doubted it. Possibly, Max Beauchamp was no longer in the high priest's confidence.

"Place them out of sight," Hatcher ordered the guards.

Someone took her by the shoulder, hustled her behind the screen, and shoved her into a chair, adjusting her cuffs so she couldn't stand. Fergal was pushed into the chair next to her but left free. He stared straight ahead.

She wanted to ask what Stefan had really wanted, but there were still guards too close.

Lots of guards.

Looking around, she realized the screen had actually cut off half the room. And sharing the space behind it with them was a whole load of heavily armed men. Certainly more than enough to take three attackers, even if they were the fiercest fighters ever.

She swallowed.

The truth was, however fierce, they wouldn't stand a chance.

In that moment, she almost hated Fergal.

Fergal caught her expression, a combination of despair and hatred. He looked away—this had gone too far to change now even if he wanted to.

The screen was slatted, and through the gaps he could see the audience chamber. The room was clearing of soldiers. They disappeared out of the side doors or behind the screen, leaving only Hatcher and two nuns who stood on either side of the priest, their heads bowed, plus a minimal number of guards, no doubt normal for these occasions.

The big double doors opened, and the room began to fill up. This was the weekly open audience where people could come and petition the high priest. It was supposed to make him look like some sort of man of the people, make him accessible to his congregation, but in fact he looked like a superior bastard standing on his dais looking down at the peasants.

A woman came forward first and spoke; Fergal didn't take in the words. He was searching the room for any sign of *The Blood Hunter*'s crew. They were hardly inconspicuous. But so far nothing.

Maybe they wouldn't come.

They hadn't heard from Daisy, so they must know something was wrong.

Hatcher replied to the woman, and she stepped back and merged with the crowd.

Two men came forward next. Fergal let the words wash over him.

Wiping the sweat from his forehead, he checked the biofeedback loop. It was holding—just. He eased back a little, and a thousand minds clamored to get in. He shut them down. A bead of sweat trickled down inside his shirt. Stefan had said he would heat up. It felt like his blood was about to boil in his veins.

And he was ravenous. Strange at a time like this, but hunger was gnawing at his insides.

He spotted Rico the moment he entered the room. The vampire was hard to miss, though at first glance he appeared human. He also appeared to be alone and unarmed. Fergal doubted that was the case—he'd never seen Rico without a weapon. But maybe everyone was searched before they were allowed into the audience chamber. Rico paused just inside the room and then wove through the crowd to stand to the side of the dais.

Tannis entered next. She looked exactly the same as usual; her only concession to a disguise was contact lenses that turned her inhuman violet eyes to a soft brown. The violet would have labeled her as Collective, perhaps not something you wanted to advertise in the present company. She stayed at the back of the room and took up position close to one of the guards.

Devlin arrived last. Like Tannis, he'd changed his eyes and also toned down his dress. Usually he looked like a soldier, in khaki combats and boots. Today he was wearing black pants and a shirt, his black-and-gold hair pulled into a ponytail.

A sound from behind him made Fergal glance back. Daisy was sitting upright in the chair. Still gagged, she managed to speak quite eloquently with her eyes.

As he gave a small nod, she blinked and swallowed.

Fergal turned his attention back to the room. It didn't look like the guards had noticed the newcomers. Was it an act?

Hatcher continued to call petitioners up. He must know they were there. Had he ordered the guards to let them in so they could be contained? It had to be dangerous with so many civilians about, but maybe Hatcher thought the sacrifice worth the risk.

Devlin had taken up position on the opposite side of the door from Tannis, close to a second guard.

Of course, they would need weapons.

He kept his eyes on Devlin, saw the infinitesimally small nod he gave Tannis, and a second later, they both exploded into action. Devlin leaped for his guard, snapped the man's neck, and drew the weapon from the holster in one smooth move. Tannis killed her man, swung her stolen laser around onto the next guard, and blasted him through the head.

They were good.

Devlin snatched up another gun, and together they moved through the room.

"On the floor," Tannis shouted.

Most of the congregation had already hit the floor anyway. She swung around and shot another guard while Devlin got the last.

Rico stood alone in the center of the room. He still appeared weaponless, but Devlin called to him and tossed the second laser pistol. Rico caught the weapon smoothly and raised it to the man on the dais.

But there were soldiers racing out from behind the screen now, filling the space between Rico and the high priest, who stood unmoving through the whole thing.

"*Mierda,*" the vampire swore. Tannis was beside him now, and they took up positions back to back, as though they'd done it a thousand times. The soldiers were returning fire, but they deflected the blasts with ease and countered with their own shots. The line of soldiers thinned, but more swarmed in from the side doors to take their place.

There were too many.

The room filled with smoke and the sickly scent of scorched flesh, moans from the injured and the occasional panicked squeal from one of the congregation. Devlin stood at right angles to the other two, shooting continuously. He took a hit to the arm but kept on firing. Then Rico took a blast right in the chest and was hurled to the floor. Without him at her back, Tannis was shot in the shoulder, and the gun went spinning from her hand.

Only Devlin was shooting back now.

"Stop," Hatcher roared.

Nobody stopped.

Rico was back on his feet. He leaped for the nearest guard, ripping his throat out. No one was going to mistake him for human now. His fangs were elongated, dripping with crimson, his eyes glowing. He pulled the gun from the man's limp fingers and tossed the body back to the ground.

But Hatcher was surrounded. No way were they getting to him, and it would only be a matter of time. The soldiers were closing in on them.

While the fight had been going on, the civilians had crawled away until only the three in the center of the room were left, surrounded by a shrinking circle of guards. The laser blasts were coming continuously. Rico and Tannis were hit at the same time, and Devlin spun as a shot took him in the back, but they all kept blasting.

Fergal was focused on the fight and hardly noticed as two guards came around the screen. He only took notice when they reached Daisy and pulled her to her feet. Her gaze flashed to Fergal, panic in her eyes.

He shook his head. "Don't fight," he mouthed the words, knowing they wouldn't be heard above the chaos.

She was shaking visibly, probably fighting to keep control. Beneath the singed flesh, the smell of blood lay heavy on the air. Her nostrils flared, but she held herself together as they half led, half dragged her out from behind the screen. At least she was protected from the shooting by the thick line of soldiers guarding the high priest. Fergal followed close behind, and no one tried to stop him.

As they reached the dais, Hatcher grabbed her arm and pulled her up. Holding her close, he took a laser pistol from one of the guards and pressed it under her chin.

Fergal stepped forward, but this time a guard stopped him with a hand on his shoulder. He held her gaze, saw her swallow but hold herself together as she took in the fight still going on.

"Stop or I kill the girl." Hatcher's voice carried above the noise of the fight. For a moment, nothing happened. The lasers continued to flare. Rico glanced up and his eyes fixed on Daisy. He stopped shooting, and a blast hit him in the leg, sending him to the floor.

Tannis whirled around, and she too caught sight of Daisy. Fury flashed across her face, but she lowered her arm and stopped.

Devlin must have realized something was up. He glanced quickly behind him and went still.

The shooting ceased. Silence fell.

"Drop your weapons."

"Great, fucking great," Tannis muttered, but she hurled the laser pistol to the floor. Rico had lost his when he fell; now he struggled to his feet and rubbed at his thigh. Devlin swore and dropped his own pistol.

"Search them, remove their communication units, and cuff them," Hatcher said.

They didn't fight as they were patted down, a scanner run over their bodies, and their wrists pulled behind their backs and cuffed.

Hatcher loosened his hold on Daisy, and she almost fell. Fergal caught her as she stumbled back, but she pulled free of him and stood on her own.

"Put her with the others." Hatcher nodded to one of the guards.

"You swore she wouldn't be harmed."

"She won't. I thought she'd like to say good-bye to her friends. Perhaps explain to them what went wrong with their plan."

Bastard.

Chapter Twenty-Two

"Well, you made a right fucking mess of this one, didn't you," Rico muttered as the guard gave Daisy a shove that put her in the middle of the small group.

She would have answered, but she was still gagged. Anyway, what could she say other than agreeing with him?

"Freaking hell," Tannis snarled at her. "What happened to keeping a low profile if you were caught?"

"Did you tell them?" Devlin asked. "Did you give us up?"

Daisy glared at him.

"Well, someone had to ask," Devlin said.

"Of course she didn't give us up," Tannis snapped. "But I'm going to make a guess at who did. Bastard."

Daisy followed her gaze to where Fergal stood on the dais beside Hatcher. Side by side, the similarities were even more evident. He was talking heatedly with his father, but they both turned to look at her.

Hatcher nodded once and stalked away to talk to the head guard, leaving Fergal standing alone.

If anything, he looked worse than the rest of them put

together. A fine sheen of sweat covered his face, and when he ran a hand through his hair, his fingers trembled.

"He doesn't look too good," Rico said. "Did they torture him? Not that I'll fucking forgive him for this even if they did."

She shook her head.

"So he just gave us up?" Tannis said. "Great, fucking great. I knew we couldn't trust the bastard. Fucking reporters. Is that why he did it—to get a story?"

Daisy glared at her. It wasn't as though she could answer.

"Well, I'll torture him myself if I ever get out of this."

Hatcher glided toward them, his eyes gleaming. "Well, we meet again. I think we'll make your executions sooner rather than later. Just a little time to set things up and make sure the world will be watching. This time you all die." He gave Daisy a dismissive glance. "Except that one. But first, call your ship. Make sure they know if they enter our airspace, you will all die immediately. Including the girl."

"No," Fergal said from behind them. "You promised she'd be safe."

"She will be, as long as her friends cooperate."

He held out one of the comm units to Tannis.

"Hit the red button," she said. "Skylar?"

"Yes." Skylar's voice came over the comm unit. "You done?"

"Not exactly. Actually, we're fucked. We're all prisoners and we're going to be executed and if you come any closer they'll do it sooner rather than later. So stay away." She looked up and raised a brow.

Hatcher nodded and tossed the comm unit to one of the guards. "Take them to the cells."

As they reached the door, Daisy twisted around to glance back. Fergal was leaning against the dais, his head bent. He didn't look up as she was taken from the room.

Would she ever see him again?

Did she want to?

Probably not, if his father succeeded in killing her friends. She would find some way to die, too, if that happened.

The prison was still on full alert, and there were guards everywhere. They were taken back to the prison and locked in a large cell with absolutely no furniture, just bare walls and a door.

As it locked behind them, Tannis turned to her. "So what the fuck happened?"

Daisy did some more glaring, and Tannis frowned at the gag. "Wait a second." She did some impressive wriggling thing and bent down, climbed over her bound wrists so they were now in front of her. Then she reached up and pulled off Daisy's gag.

She swallowed and licked her lips. Took a deep breath. Now she could speak, she wasn't sure what to say. Except maybe *sorry*, and what good would that do? She said it anyway. "Sorry."

"So you should be. Who has the lock pick?" Tannis asked. "Someone must have thought to bring a lock pick."

"In my hair," Devlin said.

He bent down, and Tannis ran her hands through his ponytail, pulling free a long, slender lock pick. "Turn around," she said, and he turned. It only took seconds, and his wrists were free. He repeated the process for Tannis and Rico.

Were they going to leave her tied up as punishment for being such an idiot? She wouldn't blame them if they did, but Tannis gestured for her to turn around, and soon she was free. She tossed the cuffs in the corner.

Devlin was pacing the room like a caged panther. Rico stood by the door, leaning one shoulder against the wall as he peered out of the small glass window. Tannis stood in front of her, her hands on her hips, her eyebrows raised.

"So," Tannis said. "You were about to tell us what the fuck happened."

"I was?"

"Yeah, because I for one would like to know how I just dived headfirst into a great big pile of crap. Is Cain working with this friend of his, with the Church?"

"No! Fergal hates the Church. He would never work with them."

"Then what is it? He wasn't a prisoner in there. It looked like he was pretty buddy with our friend Hatcher."

"He's not. He hates Hatcher as well."

"So what happened? Come on, give us something here. If I'm going to burn in Hell's fires, I'd really like to understand why."

"We were captured. Trying to find Fergal's friend. Well, we did find him, actually. He was with Hatcher, but we still would have been okay, except Max Beauchamp was there as well. He recognized me."

"Shit." Tannis scowled. "We should never have woken that bastard up. We should have left him orbiting that black hole for fucking eternity."

"Anyway, he told them who I am. And more to the point, what I am."

"Well, he never did forgive you for trying to eat his daughter."

"Hatcher was going to have me staked out in the courtyard to burn. Fergal…asked him not to."

"And why would Hatcher do anything for Fergal Cain?"

"Because…" She hesitated. It seemed disloyal to tell Fergal's secret. But they had to know. Without that, none of this made any sense. She took a deep breath. "Because Temperance Hatcher is his father."

Tannis narrowed her eyes. Devlin stopped pacing and turned to her. Even Rico straightened and took a step closer.

"Say that again," Rico said.

"Temperance Hatcher is Fergal's father. He hadn't seen him since he was twelve," she added quickly. "That's when he ran away from home. It's not as if they're close or anything. He hates him. Hatcher didn't know who he was until Fergal told him, and he only did that to save my life."

"Okay, that makes sense so far. But how did he come to betray us?"

"Hatcher decided he was going to kill me anyway. For Fergal's sake."

Rico snorted. "Don't tell me—to save him from the love of a bad woman?"

"Something like that. The thing is, he truly believes. I thought maybe he was just a madman, but he believes."

"They're the worst type," Tannis said. "But why do you think that?"

Daisy tugged down the neck of her shirt and showed the brand of the cross. "Because he did this. Rico told me that wouldn't happen except with a believer."

"Interesting. But it doesn't help us. So Hatcher was going to kill you anyway, at which point, Fergal sold us out in exchange for your life."

"I tried to tell him not to. He was supposed to kill me if we didn't get away, but he said he couldn't and…" She blinked back a tear. "I'm sorry."

"Hey, not your fault."

"Yes, it fucking is her fault," Rico said. "Falling for a fucking asshole like Cain. I always knew there was something dodgy about the guy."

"No, you didn't," Daisy said. "You practically threw me at him. Told me to let him tie me up."

"Yeah, well, what sort of decent guy wants to do that kinky stuff?"

Both Devlin and Tannis raised an eyebrow. Maybe she

wasn't the only kinky one.

"Are you okay?" Tannis asked, scrutinizing her. "Not hungry or liable to lose it in here? I don't fancy being stuck in a cell with a starving vampire. I'd rather get it over with now."

"Thanks," Daisy said. "But I'm fine. I had a guard when they captured us." It seemed like an age ago, but it had actually only been a few hours.

"Good for you." Tannis looked around the room. "So anyone got a plan to get out of here?"

Rico was back to peering out of the small window. "Even if we got through the door, there's a whole unit of them waiting outside. They'd stun us and drop us back in here."

"Well, we have one advantage," Tannis said. "I'm pretty sure Hatcher doesn't know that we've"—she waved a hand to encompass Devlin—"taken the Meridian treatment. I wonder why Beauchamp didn't tell him."

"Hmm, maybe he doesn't want anyone to know there's a source of Meridian on the other side of the black hole. Especially Hatcher, who, if you remember, went to an awful lot of trouble to destroy the Meridian in this universe."

"I think Beauchamp plans to go back," Daisy said. "Something Fergal's friend told him. Maybe he's lying to Hatcher about his reasons why."

"That would make sense, but I don't see how it will help us. Shit, you know I'm really not ready to die." Tannis went still. "Just a moment, Callum's trying to get hold of me. Let's hope he has a plan." She was silent for a minute, gazing into space, her face softening as she listened. Then she rolled her eyes. "He says he'll offer himself to Hatcher in exchange for me. How sweet is that?"

"Fucking nauseatingly sweet," Devlin replied. "And not much help."

No, because no way would Tannis allow that.

"They can bring *The Blood Hunter* down here under

cover, using the stealth control, but they've still got to get through all those guards. Chances are, they'll just end up in here with us."

"No way," Devlin said. "Saffira stays on board. She's not to set foot on this shithole."

"Don't worry, I told Callum that wasn't an option."

"What about if they get close enough to blast Hatcher from space?" Rico suggested.

"Good idea. If we weren't right slam underneath him. We'll be killed in the explosion."

"It wouldn't kill us. We'd all survive. They'd just have to dig us out."

"Or something would go wrong, and we'd be incarcerated in here for eternity. Nice." Tannis went quiet again. Her lashes flickered closed as she communicated with Callum. Finally she sighed, opened her eyes. "They're going into stealth mode. They'll take up stationary orbit close by and wait to see if anyone comes up with any bright ideas. Worse comes to worst and they'll coordinate an attack to coincide with our executions."

"That won't do us much good if they decide to stake us out in the sunlight. I might survive long enough. Daisy would burn to a crisp at the first ray."

"Except they're not going to kill Daisy. She has a boyfriend with influential fucking family. Jesus, Hatcher is really his father?"

Daisy nodded.

"Poor kid." Tannis ran a hand through her short spiky hair. "Okay, that's it for now. But search your brains, children, because dying aside, I really don't want to give Hatcher the satisfaction of killing us."

Daisy didn't want to, either. She was responsible for this, but she could see no way out. Exhaustion washed over her. She almost didn't recognize it—vampires didn't get tired. But she suspected it was more emotional than physical. Even if she lived—and she didn't want to if everyone she cared for was gone—Hatcher wasn't going to let Fergal see her. No doubt she'd live her existence in a cage. How long would she last without feeding? Vampires didn't die of starvation, but they could lapse into a coma-like state. Something to look forward to, anyway.

She leaned against the wall, then slid down so she sat on the floor, her legs stretched out in front of her. Tannis was pacing as well now, positively fizzing with suppressed energy. Devlin was the same—if they weren't careful they'd collide.

Rico was outwardly relaxed, but she could sense the tension coiled inside him.

The weird thing was she wanted to see Fergal again. She wasn't happy about it, but she craved him with a deep yearning. The hours passed agonizingly slowly. She dozed on and off, letting the conversations drift over her.

"Someone's coming," Rico said, straightening from his position by the door. "And it looks like your boyfriend."

Daisy scrambled to her feet as the lock clicked in the door and it swung inward. She tried to force down the smile that tugged at her lips; it seemed to be inappropriate. Obviously, Tannis thought so as well, from the scowl on her face.

There were two guards at his back, but Fergal stepped through the door alone and it shut behind him.

Was he a prisoner? He wasn't restrained.

A low growl broke the silence. She'd been staring at Fergal, drinking him in; now she flashed a quick glance at everyone else. The level of menace in the room was tangible.

Both Devlin and Tannis were glaring at Fergal, but it was Rico who had growled, and his lip curled up in a snarl. His whole body was tense, as if he was ready to leap. Daisy took an instinctive step forward to stand between Fergal and the vampire.

Rico raised an eyebrow. "You plan on protecting him?"

She nodded. Just hoped she didn't have to. Rico would rip her apart, but maybe that wouldn't be such a bad thing. She stood up straighter and almost dared him.

The snarl changed to a grin. "Okay. Maybe we'll hear what metal boy has to say first. Then we can decide if you're going to die protecting him."

"None of this was Daisy's fault. She would have burned before betraying you. I wouldn't let her."

"Sweet. So what are you doing here now?"

"I've come to collect Daisy to watch the execution."

"Nice idea for a date," Rico drawled.

"Hatcher insisted."

"I'll bet. The sadistic bastard. I'm surprised he let you in here."

"He's feeling merciful. He thinks he's won."

"And has he?" Tannis asked.

"Not yet."

Daisy had been keeping an eye on the others. Now she turned to study Fergal. His face was drawn, lines of pain bracketing his mouth. And his eyes were strange. Black spots whirled in the silver depths.

"Are you okay?"

Fergal almost shook his head—but that would hurt way too much. That she could still ask after all he'd done. He knew part of her must hate him, but her green eyes were soft with concern. For him.

"Fergal?"

He shook off the warm fuzzy feeling. Not because it didn't matter, but rather, he had more important things to dwell on right now.

"I'm fine," he said. Which was a total lie. His head was on the verge of exploding. Or imploding. And it was too soon.

Another hour, Stefan had said.

He just had to hold on.

He'd tried to talk Hatcher out of the execution or at least into delaying it. But there was no budging him. This time he wanted to make sure it was done. But he had settled on sunset, so Daisy could watch.

"So what happens now?" Tannis asked.

He glanced around the room. With the exception of Daisy, who looked on the point of breakdown, none of the others appeared particularly concerned. Pissed off, maybe, but not worried. Though pissed was probably too mild—the room positively pulsated with bad vibes.

"The execution is set for sundown."

"Nice," Tannis said. "I suppose the fires will look prettier in the dark."

"You'll be taken from here to the square at the front of the building."

"The one used for speeches."

He nodded. "There will be a priest present, so if you want to ask for forgiveness there will be an opportunity—I suggest you take advantage."

Tannis frowned. "You do?"

"I'm thinking between you there are a lot of things to ask forgiveness for. It will delay the execution, if nothing else."

"Good point. Rico alone could keep them busy all night."

"Exactly." He thought some more, trying to see past the headache. What else did he need to cover? "Are you in contact with the ship?"

"I've...contacted Callum." She tapped her head, and he realized she meant telepathically. "They're in orbit, waiting for..." She shrugged. "Anything, I guess."

"Good. I'm going to try and provide a diversion." That

was one thing to call it. He wished he had more idea of what would happen. Whether it would even work, or whether his brain would go up in smoke before he had a chance to do anything useful. But there was no point in worrying about that. This was the only option.

"What sort of diversion?" Devlin asked.

"I'm not sure yet, but a big one. You'll know it when you see it. Make sure your people are ready."

"They can come in and land on the podium," Tannis said. "Stay in stealth mode until we have to go. Come out when we need the extra power to take off. I take it Hatcher still doesn't know we're Collective."

"No, but your ashes will be spread to the wind. It's doubtful there will be anything left to regenerate, so I strongly suggest you try to avoid the whole burning thing."

"Fucking good idea," Rico said. "What a plan. Why didn't we think of that?"

This could really work. He was actually starting to believe it. If he could stay alive long enough, and if Stefan was right, and if Daisy would...

Daisy peered at him, her expression doubtful. Did she suspect what he was doing? How could she? Even he didn't really have a clue what he was doing. But he had to put her mind at rest somehow. He needed her cooperation, and he suspected he wouldn't get it if she knew what he was about to do and what the consequences would be. Stefan had been very clear on them. He turned to Tannis.

"Is that job offer still open?"

Her eyes widened. "Well, you've certainly got balls, anyway."

"Of fucking steel probably," Rico said.

"Yeah." He glanced at Daisy. Some of the fear vanished, and she was looking at Tannis expectantly. "So?" he prompted.

"If we all get out of this alive, consider yourself crew."

Why the hell did that make him want desperately to come out alive? Well, obviously that wasn't going to happen. But maybe if things worked out right, Daisy and her friends would. He nodded. "Good. We need to go," he said to Daisy.

No one had mentioned Hatcher. But if they got the chance, he was betting they'd kill him on the way out. Not his problem.

He banged on the door, and the guards opened it from the outside. After ushering Daisy through, he paused and turned slightly to speak to Rico, keeping his voice low. "Will you make sure she gets away safely?"

"Why don't you do that yourself?"

"I may be a little…incapacitated."

"You're not coming along?"

"I somehow doubt it."

The vampire cast him a long look. "And I take it Daisy doesn't know this is a suicide mission on your part."

"No, and I'd rather she didn't find out."

Rico pursed his lips and gave a curt nod. "Consider it done. I'll make sure she leaves with us."

"Thank you."

He released his breath, some of the tension oozing from him. Strange, but he trusted the vampire, and there were few people he had ever trusted in his life. He followed Daisy out of the cell and waited while they cuffed her again, but this time in front of her body.

Her face was expressionless, and she appeared almost serene. She trusted him to rescue her friends, thought he was some sort of fucking hero who was going to save the day.

In which case, he'd better make sure he did.

"How long until sunset?" she asked.

"Forty minutes."

Obviously, Daisy couldn't go outside until the sun had

set, but the guards led them to a small room off the main corridor of the building. There were no windows, but there were a couple of chairs.

Two guards stayed with them, positioned on either side of the door. Fergal could have taken them, but what was the point? Instead, they sat in silence. He leaned his back against the chair and closed his eyes. The loop was a constant buzz in his head, like a dam holding back the flood of awakening brains, all hammering at his skull.

"Fergal?"

Her voice was low, but he blinked open his eyes.

"Thank you."

He gave a wry smile, then glanced at the guards and spoke quietly. "I got you into this. It's up to me to get you out."

"No, I got myself in."

"Anyway," he said, "you're not out yet. Neither are your friends."

"But you'll save us all."

She sounded so sure of him. He wished he were as sure. They lapsed into silence. There wasn't much to say. Or rather, there was too much. An eternity of words that now would never be spoken. He wanted to tell her how he felt, but maybe she was better off not knowing. Maybe she would find it easier to move on. Christ, he was getting maudlin.

He was saved from sinking any further into depression by a rap on the door. It opened, revealing two more guards and behind them Hatcher and Beauchamp.

"It's time," Hatcher said.

Chapter Twenty-Three

They followed Hatcher through the building, a circle of guards surrounding them, out of a set of double doors at the back, which led into a huge courtyard area. The doors opened onto a stage at one end. Opposite was the podium Tannis had mentioned. Fergal stared at it intently but couldn't tell whether the ship was there or not.

Above them, the sky was dark crimson—the suns had set but still formed a glow. Daisy shivered beside him, and he followed her gaze. Three great pyres had been built in the center of the courtyard. They stood eight feet tall, each with a stake in the middle.

Two rows of seats had been set up on the stage. These were filled except for four in the middle of the front row. Around the edges of the courtyard, a mass of people milled restlessly. He had no doubt that this little party was also being commed to the rest of the universe.

Hatcher led them to the empty seats, and Fergal sat down beside Daisy. She was still staring with horror at the pyres, and who could blame her?

To Hell with his father. Fergal reached across, took her hand in his, and squeezed. She glanced at him. "I saw someone burned once."

"You did?" He wasn't aware there had been any public burnings—this was obviously a special occasion.

"Back on Earth. A woman. Rico shot her before the flames could get to her, though."

There was obviously a story there. One he was destined never to hear. He turned slightly so he could keep an eye on the doors to his right. He needed some sort of sign from Stefan that everything was ready.

Trouble was, he was by no means sure that Stefan would follow through. The scientist probably didn't want his success story self-destructing.

A rumble went through the crowd as the doors opened and the three prisoners were hustled out into the courtyard. They all had their hands bound behind their backs. One of the guards pushed at Tannis as she hesitated in the doorway, and she turned and snarled at him. Rico appeared cool and unbothered by the whole fiasco. Devlin bristled with barely restrained fury.

They came to a halt directly in front of the stage, only feet from where Fergal sat, and the guards stepped back. He didn't think he had ever seen his father so happy. Hatcher rose to his feet and moved to the front of the stage. God forbid, he was going to give them a speech. Rico must have thought the same.

"Save us the sanctimonious sermon, asshole."

Hatcher's eyes narrowed, but he ignored the interruption and started to speak. Fergal let the words wash over him while he kept one eye on the little group, the other on the door.

Come on, Stefan, you bastard.

He still held on to Daisy. She was gripping his fingers tightly, but she would have to let go soon. He stared at Tannis, who stood directly below his seat, and tried to work out what she was thinking. She caught his gaze and gave a little shake of her head.

No ship, then.

For a second she closed her eyes, and he guessed she was communicating with Callum—or trying to. Suddenly, she went stiff. "You're fucking kidding me." She spoke the words aloud, so presumably they were meant to be heard.

Rico swung his head around to face her. "What?"

"Freaking dragons, that's what. Shit."

Fergal turned to Daisy, who was chewing on her lower lip. Obviously, dragons were not good news.

"They've had to take evasive action," Tannis muttered.

"Well, tell them to take it quickly," Rico snarled. "Have I mentioned how much I hate the goddamned Church?"

"Frequently."

Hatcher completed his speech, and an expectant silence fell on the crowd.

"No way is anyone tying me to that fucking stake," Tannis said.

"So we fight?" Rico said.

"A little difficult trussed up like this. Ideas would be good here."

Fergal stared at the double doors, willing Stefan to appear. Tannis was right. Once they were tied to the pyres, it would all be over.

The guards approached the group almost warily. Rico bared his teeth, and they stopped.

"Come on, Stefan," Fergal muttered.

"Take them," Hatcher snapped, and the guards overcame their natural reluctance. Two grabbed each prisoner.

"Fergal, do something," Daisy said from beside him.

They were almost at the stakes now. Tannis was staring at the sky.

Then the double doors were pushed open, and Stefan slipped through. He searched the stage, found Fergal, and gave a small nod.

He squeezed Daisy's hand and tugged his fingers free. She tried to hold on, her gaze flashing to his face. "What?"

"As soon as you hear something, head for the podium where *The Blood Hunter* will land."

"And where will you be?"

"Right behind you, sweetheart. Just don't look back. Keep going. I'll catch up."

She stared into his face. Did she believe him? She glanced at her friends being dragged to the pyres, and she nodded.

"Good. Be ready."

She opened her mouth, but Fergal couldn't hear her words. A loud roar filled his mind. He was winding back on the loop, and it was disintegrating, the voices in his head clamoring for freedom. A freedom he wasn't about to give them. Not yet, anyway. He had a job for them to do first.

For a second, everything went black, then it was as though a light flicked on in his brain and he could see everything clearly. No, "see" was the wrong word. He *knew* everything. For a microsecond he savored the feeling, then he got to work.

Come, he ordered.

Daisy sat frozen in her seat, horror washing over her as Rico, Tannis, and Devlin were dragged across the ground toward the pyres.

Where was Fergal's diversion? She cast him a sideways glance. His face was white, his eyes closed, but she could see the flicker of rapid movement behind his lids. She stretched out her hand and nudged him, but he didn't respond.

Her friends were almost at the pyres now.

"Hey," Rico called out over his shoulder. "I thought we were going to get a chance to say we're sorry."

Her gaze flashed to where Hatcher stood on the stage to her right, his eyes narrowed on the vampire. He held up his hand, and the guards halted, turning the prisoners back to face them. "You wish to repent of your sins?"

"Yeah, I do. You want me to list them out?"

A small smile curved the priest's lips. "There is no need for that. I give you absolution. Now proceed."

"What about me?" Tannis asked.

"You, too, my child. And you?"

It took Daisy a moment to realize he was speaking to Devlin.

"You can take your fucking absolution and stuff it up your arse," he snarled.

Hatcher gave a wave of his hand, and the guards continued, dragging them forward. Daisy wanted to leap up, race after them, stop them, but she couldn't seem to move.

Beneath her panic, she heard something. The *thud* of many feet. The sound came from beyond the double doors and was getting closer.

Fergal still appeared out of it, but she noticed his friend standing at the side of the doors, his gaze fixed on Fergal, his face tense.

Then he too must have heard the footsteps, his eyes widening.

The people's attention shifted from the prisoners to stare at the doors. Even the guards sensed something amiss, and they stopped and turned slowly. Rico caught her gaze and raised a brow, but she could only shrug. She was pretty certain this was Fergal's diversion, but what had he done?

The doors were flung open from inside. For a second the space remained empty, then it filled with men. Silver men. This close she could see the layer of silver encasing their bodies and the blank expression in their eyes.

One of the guards opened fire, and the laser blast bounced harmlessly off the body of the man it hit. More shots, but the silver army kept coming. As one, they raised weapons and started shooting. The guards holding the prisoners went down first. Rico, Tannis, and Devlin sprinted across the open ground, heading for cover.

Fergal was still not responding, and she shook his arm. Nothing, and she swallowed down her panic.

What had he told her?

To run for the podium. He would follow. But how could he in this state?

There was total chaos now as more of the silver men swarmed into the arena. Most of the guards were down, but the audience was charging around, trying to find a way out. Hatcher still stood at the center of the stage, but no one shot him. Max Beauchamp was beside him, and a blast took him in the chest, hurling him to the floor.

"You have to go," a voice said from beside her.

She turned to see Stefan, standing behind her. "I can't. I can't get Fergal to move. They'll kill him."

"No, they won't. He's controlling them."

"What? How?"

"It doesn't matter how, just believe it."

"Will he come back?"

"I don't know. But he'll be safe. I'll look after him. You need to get out of here. If Hatcher recaptures you, Fergal will do whatever he says and this will have all been for nothing."

She nodded. She wouldn't let that happen. Not again.

"Good. Hold out your hands."

She did, and he unlocked the cuffs and pressed a laser pistol into her hand. "Fergal is doing this for you. No one else. Now make sure it's worth it."

The need to stay and the need to go ripped her apart.

She glanced up. Hatcher hadn't moved, but his focus was on them, and he took a step forward. She leaned across and kissed Fergal on the lips. No response. Then she was on her feet and running.

She passed close to Hatcher and skidded to a halt. For a second she aimed her pistol straight at his head. Her finger tightened on the trigger. She could kill him now, for all the people he had murdered. But in the end, her finger stayed steady on the trigger.

"You only live because you're Fergal's father," she said and turned away. She peered back over her shoulder. A group of the cyborgs had formed a circle around Fergal and Stefan, protecting them.

Someone grabbed her from behind. A guard. He held her in front of him as a shield. Daisy elbowed him in the gut, pulled free with ease, and broke his neck with one quick twist.

"Over here."

Through the chaos, she heard Rico call out to her and headed toward the sound. They were all crouched behind a barrier in front of the podium. Tannis was unlocking Devlin's cuffs. She glanced at Daisy and scowled. "Why the hell didn't you kill Hatcher? You had the chance."

She looked away and then back. "He's Fergal's father, I couldn't."

"Fuck that," Tannis snarled. "Give me a minute."

She stalked across the arena, picking up a laser from a dropped guard. Without a word, Devlin raced after her. The cyborgs ignored them. They were now moving methodically through the arena, picking off any remaining soldiers. Tannis and Devlin came to a halt ten feet from where Hatcher still stood on the stage. He appeared dazed at the chaos around him.

"For Janey," Tannis said.

"And Tris." Devlin spoke from beside her.

But as they took aim, a swarm of cyborgs filled the space between them, covering Hatcher.

"Shit."

"Tannis, get your ass over here, we need to leave," Rico yelled. "Now."

"Crap."

They turned and raced back to cover.

"Look." Rico pointed to the sky, and Daisy stared upward. There was a ripple in the darkness, like a tear in space. White light flashed, and *The Blood Hunter* hurtled through. "*Dios*, Saffira must have opened a wormhole."

Tannis snorted. "It's lucky we ever saw the ship again."

"Hey," Devlin said, "she's been practicing."

"I'm just grateful to see her. Let's get the fuck out of here."

The ship swooped down and landed gracefully on the podium only feet from them, and the doors to the docking bay opened. Jon and Alex stood in the doorway, blasters held at the ready.

Tannis and Devlin were already halfway up the ramp. Daisy pushed herself upright but hesitated. She glanced back over her shoulder. She could hardly see Fergal through the swarm of cyborgs.

"I'm going back for Fergal," she said. "I still have my shuttle. We'll catch up."

"Oh, no, you're not," Rico said. "I made a promise." He scooped her up and tossed her over his shoulder, his arm like an iron band holding her in place.

The ramp lifted as he ran up. Daisy had one last glimpse of Fergal surrounded by his army before the doors slammed shut behind them and they were lifting off.

Despair filled her as Rico put her down on the floor.

She hurried over to the scanner unit by the doors and switched it on, but already the planet was vanishing into the distance.

She was gone.

A thousand voices relayed the information. A thousand pairs of eyes sent back the image of *The Blood Hunter* hurtling into space.

He'd been fighting for control, trying to keep the influx of information from shattering his mind, but pain drilled into his skull. He was vaguely aware of someone beside him, talking urgently.

Stefan.

But he couldn't hear the words. His external senses were shutting down, his brain cells exploding, cutting off the nerves. He was exhausted from the fight. But Daisy was safe. This was it. The end.

He stopped fighting.

Red-hot agony poured into his skull. For a second everything was blindingly clear.

Then nothing.

Chapter Twenty-Four

A switch went on in his head.

Daisy was safe.

At least he hoped she was. He'd been off-line for a long time.

His mind blank.

Now a light flickered on, like a computer in his head, checking the systems. He remembered the pain, but right now, his brain was a beautiful white space. Empty. He wasn't sure he wanted to change that.

His eyes squeezed open, and he could see. Not a lot—he was lying on his back, staring at a white ceiling.

"About time," a voice said from behind him.

He searched his databases. Stefan.

"What the fuck happened?"

"I brought you back from the dead. Well, maybe not dead, but you were off-line. I rebooted you. Your body was fine, but your brain had shut down. Actually, it had melted."

"So where am I?"

"Still on Trakis Five."

"Hatcher?"

Stefan grinned. "Your father?"

"How the fuck do you know that?"

"He told me. Just before he was about to perform an exorcism on you."

"Shit—he's still trying to get the devil out of me."

"I told him it would kill you but I could reverse the process and hand you back as good as new. You know he loves you."

"Yeah, but he's also a complete crazy bastard." He thought about what Stefan had said. "So can you? Reverse the process?"

"Hell, no. But he doesn't know that. Wait a moment, there's something I need to do." He stepped away and pressed the comm unit on his arm. "He's awake and fully functioning."

Fergal couldn't hear the other side, but Stefan was smiling as he came back to him. "Your girlfriend was pleased."

"Daisy?" Panic hit him. She hadn't come back, had she? Everything would have been for nothing. "She's not here, is she?" He never wanted Daisy anywhere near his father again.

"No. She wanted to be. When she realized you weren't dead, she wanted to take you away. I persuaded her you were better off here, where I had all the Cybercom equipment and a functioning laboratory. I had to promise to keep her updated and inform her if there was any change. If I don't, she calls every day."

"How long?"

"Six months."

"What happened to the others?"

"Take a look."

He was almost afraid to move in case something didn't work. But he swung his legs over the side of the bed and staggered to his feet. And everything was fine. He glanced around. He was in the same room where Stefan had taken his blood, and he crossed to the big window.

Below were the other volunteers. They still stood in rows.

Unmoving.

"So it didn't work?"

"They shut down when you did. It's what enabled Hatcher to take back some semblance of control. But look…" He waved his hand toward the room below. There was some movement now, as though they were coming awake. A jerk of an arm here and there.

"Will they be okay?"

"They'll function as normal, but you'll always be able to control them…if you want to."

"My own private army? I think I'll pass. Will Hatcher let you all go?"

"I don't think he'll have a choice. A lot has happened in the last six months. The war is nearly over, and most of his remaining soldiers have gone AWOL. There's some sort of sickness devastating half the planets. No one is interested in wars or religion right now. Just staying alive. This is the Church's last stronghold, and it's only still standing because of you."

"Of me?"

"Apparently your girlfriend wouldn't let them destroy the place, because they'd have blown you up with it. And they couldn't attack for fear that Hatcher would kill you."

"He wouldn't have."

"No, I don't think so, either, but they didn't know that."

"So what happens now?"

"There's a shuttle ready for you, and your friends are waiting in orbit."

Friends? Shit, did he have friends now? For someone who was hardly human, he felt amazingly good at that thought.

Stefan brought him clothes, and he dressed quickly. Would he be allowed to leave? But the place was strangely quiet as they made their way through the building, and they saw no one.

"Where is everyone?"

"I told you the soldiers jumped ship, and Hatcher sent just about everyone else away when it became obvious the Church was going to lose this war."

"He stayed?"

"At first he went out to the other planets, trying to get support. But he caught the sickness. He's a broken man."

They were almost at the main entrance when a side door opened and Hatcher stepped out.

Fergal stopped. He'd been expecting some change, but Hatcher was almost unrecognizable. He'd always been thin, but with a wiry strength. Now he appeared frail—his skin was tinged purple and dried blood crusted at his nostrils.

"You're leaving?" Hatcher said.

"Yes."

"You could stay. Together we can cleanse the evil from your soul." For a second the old religious zeal glowed in his eyes, but it quickly faded. "The Church needs good people." His hand went to the cross at his chest. "There is darkness coming. Monsters from Hell have been seen in the skies, and a pestilence follows in their wake. Stay and do God's work."

"I can't." The old hatred rose up, mixed with the need for approval all churning inside him. He could never be what this man wanted him to be. He didn't even desire that. He just wished… Actually, he just wished he could hate him wholeheartedly. It would make things so much easier.

Hatcher coughed, a rough wet sound that racked his frail body with tremors. And Fergal realized it no longer mattered. His father was dying. Was this God's justice? He didn't think so.

Raising his right arm, he sent a signal from his brain, and silver ran over his skin. "I'll never be human. Never be what you want."

And he turned on his heel and walked away.

"How human am I?" he asked Stefan as they left the building.

"About 40 percent."

"And will that stay the same?"

"I don't know. This is new technology. You're new. We'll have to wait and see. But I'll be continuing my research if I can persuade any of the others to stay. I'll let you know what I find."

"Good."

He thought about it on the shuttle as he headed away from the planet. It had been programmed to return to its mother ship, and he had nothing to do but sit and wait.

And think.

About forty-sixty, human-cyborg. He should fit right in with crew of *The Blood Hunter.*

The ship appeared as if out of nowhere, presumably as he got past the stealth device, and the docking bay doors opened smoothly. He was out of his seat as the shuttle set down.

He wiped his hands down his pants, suddenly filled with nerves.

Maybe they'd changed their minds. Had Daisy told them about Hatcher? Probably not, if they were letting him on board. But he had to tell them. He was through hiding who and what he was.

They'd probably toss him straight out the air lock.

But when the shuttle doors opened, a single figure stood framed in the doorway.

Daisy didn't wait for him to move—she hurled herself across the space between them. Her arms twined around his neck, her legs around his waist, and she kissed him.

For a minute, he forgot everything and kissed her back, his tongue thrusting into her mouth, tasting her, breathing her in. "Thanks for waiting for me."

"I would have been there, but that bastard Stefan wouldn't let me come near. And Rico said he'd promised you he'd keep me safe. He's been a total pain in the ass."

Fergal grinned. Then the smile faded. "Do they know?"

"About you and Hatcher—yeah."

"And I'm still here?"

She took his face between her hands and stared down into his eyes. "Hey, it's not your fault."

"No, but I could have killed him."

"So could I. But his time will come. He'll have to answer for his sins."

He'd tell her later that was already happening, but he didn't want to spoil the moment. "So perhaps you can tell me a few of those long stories now."

"Hell, no. We're going to live new ones instead. *Very* long stories." She pulled back a little so she could look into his face, her expression serious. "We have forever. It's huge and it's scary and we don't know what will happen tomorrow, never mind a thousand years from now. But I love you, and I want my forever to be yours as well."

He'd never really thought about forever. Now it stretched out before him, full of adventures, excitement, new worlds to visit. All with Daisy at his side. "I love you, too. And eternity doesn't sound so scary when we can face it together."

"Good." She gave him a quick kiss and jumped down, sliding her palm into his. "Come on. We have plans to make."

"We do?"

"You're part of the crew now."

"I am?"

"Tannis said so."

"She did?"

As she tugged his hand and led him to the doorway, his nerves started to twitch. He'd never been part of anything before. What if he fucked up?

Tannis stood at the bottom of the ramp, hand on the laser pistol at her waist, the rest of the crew spread out behind her. Her face was expressionless, and then she broke into a grin.

"Welcome to *The Blood Hunter*."

Acknowledgments

To everyone at Entangled Publishing for persevering with my favorite series.

To all the great women at Passionate Critters for reading my stories and letting me know what they really think.

And also a huge thank you to my long-suffering husband, Rob, who has to put up with me regularly zoning out of the real world and playing around in worlds of my own making.

About the Author

Nina Croft grew up in the north of England. After training as an accountant, she spent four years working as a volunteer in Zambia, which left her with a love of the sun and a dislike of nine-to-five work. She then spent a number of years mixing travel (whenever possible) with work (whenever necessary) but has now settled down to a life of writing and picking almonds on a remote farm in the mountains of southern Spain.

Nina writes all types of romance, often mixed with elements of the paranormal and science fiction. If you'd like to learn about new releases, sign up for Nina's newsletter here.

www.ninacroft.com

Discover the Dark Desires series...

BREAK OUT
DEADLY PURSUIT
DEATH DEFYING
TEMPORAL SHIFT
BLOOD AND METAL
FLYING THROUGH FIRE

MALFUNCTION

Also by Nina Croft...

BITTERSWEET BLOOD
BITTERSWEET MAGIC
BITTERSWEET DARKNESS
BITTERSWEET CHRISTMAS

UNTHINKABLE
UNSPEAKABLE
UNCONTROLLABLE

RESCUED BY THE SPACE PIRATE
STOLEN BY THE SPACE PIRATE
SAVING THE SPACE PIRATE

OPERATION SAVING DANIEL
BETTING ON JULIA

LOSING CONTROL
OUT OF CONTROL
TAKING CONTROL

HIS FANTASY GIRL
HER FANTASY HUSBAND
HIS FANTASY BRIDE

FALLING FOR THE BAD GIRL
BLACKMAILING THE BAD GIRL
THE BAD GIRL AND THE BABY

HANDLE WITH CARE

BLACKMAILED BY THE ITALIAN BILLIONAIRE

THE SPANIARD'S KISS

Discover more Amara titles...

DRAKON'S PAST
a *Blood of the Drakon* novel by N.J. Walters

When Constance purchases a set of four dragon statues, she's thrust into a world of secret societies, men who think nothing of kidnapping and murder, and dragon shifters. The loneliness haunting Nic has been getting worse since all his brothers have found their fated mates. And when he finds his, and she's involved with the secret society of hunters who hunt and capture his kind, his heart and his life are in jeopardy.

THE CURSE
a *Shifter Origins* novel by Harper A. Brooks

Astrid's time is running out. If she doesn't find her soul's mate before her twenty-fifth Blue Moon rises, she will die. With only three weeks left, things aren't looking good. Lone wolf Erec is determined to stop a crazed killer from harming anyone else. Even if it means helping a rival pack. But he never expected to feel such a pull for the alpha's beautiful daughter, Astrid. Danger looms, but Astrid and Erec are willing to do whatever it takes to save the pack, even if they die trying.

BITTEN UNDER FIRE
a *Bravo Team WOLF* novel by Heather Long

The last person Bianca Devlin expected to see was Sergeant Carlos "Cage" Castillo, the member of Bravo Team WOLF that helped rescue her from a kidnapping on her vacation. But there he is, living across the street from the house she just bought. But there's something off about Cage. And how can Bianca manage her growing attraction, when everything she knows about him and his reason for being there, turns out to be a lie?